Dead Broke in
Jarrett Creek

ALSO BY TERRY SHAMES

A Killing at Cotton Hill

The Last Death of Jack Harbin

A Samuel Craddock Mystery

Dead Broke in Jarrett Creek

Terry Shames

SEVENTH STREET BOOKS®
AN IMPRINT OF PROMETHEUS BOOKS
59 JOHN GLENN DRIVE • AMHERST, NY 14228
www.seventhstreetbooks.com

Published 2014 by Seventh Street Books®, an imprint of Prometheus Books

Cover image © Media Bakery
Back cover image © PhotoDisc
Cover design by Grace M. Conti-Zilsberger

Inquiries should be addressed to
Seventh Street Books
59 John Glenn Drive
Amherst, New York 14228
VOICE: 716–691–0133 • FAX: 716–691–0137
WWW.SEVENTHSTREETBOOKS.COM

18 17 16 15 14 • 5 4 3 2 1

Library of Congress Cataloging-in-Publication Data

Shames, Terry
    Dead broke in Jarrett Creek : a Samuel Craddock mystery / by Terry Shames.
        pages cm
    ISBN 978-1-61614-996-3 (paperback) — ISBN 978-1-61614-997-0 (ebook)
    1. Ex-police officers—Fiction. 2. Murder—Investigation—Fiction.
3. Mystery fiction. I. Title.

PS3619.H35425D43 2014
813'.6—dc23

5494 5497
10/14

2014016019

Printed in the United States of America

To my incomparable sister, Sherry

CHAPTER 1

S ome people's brains shift into high gear after they climb into bed, and they end up spending the night hashing out their problems. I go on the philosophy that if there's something you can do to take care of a problem, get up and do it. Otherwise, put it out of your mind—it'll still be there in the morning. It's a philosophy that served me well when my wife Jeanne was dying of cancer.

I spend a couple of minutes lying in bed wondering how I could have handled tonight's meeting better and if there's anything to be done about it now, decide there isn't, and the next thing I know Mrs. Summerville's rooster next door is announcing the approach of dawn.

Problems usually seem more manageable in the daylight, but not this morning. While I go through my usual routine feeding and checking on my twenty head of Herefords down in the pasture behind my house, my thoughts bounce between the uproar at last night's meeting and the financial problems that are sinking Jarrett Creek. At least there's one positive development. Monday one of my yearlings looked to be developing pinkeye, so I dosed him good with antibiotics, and today the eye is clear.

I hope it isn't my imagination that when I walk back up to the house my knee seems a little less stiff this morning, despite the cold weather that has our part of Texas in its grip. I try to remind myself to do the exercises the physical therapist assigned me after my surgery, but it doesn't always reach the top of my priority list.

I've just brewed a second pot of coffee when Loretta Singletary raps on the screen door and scoots inside. I can already smell the offering she's bringing. Loretta bakes every morning and then spreads the goodies around town like she's intent on fattening us up. I tear off the foil and see four plump sweet buns oozing with dark berries. "What is this, dewberries?"

"I took some out of the freezer. I figured everybody could use a reminder that summer will come around eventually."

"Would you like some coffee?"

"I can't stay this morning. I've got the ladies' auxiliary, but I want to come back later and hear about last night's meeting."

"Free-for-all is more like it."

"Samuel, don't tease me. I've got to get out of here."

I go out on the porch to see her off, biting into one of the pastries while I stand there. Loretta has no sooner turned down the sidewalk toward her house, when a big Chevy Suburban slides to a stop at the curb. The passenger window glides down and Rusty Reinhardt, our mayor for the past six months, leans over to holler at me. "Chief, I need you to come with me. Something bad has happened."

I grab my hat and jacket, put some coffee in a thermos, and bring along the roll I was eating and one for Reinhardt. Only when I'm climbing into his truck do I realize that it didn't occur to me to bring my cane. That's good news. The doctor told me the knee he fixed up is healing exactly the way it ought to, but it seems to be taking a long time.

Reinhardt waves away the roll I offer him and roars away from the curb. He's a hefty man with a barrel chest. He wears a big, fluffy mustache that makes him look like Deputy Dawg. His eyes are hidden behind sunglasses, but I see by the set of his jaw that he's upset. "I have bad news and really bad news."

"What's up?"

"Gary Dellmore was murdered last night." His voice is pinched.

It takes a few seconds for his words to sink in. "We just saw him last night! What happened?"

"Lon Carter found him lying outside the American Legion Hall. Somebody had shot him."

"Shot him! I'll be damned. He must have stayed behind after

everybody else left the meeting." Shaken, I stare out the front window, thinking about how things unfolded last night and wondering how something like this could have happened.

Reinhardt convened an emergency meeting last night to discuss how Jarrett Creek is going to pay for a police force now that the town is flat broke. We can only pay for a couple of part-time officers. Reinhardt put me in charge of the meeting and planned to maneuver matters so that someone would suggest that I take over as chief for now, since I don't need a salary. I told him I'd go along with it. Due to a successful conclusion to an incident when I was chief of police a good number of years ago, the town still thinks of me as the best lawman they ever had. Some people still call me "Chief."

Reinhardt didn't want to railroad the idea through because everybody has had enough of that kind of strong-arming from the former mayor. He planned to be subtle. But the meeting never got that far. Gary Dellmore was determined to take over the proceedings and run the meeting his way. Dellmore's daddy owns Citizens Bank, and because Gary is the heir apparent, he seems to think he has the right to dictate how things are done in town. He ruffled a lot of feathers last night. I don't want to believe it, but it's possible he went too far with somebody and that's how he ended up dead. "How did you find out about Dellmore?"

"I was at the police station when Lon called. I figured I'd better go over to the American Legion Hall and see if there's anything I can do. I swung by your place hoping to find you home so I could get you to come with me."

"What was Carter doing at the hall so early this morning?"

"I didn't ask him. He said he found Dellmore around the side of the building." Reinhardt rolls his shoulders like he's trying to release tension.

Reinhardt is driving faster than he ought to. I watch houses slip by. In this bleak time a few weeks after Christmas, it's hard to believe there will ever be green in the landscape again. Everything is gray and brown—the grass dead from nights of hard freeze, the post oaks and pecans bare of all except curled brown leaves. Even the houses look like they've gone gray.

"What were you doing down at the police station?"

"James Harley Krueger called me first thing this morning to meet him at the station." Krueger is the acting chief of police while the current chief, Rodell Skinner, is off drying out his system from the burden of drinking a case of beer a day. Rumor has it that his liver is not recovering as well as it has in his past rehab stints.

There's something funny in Reinhardt's voice and I turn to look at him. He's got the wheel of the Suburban in a death grip. That's unusual for him. He's a mild-mannered guy. "What did James Harley want?"

"That's the second part of the bad news. He and the other two full-time deputies resigned first thing this morning. They heard they were going to be laid off because the town is broke, and they decided not to wait. I figure they were hoping to shock us into finding money somewhere and begging them to stay on."

"Apparently they don't understand that we really don't have the money," I say.

"When I got down to the station this morning, they were already cleaning out their desks. After they left, I was there with that young part-time officer, Bill Odum, when Carter called to say he'd found the body. Odum left right away to get to the scene. He should be there already."

Reinhardt squeals around the corner onto the road to the American Legion Hall. In the distance I see a Texas Ranger's car in the parking lot.

"You called the Rangers?"

"Odum did. I haven't been mayor long enough to know how it works when somebody is murdered. Odum called the sheriff's office in Bobtail first, and they told him they didn't have the personnel to handle it, that he needed to call the Texas Rangers."

I understand the sheriff's problem. Although the county is supposed to be the first responder to a crime scene, if he sent an officer out every time one of the small towns in the county had a problem, they'd be chasing their tails up one road and down another. It's almost always up to the Rangers or the highway patrol to step in if a town has a serious crime.

Reinhardt slows and turns onto the long, unpaved driveway that leads to the building. The American Legion Hall is an ugly barn-like structure with the original asbestos siding and a tin roof.

"Odum's a good youngster. He could work into the job," I say. "Besides him, who's still on duty?"

"Zeke Dibble."

"Good. Dibble has the experience to teach Odum a few things."

Zeke Dibble is a retired Houston cop who moved to Jarrett Creek, where his pension would go farther. Apparently being home all the time drove him, or more likely his wife, crazy. He managed to get hired on part-time in our police department.

We park next to the Ranger's vehicle in the parking lot on the east side of the American Legion Hall. I don't see a Jarrett Creek police car and wonder why Odum hasn't arrived yet. When I get out of Reinhardt's Suburban, the air feels so damp and chilled that it feels like it could snow, although I know it isn't actually cold enough.

We walk around to the west side and there's one of Jarrett Creek's two squad cars parked under the trees. Bill Odum is standing next to the building along with Lon Carter and a Texas Ranger I recognize, Luke Schoppe. Schoppe is one of the Rangers assigned to the region that includes our county. I got reacquainted with him a year or so ago when he was called out for a problem here in Jarrett Creek.

Lon Carter takes care of maintenance for the American Legion Hall and is the man who found Dellmore's body. He's a quiet, stoic man. He's standing with his arms crossed, staring down at the ground,

11

his face showing no emotion. The three men look over at us as we round the corner.

Schoppe walks toward us and sticks out his hand for me to shake. "I might have known you'd be in the thick of it."

Before I can reply, Bill Odum hustles over to us. He's about twenty-six, with ropy arms, intense blue eyes, and a shock of corn-colored hair that he wears as short as if he were in the military. "Hold on, Schoppe," Odum says. This is the mayor, Rusty Reinhardt, and . . ." he hesitates, unsure of what to say about me.

"I know exactly who he is," Schoppe says. "He's a helluva lawman. How'd you get roped into this, Craddock?"

"Mayor Reinhardt asked me to come out. We were both here at a meeting last night with Dellmore."

"You were with him last night? Any idea what might have happened?"

"He was alive and well last time we saw him," Reinhardt says.

I nod toward Dellmore's body. "Mind if we take a look?"

"Come on over," Schoppe offers. "We're waiting for the crime unit to show up." Odum and I follow Schoppe, Reinhardt lagging behind. I say hello to Lon Carter, who looks like he wants to be anywhere but here.

Dellmore's body is in a fetal position, facing the building. He's dressed in the same clothing he was wearing last night at the meeting, dark slacks and a tan leather jacket over a Western shirt, and black cowboy boots. He was always something of a fancy dresser. From the back there is no evidence of the gunshot wound, so it looks like he just laid down for a nap. But a dark stain of blood has seeped onto the ground around the upper part of the body. The way his legs are drawn up, he must have lived at least a short time after he was shot and pulled his legs up in pain or maybe to comfort himself. There's a vulnerable look to his body that he didn't have in life. I didn't like Dellmore, but I like even less what has happened here.

Rusty Reinhardt walks away, his shoulders hunched. Schoppe

watches him and then turns to me. "Did this man Dellmore have any problems with anybody at the meeting?"

"The meeting was contentious but not out of control. Could this have been a robbery?" I ask. "Maybe somebody was hanging around and caught Dellmore after everybody left."

Schoppe shakes his head. "I checked and his wallet is intact. Has thirty dollars in it. Looks like he knew whoever killed him. It was a close-up shot right through the heart. And no defensive wounds."

I don't like the sound of that. It is possible that somebody stayed behind and got into it with Dellmore. "What kind of evidence you find so far?"

"One bullet casing." He takes an evidence bag out of his vest pocket and shows it to me. "The ground around here is too hard to hold a footprint."

Schoppe is right. We had rain last week, but the clay soil around here doesn't hold moisture and packs up tight as soon it's dry.

"You find anything in his pockets?"

"I didn't want to mess with the body too much," Schoppe says, "so I didn't go through his clothes except to find his wallet. The clothes can be examined when the body gets to the morgue."

"I wonder what he was doing on this side of the building," I say. "Entrance is around back and the parking lot is on the other side." But I remember something from last night. After the meeting, my neighbor Jenny Sandstone and I were headed toward my pickup when we heard Dellmore's insistent voice coming from around this side of the building. At the time it didn't strike me as odd that he'd be on this side where no one was parked.

We heard Dellmore say, "This whole thing was Alton Coldwater's fault and he ought to be held accountable." Coldwater is the town's former mayor, whose big-spending ways have put the town in a financial mess.

Whoever Dellmore was talking to murmured something and then

Dellmore said, "That old fool! I don't see why he was in charge of the meeting. Just because he was chief of police back when Roy Rogers was in his prime doesn't make him any expert."

Jenny nudged me in the side and whispered, "Who do you suppose he's talking about?"

At the time I had half a mind to stomp over there and tell Dellmore off, but the smarter half of my mind told me to let it go. Besides I couldn't help grinning at the line about Roy Rogers. Now I wonder if I could have stopped whatever dust-up got Dellmore killed. The exchange didn't sound all that serious, but maybe after everyone left, the argument escalated and whoever Dellmore was arguing with pulled out a gun and shot him.

I try to remember who was still there when Jenny and I left, but like everybody else we were hustling to our cars to get out of the cold. The killer didn't have to be one of the committee members. Someone may have known that Dellmore was going to be here at the American Legion Hall and arranged to meet with him afterward.

"Does Dellmore have a cell phone on him?" I ask. Although I don't keep one myself, I'm sure the phone shows the last call made or received.

"He didn't," Schoppe says. "That's the first thing I looked for."

That's a clue of sorts. Dellmore was around forty. I don't know any man Dellmore's age—especially someone as self-important as him—who wouldn't carry a cell phone. If Dellmore had recently talked by phone to whoever killed him, it's likely that the killer took the phone to avoid having the call lead back to him.

So far Lon Carter has kept quiet, so I ask him to tell me how he happened to find the body.

He grimaces. "I came to open up the building because some people wanted to look it over for a family reunion. I went inside and straightened a few chairs and made sure the toilets were clean and came outside to empty the trash. When I was walking back from the trash bin I noticed what looked like boots, sticking out from the side of the building. I went around to see what they were doing there and that's when I found him. I don't mind telling you, I didn't like thinking that the whole time I was inside he was lying out here."

"What did you do about the people who were coming to look over the hall?"

"I called them and told them we'd have to put it off. I didn't tell them I'd found a body, though. That wouldn't sit too well."

In answer to a question from Luke Schoppe, Carter says he didn't touch anything or disturb anything around the body.

"Was the building locked up when you got here?" I ask.

"Yes, sir, it was. The lock sticks when it's cold and this morning I had the devil of a time getting it open."

Schoppe tells Carter he doesn't have to hang around any longer. He looks at his watch and says, "I hope the crime unit and the doc get here before too long."

"We're waiting for Doc Taggart," Odum says to me. His face is pale. From the way he averts his eyes from Dellmore's body, it's clear he has never seen a dead body—at least not one at the scene of a murder.

"What kind of gun you think we're looking for?" I ask Odum.

Schoppe starts to say something, but I nod toward Odum. Schoppe catches on and keeps his mouth shut.

"It's a .45 casing," Odum says eagerly, "so maybe a Colt or a Ruger. In training they told us that the Ruger is pretty popular. Or it could be a Smith & Wesson." As I hoped, being asked to contribute perks Odum up and gets his mind off the nearby body.

Schoppe smiles to himself. He probably thinks like I do that it's more likely the weapon was a Colt or a Smith, tried-and-true guns that don't cost too much. The Ruger is a little exotic for most people around here. But Schoppe doesn't correct Odum. He gets that I'm trying to help the youngster settle down.

Reinhardt comes back to join us. He looks miserable. "Who could have done this?" he says, his voice bleak.

Suddenly I think of something. "Hold on." I walk around the side of the building to the parking lot and see that Schoppe's vehicle and Reinhardt's SUV are the only two cars there. I go back and say, "Where is Dellmore's car?"

Schoppe says, "I didn't see a car. I figured he came here with somebody or left his vehicle out on the road."

"No, he had it here last night," I tell him. "It's a black Crown Victoria."

"I'll get the description from his records and alert the highway patrol to be on the lookout for it. Could be somebody shot him to get the car."

"I doubt it. Anybody who killed him for his car would have taken the money out of his wallet, too." I notice Odum looking at me. "You got something to say?" I ask him.

He ducks his head. "Probably not my place, but I'd feel better if you were back on the job."

"Yes, sir!" Schoppe says. "Smart youngster."

"I think you're going to get your wish," Reinhardt says, "as soon as I can figure out how to make it happen officially."

"Good," Odum says. "Zeke will be glad to have you on the job, too."

"Zeke Dibble said that?" I say.

He shrugs. "Not exactly. But he has good things to say about you, and I know he'll be glad if you're with us. Zeke isn't a ball of fire, but if you get him talking, you find out he's had a lot of experience, and he told me you fly under the radar, but you know what's what."

"He's got that right," Schoppe says.

Before I can let that go to my head, I remember what I overheard Dellmore say last night after the meeting, comparing me to Roy Rogers.

"Has anybody thought to notify Dellmore's wife?" I ask.

"Oh, shoot!" Odum says. "I hate to think she'd hear news of what happened by accident before somebody official can get to her."

"Is it all right with you if we notify Dellmore's wife?" I say to Schoppe. Technically it's his investigation and his call to make.

"I wish you would. I'm going to be here a while, and you know what to do."

"Why don't we drive to her place and get it over with?" I say to Odum.

"You'll go with me?"

"I know Barbara a little bit, so I'll help you out."

CHAPTER 2

"Barbara Dellmore was quite a looker when she and Gary moved here. She's originally from Bryan-College Station, and she and Gary met when he went off to college at TCU. She was there working on her master's degree." We're driving across town to a wooded area behind the cemetery that has homes on larger lots. "She's six years older than Gary."

Odum whistles as if that's an impossible span of years. If he had seen Barbara, he would have understood why Gary Dellmore was knocked off his feet. "Her dad owned a tractor/trailer business in Bryan, and when they got married Gary went to work for him. But then the business went bust and they moved back here and Gary's daddy hired him at the bank."

"They have kids?"

"No, they never did."

"Humph. I don't understand people not having kids. I can't wait for me and my wife to start a family."

He's put his foot in his mouth, but there's no reason to tell him so. My wife Jeanne and I wanted kids and then found out we couldn't have them. It almost broke our hearts. We were considering the idea of adoption when my nephew Tom fled my brother's drinking and came to live with us. We decided that Tom would be enough. Still, not having a houseful of kids left a hole in Jeanne's heart.

We turn onto the street where the Dellmores live and park at the curb. Odum says, "Would you look at that! I never saw this place. It's like a park here."

Barbara puts all her time into her yard. Like Odum said, it's more like a park than a garden. Every tree is trimmed to show off its best feature, whether it's a trunk with handsome bark or the graceful droop of the willow that spreads over the goldfish pond. This time of year there aren't many blooming plants, but pots placed around the yard display pansies and some kind of purple flowers. In beds bordered by rocks, Barbara has arranged banks of plants with contrasting combinations of green.

"There's Barbara," I say, gesturing toward the side of the house. She stands up and shades her eyes, watching us walk in through the gate. It's hard to see the attractive woman Barbara Dellmore once was. She looks dumpy and shapeless—sexless in her overalls. The sun is weak today, and she isn't wearing a hat. Her mostly gray hair is chopped off close to her head in an unflattering style. It's as if she has deliberately made herself unattractive.

She comes to greet us, slapping her gloved hands together to clean the dirt off. She's so short that she has to look up at us. "Hello Chief Craddock. Sorry I'm such a mess. I'm doing some transplanting." She gestures toward where a couple of rose bushes have been dug up and are lying on the ground. She shucks off her gloves. "What can I do for you?"

I introduce her to Bill Odum and say, "Do you mind if we go inside?"

She looks from one to the other of us. "No, of course not. But Gary isn't here."

I wait until we're seated in the drab living room that contrasts painfully with the yard before I say, "Barbara, when was the last time you saw Gary?"

She shrugs and reaches up to pluck off a leaf that's lodged at the back of her neck at the hairline. "Yesterday evening. He said he was going to a meeting—he said you were going to be there."

"You didn't hear him come in?"

She frowns. "No. I get up before dawn, so I go to bed early. If Gary's going to come in late, he sleeps in the spare room." She inclines her head in the direction of the hallway.

Odum has gone pale again, and Barbara studies him for a few seconds before turning back to me. "What's going on? Has something happened?"

"Barbara, I've got bad news for you. Gary was found dead this morning."

"What?" She claps a hand to her mouth and her chest heaves. "What happened? Did he have an accident?"

"Somebody shot him."

"Oh, my God!" Her voice is suddenly loud and seems to echo in the room. "You mean . . . what do you mean exactly?"

"It looks like he was murdered."

She falls back like somebody has shoved her. "That's impossible! Who did it?"

"We don't know that yet, Barbara. He was found this morning."

"It doesn't make any sense. Who would murder Gary? Was he robbed?" She's massaging her hands, as if they're aching. Although her expression is bleak, she isn't crying.

"No, ma'am," Odum says. "At least we don't think so. But there is one thing—his car is missing."

She shakes her head slowly. "You think somebody shot him to steal his car?"

"Could he have left the car here?" I ask. "Maybe in the garage?" Maybe I'm wrong and Dellmore's car never was at the American Legion Hall. I can't swear that it was. Maybe somebody picked him up and took him to the meeting.

"No, we leave both our cars in the driveway or on the street because the garage is full of gardening equipment. And I know he took it last night. Where was he found?"

"At the American Legion Hall, outside."

"And his car wasn't there?"

"No, ma'am," Odum says.

She's staring off, eyes unfocused as if she's trying to picture the scene. "Gary said there were supposed to be a bunch of people at the meeting. Do you suppose one of them did it?"

"We haven't had a chance to work out any suspect yet. Like I said, we only found this out an hour ago and we have no idea how it happened. We wanted to let you know right away, though." I get up and Odum springs to his feet. "Barbara, I know this is a shock. Is there anybody you want me to call to come sit with you a little bit? Or you want me to go make you some coffee or something?"

She looks past me as if I've asked her something too hard to puzzle out. Then suddenly she starts, her eyes wide. "Has anybody told Alan?" Alan Dellmore owns Citizen Bank and is Gary's father and employer.

"Not yet. We came to you first. But we ought to get on over there. You going to be all right?"

Barbara nods. "I'll call Mamma and my sister."

"Okay, then, but you let me know if you need anything."

"Do I have to go somewhere to identify Gary's body?"

"We know who Gary is."

She looks at me as if really noticing me for the first time. "Mr. Craddock, why are you here instead of the police? I mean, I know you're here with Bill, but why not James Harley Krueger—he's the one who took over for Rodell Skinner, am I right?"

"Yes, but there've been some changes."

"What kind of changes?"

"I'm sure you know the town has some financial problems—that's what the meeting was about last night. Turns out we can't pay the police, so the full-timers quit this morning."

"Well, if we can't pay for police officers, then who's going to figure out what happened to my husband?" Her voice trails away.

I'm not official yet, so I'm not going to tell her that she's looking at the answer to her question. "It will most likely fall to the Texas Rangers. But don't worry; it'll get done. Barbara, do you know offhand anybody who might've had it in for Gary?"

"Not anyone in particular." I can't decipher the look she gives me, but there's no mistaking the bitterness in her voice. I take it to mean that she can think of some people in general who might have had problems with Gary. I'll have to ask her more about that when I come back later, when she's had time to recover from the shock of finding out her husband was murdered.

She follows us to the door, and I'm surprised when she comes outside and starts pulling on her gloves. She sees me notice. "No sense in letting those roses die. I'll finish replanting them and then call my mamma."

As we're driving toward the bank, it strikes me as odd that Barbara said we needed to notify Gary's daddy. Why didn't she say "Gary's folks"?

"Hard to believe she wouldn't know her husband didn't come home last night," Odum says. He is young and newly married, and doesn't know that people who've been married a while may not maintain a close eye on each other's every move.

CHAPTER 3

In the Citizens Bank lobby little knots of people huddle around talking in low voices. There are a lot of grim expressions and a few red-eyed women. Cookie Travers, who has worked at the bank for years and is now a vice president, rushes across the marble corridor to greet us. "Samuel, I assume you've heard what happened. It's terrible." Her eyes are red-rimmed and her usually cheerful face is haggard.

I tell Cookie that I'm helping Odum and ask where we can find Alan Dellmore.

"As soon as he got the news about Gary he called us all together to tell us and then he went on home. We're going to close up the bank in a few minutes out of respect. Mr. Dellmore wanted to keep the bank open long enough for our regular morning customers to do their business."

Gary Dellmore's wife kept on with her gardening after she heard the news of his death, and now his father wants business to proceed as usual after hearing the news. Is there anyone who will be upset enough to stop their regular activities? I'm thinking that would be his mother, Clara Dellmore.

"Do you know who told Alan about Gary's death?"

"I didn't ask him. You know how things get around, though. Poor man, he was devastated. But I imagine he'll have the bank open tomorrow and you can talk to him then. The way he is, this bank is like another child to him."

I don't share her optimism that Dellmore will be up to business as usual tomorrow. But I could be wrong. Dellmore is an old-fashioned banker. He owns the bank and could leave the day-to-day business to others, but he prefers to keep his own steady hand on it. There's a board of directors, but everyone knows the committee usually follows Dellmore's lead.

I respect Dellmore, and for a long time kept my money here at his bank, but after Gary began working here, it became clear that he didn't have the discretion you want in a banker. He spread all over town how much money people had and where they spent it. I didn't want that kind of information known and slid the majority of my money into a bank over in Bobtail, leaving only enough here for daily expenses. And I know I wasn't the only one.

Bill Odum and I go back outside. Earlier in the day the air was cold and still, but a north wind is coming in and it's beginning to cloud up. I shiver and zip up my jacket.

I consider if we ought to go by to check in on Alan and Clara Dellmore, but there's nothing we can do for them. They know the basic news. "Let's go back to the American Legion Hall and see if the crime scene investigators have arrived."

When we get back, there's a crime scene van in the parking lot and an ambulance around back. The EMT duo is leaning against the ambulance smoking, waiting around for the forensics people to finish up. Reinhardt and Schoppe are watching the two crime scene investigators at work.

"They're almost finished here," Schoppe says, nodding in the direction of the two investigators. "They've got photos of the scene and blood samples and they took a couple of possible footprint samples, although they agreed that the ground isn't going to yield much."

"You missed Doc Taggart. He didn't spend much time here," Reinhardt says.

"He took the vitals and said the medical examiner will do the rest."

"Who's going to do the autopsy?" I ask.

Schoppe says, "They'll figure that out when they get the body to Bobtail. Depends on how overloaded the ME is whether they do it there or send the body on to Houston or San Antonio."

I'm hoping T. J. Sutter, the ME and justice of the peace in Bobtail, will do the autopsy at his place. Once a body gets shipped off to Houston or San Antonio, no telling what will happen to it—or when.

"Did you find Gary's wife at home?" Reinhardt asks us.

"We did."

"How'd she take the news?"

"Shook her up, but she'll be okay."

Reinhardt turns to Schoppe. "What happens now?"

"The Rangers could get somebody on this investigation right away, but . . ." He looks at me, eyebrows raised.

"But what?" Reinhardt says.

"You've got yourself a pretty good investigator right here." He nods in my direction. "We're swamped with that shoot-out that happened over in Burton last week. What's the status with your chief of police? Last I heard he was out of commission."

Reinhardt nods. "We've got us a situation." He explains about the town's financial problems and the latest development with James Harley Krueger and two other deputies resigning. "Our police force is down to Odum here and one other old boy—both of them part-time. I already had in mind putting Craddock in charge, and what you're telling me settles it."

"Good." Schoppe crosses his arms across his chest and turns to me. "I'll send over everything that comes back from the ME and the crime lab. Let me know if there's any other help we can give you."

I nod, trying to digest their easy assumption that I'll be taking over. Things are moving a lot faster than I thought they would, and with a lot more at stake.

Schoppe looks at his watch. "I'm going to have to get moving."

Right after he leaves, the crime scene technicians signal to the EMTs that they can take charge of Dellmore's body. We watch silently as they pack up their gear and the EMTs load the gurney into the ambulance.

When the crew drives away, Reinhardt hooks his thumbs in his belt and turns to me. "It already seems like it's been a long day, but I'm going to call the county sheriff now and find out what we have to do to make you temporary chief."

"That's good," Odum says, sounding relieved. The kid has been working part-time only since last fall, and my guess is that under the dynamic duo of Rodell Skinner and James Harley Krueger, he's learned zip. He'd have done as well to study old episodes of *Law & Order*.

"Odum and I are headed to the station right now," I tell Reinhardt. "Let me know when you've talked to the sheriff."

After Jeanne died, I felt like I was of no further use to anyone. Helping out in a couple of investigations in the past year kicked me back into gear, and despite the feeling that things are moving a little too fast this morning, I'm ready to get started.

Back at headquarters Odum and I sit down to talk over where to begin the investigation. "We'll need to talk to Gary Dellmore's wife again, this time with real questions. And Dellmore's folks and the people he worked with at the bank." I'm jotting down the names as I speak.

Odum sighs. "I don't see how even with both of us we're going to be able to do all this. Not and take care of regular business, too. The problem is . . ." He looks shamefaced, as if he's going to disappoint me.

"What is it?"

"I have another job. In fact, I ought to be getting out of here."

"How many hours a week do you put in here at the station?"

"I only get paid for twenty hours, and Sissy and I can't make it on that, so I've got to make an extra income. I was hoping to get on as a full-time officer, but now that's not looking good."

"What's your other job?"

"I work for my daddy. He's got a big cotton farm out between here and Bobtail. He's okay with me not keeping regular hours, but he wants me to put in the time he pays me for." He looks itchy, like he's anxious to be on his way but doesn't know exactly how to make his exit.

"I guess you better get going then. When are you due back?"

"I come in five days a week either morning or afternoon. I'll come in tomorrow morning first thing."

"Tell you what: Why don't I get started questioning people? Tomorrow we'll work out a plan."

"Sounds good. I hate to leave you to do the whole thing, though."

"Don't worry about it. We're short-handed, and we may not be able to figure this out, but there's a lot we can do. We'll probably do all the legwork and then the hotshot Rangers will take over and get all the glory."

He laughs. "That'll be okay with me. As long as I don't get shot at, Sissy will be happy."

CHAPTER 4

I stop home to grab some lunch and find Loretta waiting for me on my front porch in the sun. She's working on one of the shirts she's making for her grandsons. The shirts are the loudest red-and-blue flannel plaid I've ever seen. Her grandsons are eleven and eight, and I hope their folks have taught them the art of thanking someone who gives you a present—and acting like you really mean it.

"I thought you'd never get back here." She tucks the shirt into her workbag. "Why didn't you tell me Gary Dellmore was killed?"

"I didn't find out until after you left. How'd you hear the news?"

"How would I not hear news like that? It's all over town. That's a terrible thing, young man like that. Do you know who did it?"

"They didn't leave a calling card. Let's go inside and I'll tell you what's been going on."

She follows me inside, complaining that she was cold out on the porch. She has a key to my door, so she could have come inside and waited, but she's particular about appearances and doesn't like to if I'm not home, afraid someone will gossip. While I make a sandwich and coffee, I fill her in on the visit to Barbara Dellmore.

"How did she take it?"

"Pretty shocked, but she'll be okay." I tell Loretta I was surprised that Barbara went on with her gardening after hearing that her husband had been murdered. "She said she had to finish up transplanting and then she'd call her mother."

Loretta says, "I've always found Barbara a little standoffish, but her going back to her gardening doesn't mean anything. You not being a gardener, you don't know what a comfort it is to work in the garden when you're upset. I'll take her some coffee cake tomorrow morning."

She frowns and sets down her coffee mug. "What was she transplanting this time of year?"

"Roses."

"It's not the right time to move roses, but I guess you can't argue with success. I never was much good with roses." I hear a tinge of jealousy in her voice. Every year Barbara enters her roses in the county fair contest and almost always wins.

"What do you know about Gary Dellmore's folks?" I ask.

She puts a finger to her lips and ponders. "I don't know Clara. They're Episcopal. She's quiet. Not in a standoffish way like Barbara, just doesn't say much. But I do my banking with Alan Dellmore, so I know he's a fine man. He and Clara will be devastated. Their only son."

"They have a daughter, too, I recall."

"Yes, she's older than Gary. She married a man in the insurance business in San Antonio. I think they do pretty well. Not that I know anything but what I've heard. Now, you haven't said a word about last night's meeting. You said it was a free-for-all. You think somebody got riled up enough to shoot Gary Dellmore?"

"There were some hard words, but it was mostly hot air. I can't imagine anybody shooting anybody over it." The meeting seems like it was two weeks ago instead of last night.

"How many people did you have there?" She pulls one of the shirts back out of her bag and starts working on it again.

"There were eight. Besides Rusty, Gary Dellmore and me there was Marietta Bryant, of course." She's the city administrator who discovered the disastrous state of the town's finances. "And Jenny Sandstone."

She looks up. "Why Jenny Sandstone? She grew up in Bobtail."

"You don't have to have been brought up here to understand the problems. Jenny being a lawyer, I thought she'd have something to contribute." Jenny is also my next-door neighbor and a good friend. She and I had a disagreement over her horses for a time after she moved next door to me, but that has been smoothed over and I've come to appreciate her wit and wisdom.

"Who else was there?"

"Oscar Grant. We figured the Two Dog Bar needs more than its share of law enforcement, so Oscar ought to be on the committee. And Jim Krueger, since he's the school principal." Jim is the father of James Harley Krueger, acting chief of police. The two men couldn't be more different. "Jim will be an asset to the committee."

"That's only seven."

"Slate McClusky was there, too, although I can't say he contributed much. He mostly grinned and tried to agree with everybody."

"Why did you ask him? He only lives here part-time."

"He's a successful businessman, so we thought he might have some ideas." My motives weren't pure. I thought since McClusky was the richest man in town he might be willing to chip in a little extra money for law enforcement. I could put money in, and I know a couple of other people I could count on, too. But the committee didn't get that far.

"Was he above it all?" She's not looking at me; she's busy making little stitches, but I know she's concentrating on what I'm saying.

"Nothing like that. Everybody got in an uproar arguing whether we even need law enforcement. Dellmore had the bright idea that we ought to try to get along with a volunteer force to back up the two part-time officers we're able to pay, and he didn't want to hear any argument."

She sets her work down on her lap. "That's ridiculous! We can't make do with a bunch of amateurs who don't know a thing about how to handle a criminal. Next thing you know someone will shoot somebody by accident. It's bad enough that everything else in town is falling apart."

"Nothing is falling apart. There will be volunteers to take care of things. You know the fire department has always been a bunch of volunteers."

"Yes, but I don't like the idea of volunteer police."

"Neither do I, but there were some who wanted to try it."

"Who besides Gary Dellmore?"

"Oscar Grant, for one. You know how Oscar is, though. He's pretty independent. He said he could take care of problems at his bar, and for any other problems we only need a couple of part-time officers. And Dellmore only needed one person on his side to think he had a majority."

"Nobody would argue with him? You didn't disagree?"

"Of course we argued. Rusty Reinhardt pitched a fit, but it was hard to reason with Dellmore. It was my fault for not having an agenda for the meeting. Reinhardt had a plan, but I hadn't counted on people having such different ideas."

Loretta picks up her work again. "With Gary being killed, that's pretty good proof that we need a police force. Until we get one, who's going to investigate his murder? Somebody has to."

"Like I said, Rusty has a plan. He's off taking care of it right now."

"What plan?"

"Let's hold off until it's official."

I don't want to tell her that Reinhardt has me in mind. It may turn out that the sheriff in Bobtail doesn't like Reinhardt's plan and will come up with another idea.

"Shame for that boy to be killed. Such a good-looking boy. But he knew it. I hear he catted around a good bit. You think maybe Barbara had enough of it and killed him?"

"Loretta, don't go make accusations like that!"

"All I'm saying is it must have been awfully hard on her having him run around the way he did, especially her being older—and you know as well as I do she's not holding on to her looks."

"She looks okay to me." I speak more sharply than I intended to and she looks surprised.

She sniffs. "I don't know what's gotten into all these married men around here anyway, carrying on the way they do."

"You mean Gabe LoPresto," I say.

"Of course that's who I mean."

LoPresto has scandalized the town by taking up with a young girl who works at Citizens Bank and moving out of his house. He's in his fifties and the girl is in her twenties. I figure LoPresto is making a last-ditch effort to capture his youth, but what I don't understand is what the girl gets out of it.

"I'll tell you what's gotten into Gabe LoPresto," she says, "That little Darla Rodriguez is a troublemaker. You know she and Gary had a little thing going before she took up with Gabe."

"Loretta, how would I know that?"

"Because everybody else does. You haven't been paying attention. Maybe Gary wouldn't leave Darla alone, and Gabe shot him."

I stand up. "It may be that you're right, but I'll reserve judgment until I know more about it. And you shouldn't go around spreading that kind of gossip."

CHAPTER 5

L oretta is leaving when the phone rings. It's Rusty Reinhardt with
news that sends me out the door ten minutes later.

"You all know why I've called you here." Reinhardt's mustache is drooping as if he's been pulling the ends of it down to match
his mood.

He's called an emergency meeting of the committee that met last
night, and we're back at the American Legion Hall. Everybody but
Jenny has managed to make the meeting. She's in court today and
couldn't be reached. The six of us have gravitated to the same seats we
sat in last night, which means we are all acutely aware of Gary Dellmore's empty seat.

It would be nice if the meeting was in a more agreeable spot. The
American Legion Hall is convenient, but that's the only thing to say
for it. We're sitting on hard metal folding chairs around a long rect-
angular table scarred with use. The lighting makes all of us look like
we've got green-tinted skin. Worse, the place smells of mold and the
accumulation of years of people holding their family events here. I can
pretty much guarantee that last weekend somebody served barbecue
and potato salad and beer. And if I'm not mistaken, the toilets have
backed up recently.

"Seeing what happened to Gary, we've got to get some law established in town," Reinhardt says.

Heads nod. Everybody looks distressed and a little guilty at all the
fuss they made last night, even if it was mostly Dellmore who stirred
everybody up.

Reinhardt tells them that as of this morning James Harley Krueger
and two of the deputies have resigned.

"You can hardly blame James Harley," Jim Krueger says. The school principal, he's also James Harley's dad. There's a trace of anger in his voice. "He knew he was going to be out of a job. He had to find work. He doesn't have the luxury of giving away his time."

"No one blames him." Marietta Bryant reaches over to pat his hand. Marietta is the city administrator who took office six months ago and discovered the disaster. A part-time realtor who wears crisp suits and neat little earrings, she has perfect posture. Usually warm and friendly, she had a few sharp exchanges with Dellmore last night when he questioned whether the town's finances were as bad as everyone said. "You better believe it's that bad," she said. "Alton Coldwater should have known better than to invest in that water park."

Reinhardt says, "Jim, no one is sorrier than I am that we can't pay James Harley, but we simply don't have the money."

Slate McClusky was so quiet last night that everybody's a little startled when he pipes up. "I wonder if the city council ought to be in charge of this?" As usual, he asks this with a bright-eyed smile. In his late forties, he's a well-kept man, tall and rangy, with a thick head of hair that has a good bit of gray in it. Today he looks a little rumpled. Even his usually carefully groomed hair looks untended. I don't believe I've ever seen McClusky frown. He always seems eager to shake hands and tends to step in a little too close when he talks to people.

"We discussed this matter last night," Reinhardt says, "and if we turn it over to the city council, they'll have to start from the beginning. Now I've got a proposal to make." Reinhardt looks over at me, so everybody else looks my way, too. "I propose that we ask Samuel Craddock to become temporary chief of police on a one-dollar-a-year salary until such time as we have the money to pay a police chief." He glances over at McClusky. "If the city council goes along with it, of course."

McClusky claps his hands, beaming. "That's the best idea I ever heard."

Krueger glares at Reinhardt. "Looks like you two have this plot all worked out."

"Now, Jim, I wouldn't call it a plot," Reinhardt says. "It makes it sound like we were going behind everybody's back. I did ask Samuel if he'd be willing to help us out and he said he would, but that's all the plotting that went into it."

"Must be nice that he can afford to step in when my son is out," Krueger says.

"I'd say that's a reason to rejoice." Marietta's voice has an edge to it. "Especially if Samuel agrees to do it."

"Do you all want me to leave the room while you discuss it?" I half rise from my chair.

"Samuel, sit down!" Reinhardt says. "You don't need to go anywhere." His eyes are flashing. "Any of you have any better suggestions? Like Marietta says, we're damn lucky to have Craddock."

Everyone perks up. Reinhardt is not usually one for cursing.

"I don't believe she put it exactly like that," I say. Everyone chuckles and the tension is broken.

"Seems to me Craddock is making a sacrifice for the town," McClusky says. He opens his hands wide. "I know personally that when money gets tight, it's up to those of us who are well-off to step in." By far the wealthiest man in our community, McClusky probably gets hit up for money every time there's a fundraiser for the football team or the senior center or the charity rodeo.

"If we do okay this, how is it going to work?" Krueger asks. "Don't you have to pass it by the powers-that-be in Bobtail?"

"I talked to the sheriff only an hour ago," Reinhardt says. "He said as long as a citizen's committee gives the okay, he'll rubber-stamp it. The county has an emergency provision that he can use."

Oscar Grant nods over at me. "I say we're lucky to have Craddock. And I move that we take up Rusty's suggestion."

"Any discussion?" At last night's meeting Reinhardt was hesitant and unsure of himself. He seems to have suddenly found the gumption to be mayor.

No one says a word.

"All right. Let's take a vote, asking Samuel Craddock to take over as chief of police until the town can start paying somebody again. Everybody in favor?"

It's unanimous, although it takes Jim Krueger a few extra seconds to raise his hand.

People start to shuffle in their seats as if they're ready to rush out of here. "Hold it," I say. "Before you go, I want to ask a couple of questions. Did anybody see Dellmore leave last night?"

People dart glances at each other. A couple of them say he was here when they walked out.

"Anybody notice his car in the lot?"

"I saw his car when I left," Jim Krueger says. "He was parked a little too close to me." Krueger has a nervous habit of slicking back his thinning hair. "Why is that important?"

"Dellmore's car is missing," I say. "It wasn't parked here when Carter found him this morning."

"Whoever killed him must've taken the car," Oscar says.

"Could be. But I'd appreciate it if you all would talk it up around town that if anyone sees Dellmore's car, they should give me a call. One more thing. I want you all to think back if you heard or saw anything unusual last night. I know we were all in a hurry to get out of here, but give it some thought and let me know if something didn't seem right to you."

"You're thinking somebody was hiding out there, waiting for Dellmore?" Oscar says.

"It's as good a theory as any at the moment." I don't say what I expect most everybody is thinking—that it could also have been somebody in this room who killed Dellmore.

I walk out into the crisp winter air with a new purpose, remembering what always struck me as strange about being chief of police. Suddenly I'm set apart from the people I came in here with. It's a lonely position in some ways. People aren't as comfortable in your presence because most people have a little something to hide, even if it's only that they are careless about stopping at stop signs.

Before when I was chief, I had Jeanne to go home to, always on my side whatever happened. With her gone, I'm going to be glad to have my friends Loretta and Jenny. As a lawyer, Jenny understands the sacrifice the law asks of you. And Loretta wouldn't think of not stopping at stop signs.

Reinhardt comes out, locks up the building, and walks over to my pickup. "Let's drive on over to Bobtail and get you sworn in."

CHAPTER 6

I t's my turn to bring the wine to Jenny's house for our weekly date. Since Jenny introduced me to the pleasure of good wine, I've joined a wine club and enjoy the selections they send me, although I stick with the reds. I take a nice California pinot noir and some salami over to her place, to go along with our usual fare of cheese and crackers.

"Oh, Lord, what a week," Jenny says. Her mass of red curls is loose for once and that makes her look younger. She has added a sweater to her customary after-work T-shirt and jeans and could be taken for a college student. She's a big woman—not overweight—just tall and substantial. "I think there's a good chance my client has been lying to me."

We usually sit at the kitchen table, but tonight I feel the need to prop my knee up. I've overdone it today, and the knee feels sore. I sit in her big, stuffed easy chair with a footstool, and she settles back on her leather sofa.

We kick around her woes with her wayward client and then I fill her in on everything that happened this morning after Gary Dellmore's body was discovered and the results of the afternoon meeting.

She tells me the news of Dellmore's death was all over the courthouse in Bobtail. "How does it feel to be chief again, knowing you have to face that investigation?"

I know Jenny well enough that I trust her, but I'm not ready to admit to the way I really feel—past my prime and maybe biting off more than I can chew. I keep reminding myself that murder doesn't happen all that often in a small town. But maybe I'm remembering the way things were in the past. In the last few years we've had quite a bit of mayhem. Greed, jealousy, and fear have always been around, but there seems to be more willingness to bring violence into the mix these days.

There are twice as many people in the county now as there were when I was chief the first time. People have moved in from Houston, bought big pieces of land out on the far side of the lake, and set up some fine houses. And maybe they've brought some of their city ways with them.

Jenny cups her ear and leans forward. "I'm not hearing words coming out. Or did you not hear the question?"

I laugh. "I heard you. I'm not sure I can answer yet."

"Fair enough. I'll rephrase my question. What's your plan for figuring out who killed Gary Dellmore?"

Jenny pours us both a little more wine and then sits back and props her feet on the coffee table.

"Not much of a plan yet. Sort of playing it by ear. My first thought was that it was somebody who got bent out of shape at the meeting the other night. I'll know more after I question everybody. I hope I can rule you out since you rode home with me. I suppose you didn't walk back over there and kill him and steal his car."

"What do you mean 'steal his car'?"

I tell her about his missing car.

"I can't say I liked the man, but he and I didn't cross paths enough for me to have a reason to kill him, and I have a perfectly good car of my own." Jenny drives an SUV that's a lot newer than mine.

I'm only half-joking when I tell her Loretta's suggestion that Gabe LoPresto shot Gary. "She said maybe Gary was sniffing around Gabe's girlfriend. At first I made fun of her for jumping to conclusions, but I've had second thoughts."

"What second thoughts?"

"Remember we overheard Dellmore arguing with someone after the meeting? I couldn't hear clearly, but that voice could have been LoPresto's."

"When have you ever known Gabe LoPresto to speak quietly? If it was him, he would've been talking as loud as Dellmore."

I reply with a grunt. I'm annoyed with myself for not paying more attention to my surroundings when we left the meeting. I should have noticed who was leaving when Jenny and I did—then I'd know who Dellmore was talking to. Of course, at the time I didn't realize it would be important.

"Come to think of it, I'm surprised you didn't ask LoPresto to be on the committee," Jenny says.

"Even at his best, LoPresto can be pushy. I thought one person like that on the committee was enough. Besides, with LoPresto leaving his wife and taking up with Darla Rodriguez, I'm beginning to think he doesn't have good sense."

"I'd be inclined to agree with you," Jenny says.

"Tell you the truth, I wouldn't really have thought that Gabe would take up with a young girl like that. Or her with him. What she sees in LoPresto is beyond me."

Jenny laughs. "As I recall he struts himself around like a rooster."

"That would pretty much describe him."

"I don't know Darla Rodriguez, but I'll bet I can guess what attracts her to him. He owns that big construction company, and she may think he's a good catch. Bottom line, she's after his money."

"He does pretty well, but his wife, Sandy, has let it be known that if he divorces her for Darla, he's going to walk away without a dime."

This sends Jenny into a fit of laughter. I can't help laughing with her. "Why is that funny?" I say.

"The idea of those two women fighting over Gabe LoPresto. Now if they'd been arguing over Gary Dellmore, I could see it."

"You and every other woman in town."

"So why didn't Darla go after Dellmore? He's got money, too."

"I couldn't tell you."

"Or Slate McClusky? He's the one with real money."

"You'd have to ask her all these subtle questions."

Jenny asks me for the specifics of what happened to bring Jarrett

Creek to the edge of financial ruin. "I was surprised when Marietta Bryant told us how bad it was," she says. "But she didn't say why."

"It's not hard to follow. Same thing that happened to a lot of small towns in the last few years. When the economy went bad, some businesses went under, people lost their jobs and couldn't pay their mortgages, and they lost their houses, so the tax base contracted. Alton Coldwater thought he could attract some new business by renovating those streets downtown—and that cost money."

"It actually looks nice, though."

"Yes, and it has brought in a few new stores lately, but not in time to shore up the city's finances."

"So that's when somebody had the bright idea to build a water park out at the lake?" She shakes her head. "What a hare-brained scheme!"

"You think so? Everybody was all excited about it at the time, but maybe that's because Coldwater talked it up big."

"Seems to me somebody would have figured out that the town didn't have the money to service the loan and keep paying its employees at the same time."

"Well, that's all water under the bridge. We're in trouble now, and it's going to take a while to recover. I admire Rusty for trying to figure out a way to keep city services going with volunteers. I hope it works."

Before I know it, it's late and I'm yawning. I get up and realize I've made a mistake that my doctor warned me against—I've been on my feet way too much today. My knee has swelled up, and it hurts to put weight on it.

"What's the matter with you?" Jenny says.

I tell her my knee is flaring up.

"You can stay here. It won't be the first time." I stayed at her place for several days after someone tried to burn down my house last year. She saw the flames and called the fire department before the fire could get too far, but not before my house was so smoked up that I couldn't stay there for a while.

I pick up my hat. "I'd better get on home, if you can lend me a hand. Tomorrow morning I've got a job to do."

It's a good thing she's got some heft to her, because I have to lean on her to get back to my house. She fetches me an icepack for the knee and I take a couple of pills for the swelling. When I lie down with my knee all trussed up, I feel pretty sorry for myself.

CHAPTER 7

"You've got some nerve coming over here gloating. I heard about that secret meeting where they decided you'd take over the police department. You've always wanted Rodell's job. Now see how you like it. Nobody appreciates anything the chief of police does."

Rodell Skinner's wife, Patty, hasn't invited me in, so I'm standing on her porch, hat in hand. I've come here to see if she knows how long Rodell will be out of commission and to tell her I've been temporarily appointed to Rodell's job. I was hoping to smooth things out with Rodell, but it's not going quite as I'd planned.

"Patty, I'm sorry I upset you. It's a hard situation. The meeting wasn't meant to be secret, but something had to be done—and it had to be done fast. The town is flat broke. A lot of people are being affected by this."

"That's what you say. But you watch—Rusty Reinhardt will find the money to do what suits him. That's the way government always works. They take hard-earned money from people who work for a living and use it for whatever suits them."

I don't bother to tell her that the salary I'm getting is a token dollar a year. Finding that out would stir her up more. I don't know what more I can do here. "Patty, my intention was to extend a hand to Rodell," I say. "I'd appreciate knowing when he gets back from rehab." I turn around, clapping my hat on my head. I'm barely two steps away before the door slams behind me.

The way Rodell has always carried on, I don't know why Patty is such a big defender of his. I suspect she's so mad at him she can barely see straight and thinks if she doesn't defend him everybody will guess how mad she is.

Alan Dellmore's house, one of the oldest and grandest in Jarrett Creek, has a sedate, comfortable feel to it, with rocking chairs on the wide porch and potted plants in the corners. The Dellmores both grew up in Jarrett Creek and are not inclined to put on airs.

I raise my hand to knock on the door, but I hear loud voices inside—angry voices. I hesitate, not wanting to intrude on a family argument, but I remind myself that I'm no longer a private citizen. I'm the chief of police. I have to do the job even if I'm walking in on an embarrassing situation.

Before I can knock, though, the front door opens and Barbara Dellmore shoves open the screen door. I dance backward to avoid her running into me.

"Oh! You startled me. I'm just leaving." Barbara's face is flushed and her voice is sharp. She barrels past me and down the steps to her car.

I don't try to stop her, but I do wonder what has her so flustered. I hold the screen door open and call out, "Hello? Clara, Alan?"

When Alan comes to the door, he's a pitiful sight. His face looks like somebody has gouged furrows in it. His wrinkled corduroy pants and baggy sweater look like they've been slept in. "Come on back," he says. "Clara and I are in the den." I follow him inside and he shuffles in front of me like an old man. He's several years older than me, but I wouldn't have thought of him as old until today.

The den is a big TV room with a picture window that draws my eyes out onto the bleak-looking backyard with its patchy stubs of dead grass and stark, bare trees. There are a few bushes along the back fence, but no garden.

Clara is sitting on a plump sofa. She's a small woman. I've known her since we were young. A few years older than me, she was a pretty girl with an unexpected deep dimple when she smiled. She's not smiling now. Her face is gray, her eyes puffy, but she still manages to convey dignity.

I lean down to take her hand and tell her and Alan how sorry I am about Gary. "I'm intruding, but I have to ask you some questions."

I explain that as of yesterday afternoon I'm acting chief of police. "It's up to me to find out who did this to your son."

Alan starts to speak, but it comes out as a croak. He clears his throat before he starts again. "Thank you for coming. It's been a terrible shock."

Clara gestures to an armchair. "Samuel, why don't you take a seat. Can I get you something?"

"No, no, you stay there. Don't get up. I'm fine." I sit down facing her.

Dellmore lowers himself onto the sofa next to his wife. "What kind of questions do you have?" he says.

"Let me get a little background. When did you last see Gary?"

Clara puts a hand to her lips and closes her eyes. Alan answers. "I see Gary every day at work, and Clara saw him over the weekend. He stopped by."

"Did everything seem all right with him?"

Alan hesitates but then nods. "Same as usual." He glances at Clara. There's something he's reluctant to say, but I'll get at it.

"Do either of you know if Gary had a falling-out with anybody recently?"

Clara draws a sharp breath. Dellmore takes her hand. He looks at me, his eyes full of pain. "You might as well hear it from me. Gary and I didn't always see eye-to-eye on things, and . . ." he pauses and swallows. "We had a fight last Friday, and then again Tuesday. I shouldn't have been so hard on him!" He hangs his head.

Clara puts her other hand on his arm and squeezes. "You can't blame yourself, Alan. People have arguments all the time. You can't keep things to yourself for fear that somebody might . . ."

Dellmore puts his hand up to stop her. "The problem was I flew off the handle and called him out right in front of everybody at the bank. I should have talked to him privately."

"What was the argument about?"

Dellmore looks off in the corner and runs a hand over his mouth hard like he's trying to wipe away the words he has to say. "Cookie Travers told me last week that Gary was paying one of the girls the wrong kind of attention. Flirting with her. Could be considered harassment, she said, and it needed to stop. Friday I confronted him."

"Who was the girl?"

"A teller. New girl. Rusty Reinhardt's daughter Jessica. She started working for us last summer, straight out of junior college. Nice girl, pretty. Made me mad that Gary would do such a thing. He's a married man and everybody knows it! He was making of fool of himself, not to mention the girl and the people who saw what was going on and had to pretend they didn't notice." His voice grows more vehement the longer he talks.

Clara has been sitting frozen, but she gives herself a little shake and says, "Now Alan, you're going to get your blood pressure up. There's no need to go over this again."

Dellmore lowers his head into his hands and shudders. "You're right. But I hate to think . . ."

"Stop," she says firmly.

I wonder what he was going to say—does he hate to think their argument was one of their last exchanges or that his son had flouted the rules? "You said it could be considered harassment. Did Jessica threaten to bring any charges or anything like that?"

Dellmore manages a tired smile. "No, according to Cookie it was a mutual flirtation. Like I said, Jessica is young. I guess she didn't realize how it looked. Cookie said she had to bring it up because people were starting to gossip. Apparently Jessica told Cookie that it was no big deal, that Gary was simply being friendly."

"You said you had another argument Tuesday?"

Dellmore hits his knee with his fist. "Gary was right back at it. Tuesday morning I walked in, and there he was in her cubicle again like some teenager with hormone problems. I told him I wanted to talk to him in my office, he gave me some back talk, and it escalated from there."

Suddenly from the doorway, a woman's voice says, "What's going on? I thought you two were going to lie down for a while. We've got people coming into town once we make funeral arrangements. You're going to need your strength."

A young woman who's the image of Clara is standing in the doorway.

Alan says, "Annalise, come on in here." The girl walks a few steps into the room. "I don't know if you remember Mr. Craddock. He's been appointed temporary chief of police. He's investigating your brother's death. Samuel, this is our daughter, Annalise Whittier. She lives in San Antonio with her husband."

Annalise strides over to me and shakes my hand. She has a more confident manner than Clara. "I remember your wife from the front office at school. She was always so nice. I was sorry to hear she passed away."

"Thank you. She did enjoy the students. I'm glad you remember her. And I'm sorry about your brother."

"I couldn't believe it when Daddy called me. I still can't believe it. As soon as I heard, I came home to help Mamma and Daddy." With her brisk tone, she strikes me as the kind of person who will always take charge in a crisis.

"Where's Mikey?" Clara asks, rising from the sofa.

"He's having a snack in the kitchen."

"He shouldn't be left alone when he's eating," Clara says, moving toward the door. "He might choke or fall out of his high chair."

"Mamma, he's fine. He's all strapped in, and you know how he likes to eat."

In the doorway, Clara pauses. "Samuel, do you need me for anything more?"

"No, you go on and see about the baby. I'll talk to Alan a few more minutes."

I ask Dellmore if there were any other incidents between him and his son, and he hesitates. "Not really incidents."

I wait. He'll tell me.

Dellmore studies his hands, gathering his thoughts. "You know, Gary didn't plan to come back here and work for me. You may remember that Barbara's daddy had a tractor/trailer business over in Bryan-College Station. When she and Gary got married, her daddy hired Gary to handle the financial side of things. Said he was grooming Gary to take over. But somewhere along the line, things took a downturn and the business went under. After that, Gary had trouble finding another job. He didn't want to come back here, but I offered to hire him, and frankly I was surprised when he said yes. He never thought he was cut out to be a banker, and I'm afraid I have to agree."

"I was under the impression that your son was going to take over the bank when you retired."

He sighs. "I always hoped that would happen. But when it came down to it, Gary didn't have the right attitude to go into banking. He didn't always do things the way I thought they should be done."

"So the flirtation with Jessica Reinhardt wasn't the first time you two had words?"

"No." He draws a deep breath. "And I had to defend him to the board more than once. They weren't satisfied with the way he handled business. I kept hoping I could guide him, and I thought I was making some progress."

He gets up and walks over to a wall covered with pictures of the family and looks at them for a few seconds before turning back to me. "Gary was a good uncle to Annalise's kids and I think he would have been a good father. Maybe that would have settled him down. But Gary said that's one thing he and Barbara agreed on, that they didn't want kids."

"You get along okay with your daughter-in-law?"

"Who, Barbara? We get along fine with her." He glances toward the kitchen and then says in a low voice. "I should say *I* get along with her. Clara and Annalise . . ." He shrugs. "They never took to her. They say she's hard to get to know, but I don't have a problem with her. She's always friendly to me."

"When she left just now, she was upset."

"She and Annalise had words. Annalise . . . let's just say sometimes she has strong opinions and doesn't mind letting people hear them." Interesting that both Gary and his sister were outspoken when their parents are self-effacing people.

"Grief doesn't always bring out the best in families. What were they arguing about?"

He shoves his hands into his pockets and takes a turn around the room. "She was put out because she said Barbara didn't seem upset by Gary's death."

"Barbara seems like the kind of person to keep her feelings to herself. Sometimes people can take that the wrong way."

"You're right. Barbara has never been one to let her feelings show, but she was pretty offended when Annalise said what she said. She told Annalise it was nobody's business how she mourned. And then . . ." He glances at me and ducks his head, looking at the floor.

"Then what?"

"Barbara got a little ugly. She said that Gary was unfaithful to her and if he had been a better husband she might have been more broken up." He sighs. "It escalated from there. Annalise said something she shouldn't have. She said that Barbara let herself go and if she had kept herself up better, he wouldn't have been interested in other women. It was a bad fight. Both of them were way off base."

"Did Clara get involved in the argument?"

"No, she stayed out of it. As I said, she never took to Barbara. But I'm sure she didn't approve of the way Annalise talked to Barbara today."

"Do you know of any problems Gary had with anyone else lately? Anybody who was especially upset with him?"

He thinks for a minute and shakes his head. "I can't think of anybody. Gary confided more in Clara than he did in me. Maybe she can help you out. You want to talk to her?"

"I'll have a quick word with her."

"Why don't we go in the kitchen? You can meet the wild man." It's the first time there has been a light in Alan's eyes since I got here.

I ask how old his grandson is.

"He's two. Cutest thing you ever saw. And smart! But he's giving Annalise fits. Her two older ones are in school, and between them she didn't have half the trouble that little pistol is giving her."

In the kitchen it's taking the efforts of both his mother and his grandmother to keep little Mikey from pulling everything he can reach out of the cabinets. "I don't mind a bit," Clara is saying to her daughter. "After you leave, I'll have plenty of time to put things away."

"Mamma, I don't want to give him the idea that it's okay to make such a big mess."

"I understand. You have to discipline him. But I'm his grand-mother and I can indulge him if I want. He's so darling."

The little darling starts running around the kitchen, roaring, holding a pan over his head like a club. I make the appropriate noises, saying how smart he is while dodging his efforts to hit me with the pan. I can't help being skittish that he might clobber my knee.

I tell Clara I need to be on my way and ask her if she'll walk out with me.

At the front door I ask if she knows of any problems Gary was having with anyone.

She holds herself straight, and despite the misery in her eyes, her voice is clear and strong. "It's no secret that Gary wasn't as discreet as he could be with bank business. Alan was always on him to do better, but I chose not to bring it up with Gary." She falters. "I wish I had tried to talk to him. I wish I had told him to shape up." She shakes her head. "I indulged him."

"Clara, you know as well as I do that he probably wouldn't have listened to you."

She puts her hand on my arm. "Alan told me Gary's car was missing. Has anybody found it?"

"Not yet, but we will."

She frowns. "I wonder if somebody from out of town killed him to get his car? If so, they'd be long gone."

"The highway patrol is on the lookout for it. It'll turn up. Meanwhile, I want you to think over the conversations you had with Gary in the past couple of weeks. Call me if you think of anything that seems off, even if you don't think it's important."

"Where do I reach you, at your house or your cell phone?"

"Try the house," I say weakly.

I'm going to have to break down and get a cell phone. Everybody will expect me to have one if I'm going to be police chief. Recently a new tower has gone up between Jarrett Creek and Bobtail, and they say it's easier to get service now, so I don't have that excuse for not getting one anymore.

CHAPTER 8

I head for Citizens Bank to see what Cookie Travers can add to Alan Dellmore's version of the argument between him and his son. Cookie is standing next to her desk in the carpeted area of the bank where loans and new business get handled, talking to a woman I don't recognize. She spots me and waves me over. "Here's Samuel Craddock right now," she says to the woman. "He's the one I was telling you has a big art collection."

The woman who turns toward me is in her fifties, with a fine figure, dark eyes, and an uncomplicated chin-length hairdo. She has an anxious look, but when she smiles her expression lightens.

"Samuel, this is Ellen Forester. She's just signed a lease to bring a new business to town."

I shake her hand. She has a firm handshake and looks me straight in the eye.

"That's good to hear," I say. "We can use some new business." I'm wondering if anybody told her the town is insolvent.

"Guess what kind of business?" Cookie says.

I'm surprised at the hint of conspiracy in her voice, as if the business has something to do with me. "I couldn't begin to guess."

"She's opening an art gallery and workshop."

Ellen gasps and slaps her hand to her mouth. Her eyes are dancing. "Oh, dear," she says. "Hearing you say it out loud makes it seem real."

"Anyway, I told her you collect art. I hope you don't mind me gossiping."

"I don't mind at all." Sometimes it surprises me that anyone in town knows I collect art. It's not what most people expect in a small town. My wife Jeanne and her mother were passionate art collectors, and after a while Jeanne got me interested in it, too. Luckily, Jeanne's family had the money to buy art, and Jeanne and I bought a few things, ending up with a nice little collection.

"What kind of art are you going to carry?" I ask. I expect it will be the kind of paintings you find in most Texas galleries, the three "Cs"—countryside, cows, and cactus. It's a far cry from the art I appreciate.

"I'm still working on that," she says. "Nothing too unusual. I'll show some of my own work, and I hope to find some local talent. But I'm also going to have a workshop where I can offer painting classes."

"You think there's some untapped talent here?"

"You never know. I think it's good for people to have a creative outlet." She glances at her watch. "I better get going. I'm supposed to meet the contractor at the new site." There's excitement in her voice. "It was nice to meet you. I hope I get to see your collection sometime soon."

When she's gone, Cookie says, "She ought to perk things up around here. A new business and a little more tax revenue is exactly what this town needs. Now I expect you've come to talk about Gary."

We sit down at her large, tidy mahogany desk. As a bank vice president, her desk is positioned so she can see everyone who comes and goes. Cookie is pushing sixty and is working hard to pretend the years aren't piling up. Her hair is blonde, though I know for a fact it used to be dark. She's wearing a shapely pink suit that would look good on a younger woman, and she uses makeup with too heavy a hand, her eyes surrounded with dark eyeliner. I don't remember whether Cookie was ever married, but I know there isn't a Mr. Travers currently.

"Cookie, Alan Dellmore told me he and Gary had an argument over an incident between Gary and Jessica Reinhardt. Can you tell me more about that and introduce me to Jessica?"

Cookie shifts in her chair. "She didn't come in today. She was pretty upset yesterday when she heard what happened. Tell you truth, I wouldn't be surprised if she quit."

"Really? Why is that?"

"I might have been a little hard on her." She sniffs. "But it's my job to keep things running smoothly here. I've got standards that I demand the employees hold to, and I expect the women to behave well. It might have been Gary's fault, but it takes two to have a flirtation."

"Surely with Gary being the boss and being older, most of the blame fell to him?"

"Maybe so. Alan thought so. Gary is a good-looking man, and the girl was probably flattered, but I still say that's no excuse. I spoke pretty sharply to her and told her to see to it that it didn't happen again."

"Who told you they were flirting with each other?"

Cookie's penciled eyebrows shoot up. "Saw it with my own eyes! It had been going on for a while, but last week it got out of hand. One night—I guess it was Wednesday—Jessica stayed behind because she found an error when she was tallying up and had to go back over everything. I went out on an errand and came back to lock up after her, and when I walked in, I saw the two of them in one of those cubicles." She gestures across the bank lobby to where a teller is counting out money to someone.

"Looks crowded for two people."

"Yes, it is. That's the way these types of situations get out of hand. Close quarters. But I was surprised anyway. When I walked in, Gary had his arm around her and then..." Cookie draws a sharp breath. "Well...his hand dropped down...toward her rear end, and she giggled. What kind of behavior is that! Even if he did like her, and even if he wasn't married, that's no way to behave in a professional setting."

"Did you say anything to them?"

"I asked what was going on. Gary laughed, and Jessica said it was nothing. She can be a snippy little thing, and I didn't like her tone, which I pointed out to her when I talked to her Monday."

"You felt you needed to tell Alan about it?"

"Yes, I did. It upset me. Gary is his son!"

"Is this the first time something like this had happened?"

Cookie grimaces. "I know of one other girl Gary flirted with. I was thinking of asking if any of the other women had problems with Gary—if he got fresh with them. I'm not a prude, but laws being the way they are these days, if Gary made a move with the wrong person, somebody might bring a lawsuit."

"I'd like you to do that. Find out if anybody else had a problem."

She puts a hand to her chest. "You don't really think somebody killed Gary because he was fooling around, do you?"

"I'm trying to get the situation here at the bank clear in my head. Did the employees like Gary? Did they respect him?"

Cookie pauses, her hands tightly clasped. "It's hard to measure how much people respected Gary for himself, and how much because he was Alan's son. I don't know of anyone who had any particular problem with him. I do know that no one looked up to him the way they do to Alan."

I glance over at the two women within my line of vision. "You said Gary flirted with one other woman. Who was it?"

She grimaces. "It wasn't exactly the same thing. It was that little Darla Rodriguez. She flirts with everything in pants who comes through the door, and I guess she finally nabbed Gabe LoPresto, though he's no prize. That poor fool! She's going to run rings around him and then drop him. You watch."

I stop by Town Café for some enchiladas, hitting the place at lunchtime, so it's crowded. I hesitate in the doorway, the same feeling coming over me that I had yesterday. I don't have the same relationship with people that I did before. I hope it's my imagination that the room gets quieter with my standing there.

Town Café wouldn't win any award for decor, being a big tin Quonset hut reinforced with knotty pine paneling and linoleum tile floor. The walls are hung with neon beer signs, old photos from Jarrett Creek's past as a thriving railroad town, and photos of winning football teams. Christmas was several weeks ago, but they haven't taken down the decorations, which consist of worn-out gold and silver garlands and a tiny artificial tree hung with miniature candy canes. Despite the haphazard decorating, the café is a popular place because the food is good.

A couple of the old boys I frequently have lunch with wave me over and I sit down with them. One is Gabe LoPresto, who is either behaving in a scandalous way or making the most of life, depending on who you talk to. LoPresto's construction company has pretty much tied up business in the county. He's a little hard to take sometimes because he brags and struts himself around, but his company has a reputation for quality work. Today he's wearing a suit with a string tie, snakeskin cowboy boots, a black suede hat, and a big self-satisfied grin. He has been more or less insufferable since he took up with Darla Rodriguez. It makes it hard to talk to him like he's a reasonable person.

"I hear you're the Big Chief again," LoPresto says.

"At least for a while," I say. "Until we can get the city finances under control."

"That's not likely to happen anytime soon," LoPresto says. "You're in for the long haul." He gestures toward my knee. "At least it looks like the knee is doing pretty well."

"It's getting there." I don't know why it makes me skittish to discuss the knee, even though it's healing fine. Remembering what it's like having it so banged up reminds me of how vulnerable I can be.

"I hope it's not going to take so long for the city to get back into financial shape," one of the men says to LoPresto. "My wife was already complaining that the library is only going to be open a couple of afternoons a week. And that's only because Mrs. Cutter is willing to volunteer her time."

"I'm afraid your wife is going to have to get used to it," LoPresto says.

"You've got your hands full being chief again at your age," Harley Lundsford says, looking me up and down. He's a rough-and-ready kind of guy, face as weathered as a lizard from farming. "I wouldn't want to take on the job right after somebody got shot."

"That does make it something of a challenge," I say.

"If Dellmore had carried a gun on him, he'd be walking around right now." Lundsford is a fierce advocate of everybody carrying a loaded gun in plain sight. So far he hasn't gotten enough people to agree with him that it's been made into law, but he takes every chance he gets to poke people with his opinion.

"Could be," I say, not wanting to open that particular can of worms today.

I give Lurleen my order and then field questions about Dellmore's murder until the conversation veers to the surprising success of this year's football team. The season is long over, but the season for discussing football is year-round. I'm finishing up my lunch when Alton Coldwater walks into the cafe.

"There he is," LoPresto says under his breath, "the head crook himself." LoPresto's company was slated to build some of the structures for the water park before the project went belly-up. No wonder he's mad at our former mayor.

With Coldwater standing in the doorway surveying the room, there's no mistaking the hush that falls. Everybody knows he's saddled Jarrett Creek with crushing debt. He should know he's not too popular right now and should have stayed away. But Coldwater never was known for being perceptive. He comes over to our table, grinning like a fool. He sticks his hand out to shake mine. "I understand we've got ourselves a dollar-a-year man."

It's just like Coldwater to make a public spectacle of the fact that I'm not getting paid. It makes it seem like the only reason I got the job is that I don't need the money. I can't begin to think what to say to him. Lundsford saves me by pushing his chair back and saying to nobody in particular, "I've been sitting around here too long. Better get back to work." All the other men at our table get up, including me.

"I'll catch up with you boys later," Coldwater says. His voice is pleasant enough, but his face has hardened as he gets the message. I don't have the heart to leave him to swing in the wind.

"Alton, can I have a word with you?"

"Why sure!" Louder than it needs to be.

"Outside?"

"Okay, let me tell Lurleen what I want to eat."

When Coldwater comes outside and it's the two of us without an audience, he's deflated and looks at me with hangdog eyes. "You don't have to say a thing," he says. "I know what people are saying. But I can't just hide at home. I'm not built that way. I'd go crazy. I figure if I keep showing up, people will get used to seeing me and eventually they'll forget what happened."

His assessment strikes me as being too optimistic, but I feel sorry for him. Everybody makes mistakes at one time or another—his happened to be public. "I understand, but everybody is on edge right now, Alton, not just about our financial situation but because of what happened to Gary Dellmore."

He glares at me. "Everybody thinks I played fast and loose with the town's money, but I really believed in that project out at the lake. I put up a lot of my own money. It wasn't only the town that lost out; it was me, too. And let me tell you something else: everybody can cry crocodile tears over Gary Dellmore, but if they knew the way he pushed for the deal out at the lake to go through, they might have second thoughts."

CHAPTER 9

I thought I could eliminate Rusty Reinhardt as a possible suspect until I heard that his daughter had a public flirtation with Gary Dellmore. No telling what a man will do if he thinks his daughter is being interfered with.

I track Reinhardt down at his grocery store, the Qwik Mart, the biggest grocery store in town. He's stocking cans of tomatoes, and as I walk up he hoists another box off the pallet with a grunt. He's dressed in blue jeans and a sweatshirt, and you wouldn't guess that he was the owner of the store.

"Rusty, seems like you could hire somebody a little younger to do this job."

"You find somebody, I'll hire him! Boy walked off the job this morning like he had a whole pack of jobs lined up. They say the economy has gone bad, but these kids think they can get another job just like that." He wipes his forehead with his sleeve. "What can I do for you?"

"I need to have a word with you."

"Come on to the back room. I need a break anyway." He pushes the pallet to the end of the aisle and against the wall.

I follow him through the swinging metal doors, across a cold concrete floor stacked with boxes of goods, and into a cramped office. He parks himself behind a desk strewn with receipts and bills and points me at the chair facing him.

"Rusty, I guess you know why I'm here. I have to question everybody who was at the meeting the other night."

"You mean to find out if I heard a gunshot?" he says dryly.

I give him the benefit of a laugh and then continue. "From my end, I can tell you that I overheard Dellmore having an argument with somebody after the meeting. But I didn't see who it was. You have any idea who he was talking to?"

Reinhardt frowns and shakes his head. He rears back in his chair and folds his hands over his belly. "I don't know what I could say to help you. I didn't see or hear anything out of the ordinary."

"You know Dellmore's car is missing. Did you see it when you left?"

He thinks it over. "That's the damnedest thing. You'd think I would have noticed if the car was there, wouldn't you? Krueger said he saw it, though."

"Couple of other things." I tell him that I ran into Coldwater at the café. "He implied that Gary Dellmore pushed the city's involvement in the water park investment. Citizens Bank did the loan on that project. Is that right?"

He ponders my question. "Marietta and I went through the numbers and I think it was Citizens that made the loan. Marietta is the bookkeeper, so she knows more than I do. Coldwater didn't mention that Dellmore was involved. Bottom line is, Dellmore didn't force Coldwater to make that investment. I expect Coldwater is looking for somebody to take some of the heat."

"There's one other thing, and it troubles me to have to bring it up. Did your daughter tell you she got in trouble at work because she and Gary Dellmore were carrying on?"

His face darkens. "She mentioned it, but she said he was just flirting with her—that it was nothing more than that. Needless to say, I was pretty put out with him. After all, he's her boss, and married besides. But if you're suggesting I killed Gary Dellmore because he was making improper advances to my daughter, think again. I would happily have horsewhipped him in public, but my daughter said she'd be humiliated if I made a fuss over it."

It's no surprise that, unlike Cookie, Reinhardt put the blame for the flirtation on Gary Dellmore. I need to dig a little deeper and make sure it was only a flirtation and that Dellmore didn't pursue her after banking hours. "Cookie Travers said Jessica was really upset when she heard that Gary was dead. Do you think there was anything more to their relationship?"

"What are you suggesting? That my daughter would date a married man?"

"It wouldn't be a reflection on your daughter, Rusty. Like you said, he's her boss, and she might've worried that her job was at risk if she didn't go along with him."

He brings his chair forward with a sudden jerk, glaring at me. "My daughter was brought up right. If Dellmore tried anything with her, she would have put a stop to it right off. She knows there's no job worth a sinful relationship." He stands up. "I've got things to do. Is that all?"

I rise. "Rusty, you understand I need to clear this up. It's nothing personal."

"I understand. But it's hard to think of that man putting hands on my daughter and then having you question her morals."

He sees me to the door of his office but is still huffy, and we part awkwardly.

Reinhardt has given me two new perspectives. People have suggested that Alton Coldwater be prosecuted for mishandling the city's funds. But with Dellmore dead, he can shift the blame. Would he have been desperate enough to murder Dellmore to do that?

The other thing is that, according to Reinhardt, his daughter made light of her flirtation with Dellmore, while Cookie seemed to think Jessica was partly to blame in the matter. I have a feeling that Jessica Reinhardt isn't telling her daddy the whole story.

I'm walking across the parking lot to my truck, not paying attention, and nearly run straight into Sandy LoPresto. She's a lanky woman with a wide-mouthed smile and a significant bosom. I've never seen her dressed like she is today, in a low-cut sweater and a tight skirt just above her knees and high-heeled boots. She has a wild look in her eyes that's a little dangerous. She glares at me as if I'm partly responsible for her husband running off with Darla Rodriguez.

"Sandy, how are you doing?"

"How do you think I'm doing?"

"Probably not too happy at the moment."

"I imagine you're like every other man in town, wishing he could be in Gabe's shoes screwing around with that little hussy."

I hold up my hands. "Don't look at me! That's the last thing I need."

"You're the only one then." Sandy comes by her feisty disposition honestly. Her dad, Carl Filson, always had a ready temper.

As wound up as she is, I know it's best for me not to tangle with her. "What do your kids have to say?" Her kids are both in their thirties. Their son is a dentist who lives in Bobtail with his family. The daughter has proven to be something of scholar. She's getting her PhD at the University of Houston.

"They think Gabe has gone off his rocker. I told them I'm ignoring him, and they should too."

I almost laugh when she says she's ignoring Gabe. Sandy has been stalking Gabe since they split up. She sits outside the little house he rents and follows him to his girlfriend's place, sometimes sitting in the parking lot if Gabe takes Darla out to eat.

"I assume you at least talk to Gabe."

She casts a critical eye at her bright-red fingernails. "Our conversations are strictly business. And if his friends had any respect for me, theirs would be, too."

Her glare at me is so intense that I have to tamp down an impulse to take a couple of steps back.

"Well, I hope things work out." I tip my hat and scoot out of there.

Cookie Travers gives me Jessica Reinhardt's address and tells me she rents a house with another girl. When I arrive at the house, Jessica comes to her door barefoot, wearing baggy sweatpants and a sweatshirt. Her face is blotchy and her eyes red and weepy. Her limp hair is pushed behind her ears.

"Why do you want to talk to me?" Her voice is dull and hopeless.

"I understand that you worked for Gary Dellmore. I'm hoping you might be able to give me a little background."

She shrugs. "Come on in."

The living room is a girl's lair, the coffee table strewn with fashion magazines and dirty dishes. An open box of cookies sits next to paraphernalia for doing nails. Jessica plops onto the sofa, reaches over, and closes a bottle of nail polish. The TV is turned to a soap opera, and she grabs the remote and turns it down.

"What do you want to know?"

I take a saggy armchair near her. I suspect most of the furniture is cast-offs from the girls' families. "Tell me what Gary was like as a boss."

Her eyes fill with tears. "I could never imagine a nicer boss. He was so wonderful."

"Cookie Travers said you had a problem with him."

"What? I didn't have any problem at all! He was really sweet to me."

"But there was a question of him harassing you?"

Outrage wipes away her pain. "That's ridiculous! Cookie seems to think she's my mother. Gary didn't harass me. So what if he paid attention to me? I don't see what the big deal was."

"Cookie told you that your behavior wasn't suitable for the office, though."

Her eyes widen. "God! I can't believe she told you that. She's such a frustrated old maid."

"Did you and Gary see each other outside of work?"

Her eyes are suddenly guarded. "No. I mean . . . like, okay, once, but nothing happened."

She doesn't even realize how inappropriate it was for Dellmore to see her outside work. He had at least twenty-five years on her and was married to boot. "Did he come here?"

She presses her knuckles to her mouth and nods.

"Did you invite him or did he show up?" I keep my voice gentle.

She starts to chew a nail and then grabs it away from her mouth with her other hand. "I don't want to get Gary in trouble."

He can't be in any worse trouble. "He came by here?"

She nods.

"He was friendly."

"Yes, he was so sweet." Her lips are trembling. "I can't believe he's dead."

"What did you two talk about when he was here?"

"Nothing. Work. He asked me if I was happy at work, if I liked it there. He was always interested in what I had to say." She sits forward, eager to convince me of his good intentions. "He liked to kid around, you know? He made me feel . . . valued." In that moment, I see what appealed to Dellmore. Animated, her face is pretty, her blue eyes round and innocent.

"I have to ask you: Were the two of you involved sexually?"

She jerks back as if I've slapped her. "No!"

"When you talked, did he seem worried about anything?"

The momentary light in her eyes flickers out. She shakes her head. "No, and . . . he wouldn't have told me anyway. We just goofed around. My roommate was in her room, so . . ."

I can't help thinking she was lucky her roommate was here.

She glances over at the TV screen. The sound is muted. On the screen a man and woman are standing too close together for real life, and by the look of it they are angry with each other.

"Did Gary flirt with other girls at the bank?"

Jessica pulls her attention back away from the TV. "He was friendly to everybody. Everybody liked him."

Somebody didn't. "Were you jealous of him flirting?"

She picks at her nails, catches herself again, and balls her hands into fists. "Why would I be jealous? It wasn't like we were dating or anything . . . like, you know, he was married."

CHAPTER 10

Marietta Bryant is walking out the door when I pull up at Grange Realty. "I've got to drive out to look at a lot ten miles outside of town. Why don't you come with me and we'll talk on the way?" I've never seen her dressed anyway but "up." Today she's wearing a white blouse with the collar turned up and a modest black skirt and high heels. She always wears gold jewelry: chains and small button earrings.

She drives a big SUV that she has to hoist herself up into, and she looks like a doll behind the wheel. "My husband usually drives this. It's a gas hog and he had to drive to Houston today, so he took my Toyota." She says she's gotten used to the big car. She and her husband live on a little farm on the outskirts of town and they need a big car to haul things around in.

I tell her it's hard for me to imagine her mucking around on a farm. She turns sparkling eyes to me. "Oh, I can wear jeans and a sweatshirt with the best of them. But mucking around? Forget it! I told my husband when we got married that I wasn't doing anything that would break my nails." The glee in her eyes tells me she's probably teasing.

She's equal to the task of driving the SUV, wheeling out of the lot like it's a sports car. We head across the railroad tracks and into pastureland studded with the occasional rustic home. Before we've gone half a mile, her cell phone chirps. She glances at it, pushes a button, and slips it back into the holder between the seats like a gunslinger.

It's relaxing to be in the passenger seat for a change, and Marietta points out various lots for sale and talks up plans people have for upgrading the area.

I ask her the same thing I asked Reinhardt. Did she hear or see anything suspicious when she left the night of the meeting?

75

"It seems like I'm always in a rush, and that night I left there like I was driving to a fire. I had to meet a client and sign some papers before it got too late. There could have been twenty extra cars there, or none at all, and I wouldn't have paid any attention."

"Fair enough. Now let me ask you something. Did you see this thing coming with Alton Coldwater?"

She glances over at me. She's driving fast, but she knows what she's doing. "No way I could have. I only got my hands on the books a few months ago and by then the damage was done. Alton kept dancing around, putting Rusty and me off until Rusty insisted he turn over the books. When I got them in front of me, I realized why he was reluctant."

She slows down and turns onto a gravel road. There's a lot of scrub brush here and few trees, but farther up the road I see a stand of post oak.

"Anyway, I tried juggling numbers every way I could, but last month I had to tell Rusty the town was going under."

"Some people think we should be charging Coldwater with a crime," I say. "What do you think?"

The road is rough, so she slows down. She glances over at me again. "We could probably make a case that he was negligent, but nobody has the heart for it. What good would it do? It's not like Alton is rolling in money. Do you really want to see him go to jail?"

"I guess not. But I want to know why Coldwater put the town's money in such a cock-eyed idea as a water park."

She slows down and pulls over to the side of the road, then puts the car in idle. Turning to face me, she says, "That was my first question, but it's pretty clear what happened. When tax revenues got so bad, he was looking for a way to make some money."

"Why did he think a water park would help? Seems to me it was a big gamble."

"The only thing I can think is that Alton was running scared and he ignored the risk because the possible returns seemed big enough to take care of our problems."

"Whose idea was it? And how did he persuade the city council to go along with it?"

"I don't really know. You'll have to ask Alton."

"Can you tell me who handled the sale of the land?"

"I did. I've got all the contracts back at the office, if you want to see them. Now let me look at this property so we can get on back. I've got an appointment in a little while."

She takes a hand-drawn map out of the side pocket of the door and studies it. "I think that's the gate right there." She points a hundred feet up the road and slowly pulls up to it. "We'll see if the combination I have opens this lock." She hops out before I can offer and within minutes she swings the gate open. When she drives through, I get out to close the gate, glad I don't have to favor my knee like I used to.

We drive down a rutted road. "Would you look at that!" She points to the right of the car. "These oil companies come in here like they own the whole world. They drill test wells and say they're going to put in roads and clean up after themselves. And they leave a big mess."

I wouldn't call it a big mess, but there is a pile of scrap metal and PVC pipe. And the road is not much of an improvement over bare ground.

"What do you think of this acreage?" she says. She tells me it's thirty acres that's never been farmed or had cattle run on it.

There are a lot of trees on the land, and it would take some clearing if somebody wanted to use it. "I don't know why somebody would want it," I say. "You sure wouldn't be able to feed cattle on it. Goats, maybe. And it's pretty far from town."

"My thinking exactly." We get out and walk around. The soil around these parts has a lot of clay in it, not the best soil for farming. To put in any kind of crop at all, you'd have to haul rocks out and supplement the soil. After fifteen minutes she says she's seen all she needs to see. "The old man who owned this died last year. I expect the son will be disappointed that it isn't going to be worth as much as he thought."

"I thought there were going to be some homes put in out here. That could make it worth something."

"Could be." She smiles. "Where'd you hear that?"

"I couldn't tell you. Are you holding out on the seller?"

Now she laughs. "Everybody thinks we realtors have something up our sleeve. For ten years or more I've heard rumors that a development is going to be built out here, and nothing has come of it yet. It goes to show you, everybody's always trying to make something out of nothing."

When we're back in the car and on our way, I say, "I have one more question about the water park. It seems to me the state would have to okay something like that. Did you run across any information about permits or licenses?"

She frowns. "I don't remember anything like that, but I was going over the financial end of things. It's probably in separate folders. I expect Rusty can find that for you."

Marietta glances at her dashboard clock. "Oh, shoot! That took longer than I thought it would. I'm supposed to meet a client for a signing. It's kind of exciting. She's moving here from Houston to open a store in that new block downtown. I guess poor Alton was right to put money into street renovations. She's the third new business that's coming in."

"You mean Ellen Forester? I met her at the bank this morning. She seems excited to move in and get started."

"Yes, but I'm worried she's picked the wrong town for her store."

"Why do you say that?"

"Because she's doing some kind of arty thing. I don't know how much business she'll have here. But you're right—being in real estate, I ought to be happy for new business of any kind. Between you and me I'm not sure she's in it for the money anyway. Seems like she has plenty."

A small Honda ahead of us pulls into the Grange Realty parking lot. "There she is," Marietta says.

Marietta parks and starts to open her door but pauses and looks back at me, her sudden good cheer gone. "Samuel, I don't know if I should tell you this, but Jim Krueger has been talking behind your back."

"He's mad that James Harley is out of a job," I say. "Can't blame him."

"I suppose, but he seems to have built it into some kind of personal grudge. You might want to tread softly there." Then her smile lights up again. "Listen to me! Telling you how to do your business. You let me know if you want to see the contracts on that land deal."

CHAPTER 11

Marietta's words send me straight to the high school to nose out Jim Krueger's complaint. When you're investigating a crime, you don't let sleeping dogs lie. A police chief is obligated to poke sleeping dogs.

It's after hours, but I suspect that high school principals don't keep banker's hours. Krueger's receptionist is packing up for the day, but she buzzes him for me. Being in this office gives me a touch of nostalgia. Jeanne worked here for twenty years as a receptionist while also being a sounding board for kids who needed an ear.

At least Krueger doesn't play the game of keeping me waiting. I've barely sat down in one of the uncomfortable straight-backed chairs designed to intimidate wayward students when two hangdog teenage boys come slinking out of Krueger's office and he motions me inside.

Krueger's shorter than his son, with thinning hair that he wears a little too long. James Harley already has a bowling ball gut, and when you look at his daddy you can see who he inherited it from. Jim's gut pokes out over his pants and strains the buttons of his shirt. He peers out of his dark-rimmed glasses like he's lost his way. Although he looks like somebody teenagers would make fun of, people say he's popular with the high school kids. That probably means he's fair. He points me to a chair and sits down behind his desk.

Normally, I'd lead in with a little small talk, but Krueger's tight manner with me discourages chat. As soon as we're seated, I say, "Jim, I wanted to follow up on our conversation yesterday. I've taken this position as police chief as a temporary fix to the financial situation. I have no intention of beating your son out of his job."

Krueger's shoulders slump. "I know that. I had a good, long talk with myself last night when I got home. It wasn't right for me to take it out on you. Like everybody said, we're lucky to have you. And quite frankly I'm not sure James Harley is cut out for police work anyway. I think he ought to look into other jobs."

I can't put up a big argument to that. "He's young. He'll find his place before too long."

"Not that young. He's over thirty."

"Knowing he was going to lose his job, James Harley's ego is probably a little scalded. If you think it might help, I'll be glad to talk to him."

"I doubt that would work out, but I appreciate the offer."

I nod. "Down to business: I'm trying to get to the bottom of what happened to Gary Dellmore."

Krueger sits back. "And you think I can help you?"

"I'm questioning everybody who was at the meeting the other night." I ask if he remembers hearing or seeing anything notable after the meeting.

He shakes his head. "I had James Harley's situation on my mind and I wasn't thinking about anything else."

"I heard Dellmore talking to someone around the side of the building when I was leaving, but I don't know who it was," I say. "Any ideas?"

"Hold on a minute." Krueger leans back and looks at the ceiling for a couple of seconds, smoothing his belly with his hands. "As I was walking out, I heard Rusty Reinhardt say he'd like a word with Dellmore. But whether or not they went outside to talk, I don't know. Have you talked to Reinhardt yet?"

Reinhardt didn't mention that he met Dellmore after the meeting, so I dodge the question. "I'll have to ask him whether they talked. If you think of anything more, let me know."

I get up. We shake hands, and Krueger sees me to the door, friendlier than when I walked in.

As I put my hand on the knob, Krueger says, "There is one more thing. I don't know if I should even mention it. It's something my wife heard in confidence. But with Dellmore being killed, you ought to at least be aware of it."

I turn back to him. "I appreciate any help you can give me."

"My wife is friends with Cookie Travers, who works down at the bank. Cookie told her that Alan Dellmore had had it with Gary. Ever since Gary came to work for his dad, the bank has steadily lost customers."

"That's been several years." Since I'm one of the customers they lost, it's no surprise to me.

"Yes, Cookie said it's a steady trickle. Apparently she had private talks with some of the customers who left. They said Gary didn't keep their financial affairs confidential. Cookie said she was worried the bank was losing too many customers."

"Well, I'll look into that. Thank you for mentioning it."

It's possible that Alan and Gary Dellmore had an argument that got out of hand, but it's hard for me to picture Alan pulling a gun on his son and killing him, no matter how mad he was.

Zeke Dibble came on duty at noon, so I swing by the station to see how his afternoon has gone. I meant to check in earlier and haven't made the time.

Zeke's playing solitaire, cards laid out on the desk. He doesn't pick them up when I walk in.

"Something tells me it's been a nice, quiet day," I say.

Zeke is only a few years older than me, but he looks like life has used him a lot harder. Deep lines etch his pale face and his hair is a dull color of gray, giving him a sickly look. If you were meeting him for the first time, you'd want to send him to the doctor—but he's looked like that ever since he moved here.

"Quiet except for Plymouth O'Connor calling to complain that neighbor boys are tearing up her yard." Plymouth is one of three maiden sisters, all named after cars, who live together. One of them always has a complaint. Often over the years when they have gotten no satisfaction from the police, they've called me. I think their complaining is a way of passing the time when they get bored.

"What did you tell her?"

"I told her you'd call her back, but that you had a lot on your hands right now and it may take some time."

"Zeke, you think this is something you can take care of tomorrow?"

He chuckles. "I don't see why not." He picks up his cards, slips the deck into his desk drawer and gets up from his chair. "I ought to be heading home. My wife will have a fit if she has to keep dinner waiting."

After he leaves I look around at what I've inherited. I've been here off and on since they built the new station, but I never noticed how much Rodell had let it run down. There's a bank of file cabinets against one wall, but there appear to be more files stacked on top of the cabinets than inside. The desks are metal and should have stood up to the wear better than they have. They could use a good scrubbing—or maybe they could use replacing. Except the city is bankrupt, and I bet new desks for the police station is pretty far down the list of necessities. I lock up and head for the Walmart, twenty minutes away, on the outskirts of Bobtail. That's as good a place as any to find a cell phone.

CHAPTER 12

A ngel Bright, Slate McClusky's wife, answers the door when I stop by at seven thirty. When Slate married Angel she was a country-and-western singer of some success. She kept her stage name when she married. I suspect it's a made-up name, but you never know.

"Hey, Samuel, what a nice surprise." She hasn't lost the flat, nasal accent of a west Texas gal. And she hasn't changed her looks from when she was on stage. She's wearing tight jeans and a rose-colored Western shirt with pearl snaps. Her long mane of fluffy hair brushes the tops of her breasts. "Come on in. It's time for a cocktail, and you look like you could use one."

"I could have a glass of something. Is Slate around?"

"He should be home any time now. He called me when he left the resort an hour ago." McClusky owns a resort west of here, in the hill country, that stocks exotic game and puts up hunters in fancy surroundings. They say he gets a lot of clients from all over the country willing to pay his prices.

I follow Angel into the living room, aware of the way she swivels her hips as she sashays across the room. I catch myself staring and make a conscious effort to look elsewhere.

There is a fire going in the huge fireplace, and hanging above it is a painting that immediately draws my attention. I move close and see that it's a Frederic Remington. I assume it's real because it's got a substantial frame and a little light shining on it. Even though I long ago turned my interest to modern art, I still like the Western painters. This is a good example of Remington, with the horses and cattle and riders all looking like they could step out of the picture and ride into the sunset.

"You like that picture?" she says.

"I do. Remington has such a good touch with the brush that he makes it look effortless. And he has a keen eye for a scene. Gives you a real feel for the Old West."

She looks surprised and inspects the picture as if it never occurred to her that someone actually painted it. "I like it too. I don't know anything about art, but Slate told me that picture is worth a pretty penny."

I've never been to the McCluskys' house before. The room looks like a decorator's idea of a Western home—two big puffy sofas covered in a fabric with a cactus theme sit on either side of the fireplace. A coffee table as big as a car, set on wagon wheels, separates the two sofas. Angel goes over to a massive piece of furniture that, when she opens the door, turns out to be a bar. "I'm having Scotch," she says. I tell her I'll take a little bourbon. "Just two fingers. I'm not much of a drinker."

"Me neither. It's bad for the voice." I don't know why she'd care since as far as I know she hasn't sung in several years. She pours both of us a lot more than two fingers and reaches into a little refrigerator inside the cabinet and adds ice to the drinks.

She hands me my glass and then clinks hers to mine. "Let's sit down and get to know one another better while we wait for Slate."

I like women and usually don't have any trouble talking to them, but for some reason I feel awkward with Angel. She has a sort of sly way of looking at me, with a lazy, knowing smile that unsettles me.

We sit down across from each other on either side of the fireplace. She tucks her legs up next to her, thrusts her chest out, and tosses her hair back behind her. I can imagine her up on a stage, calculating her moves to draw the interest of her audience.

"I don't know why me and Slate have never gotten to know you." The words are friendly, but the way she looks at me, I'm aware that my pants and shirt are a little worn and my hat is a little the worse for wear.

"You all travel around a good bit, and I guess we don't cross paths. Remind me: how long have you had this place in Jarrett Creek?"

"Ten years."

"You're from west Texas, right?"

"Lubbock."

"And where did Slate grow up?"

"Midland." I recall that Slate's mamma left his daddy when Slate was a little boy and took Slate out west. Slate's daddy stayed on in Jarrett Creek. When his daddy died everyone expected Slate to sell the old house. But he sent out a construction crew to renovate the place, and since then they've come here for several months every year. They usually spend winter in their place in Vail. I don't know what's keeping them here.

"How did you two meet?"

"He wangled a backstage introduction after one of my concerts. Now that's enough about us. It's your turn."

"Not much to tell. I grew up here, went to college at A&M, spent a couple of years in the air force, then moved back and settled down with my wife."

"Oh, that's right. Your wife died a while back. I'm sorry. What was she like?"

Angel's got a trick of conversation that would suit a police investigator, asking open-ended questions. But when I ask her anything, she replies with the shortest possible answer. My guess is she developed it when she was well known, as a way of protecting her privacy.

"She was a fine woman. I think you would've liked her," I say.

She rakes her hair back in a careless motion. "I imagine so."

I can do open-ended questions, too. "What drew you and Slate to put down some roots here? I would have thought you might want to stay around Lubbock, where you've got family."

"Family." She says the word like it's got a sour taste to it. "Yeah, I've got family, but not much of anybody I wanted to spend a lot of time with. Slate wanted to come back here, and that was fine with me. You need a refresher?"

"I'm good."

"If you don't mind, I'm going to have another one." She slides off the sofa and heads for the bar.

"Slate's dad had another son by his second wife," I say. "Do you and Slate keep up with him?"

"Yes, we do. He actually runs our game resort out near Blanco."

"What's his name?"

"Harold. He's several years younger than Slate. They don't have a lot in common." I recall that something was not quite right with Harold and he got shipped off to a special school when he was a boy.

I glance at my watch. "Maybe before Slate gets here, I can ask you a couple of things. I'm here because I'm investigating Gary Dellmore's death."

Angel is turned away from me, refilling her glass. Her shoulders go rigid. "Oh, that was awful." She turns around but stays standing by the bar, stirring her drink with her finger. "Why would somebody shoot Gary? He was a really sweet man. Was it a robbery? Was he carrying a lot of money?"

"It doesn't appear to be a robbery."

She frowns. "You wanted to talk to Slate? What would he have to do with it? He hardly knew Gary."

"Slate was at the meeting we had the night Dellmore was killed."

"Oh, that's right." She rattles the ice and downs her second round of Scotch.

"Dellmore was killed sometime after the meeting, and I'm checking with everybody to see if they might've noticed anything unusual."

She swirls the ice cubes in the glass. "Slate isn't exactly the type of person to notice much." She looks over at me with an eyebrow arched. It's pretty clear that she's telling me Slate doesn't pay much attention to her. That's not a street I'm willing to travel down.

I push myself up from the sofa over the protests of my healing knee. This time of night, after as much activity as I've had today, the knee has had enough. "It's getting late. I'm going to go on home and catch up with Slate later."

"Oh, don't go." There's a kind of begging sound to her voice, but she takes a few steps in the direction of the door, as if inviting me to leave.

I leave my drink on the table. "I'll tell you what. When Slate comes in ask him to call me, even if it's late."

"I could call his cell phone and see where he is. He might've had to stop somewhere." I think of my new cell phone waiting to trip me up with instructions when I get home.

"That's all right. No need to bother him. Just ask him to call."

As I pass through from the living room into the foyer, I notice two framed gold records on the wall, more discreet than I would have expected. There's one for each of Angel Bright's two hit recordings, "I Just Called to Say Remember When" and "Too Late to Head Home." Next to them hangs a framed poster, announcing a comeback tour to be kicked off in Nashville, dated last spring. I don't remember hearing about the tour. Although I don't keep up with celebrities, I'm sure it would've made a big stir in Jarrett Creek, and I would've heard about it if it had taken place.

Back home I feel restless, even though it's late. I sit down at my kitchen table, determined to decipher the instructions to the cell phone and learn how to use it. It's not as daunting as I thought it might be, although I'm prepared for it to surprise me in the future by doing something I hadn't planned for.

When I'm ready for bed, I sit on the side of the bed and try to confront the unsettled thought that has been poking me at odd times during the day. Something about these fellows cheating on their wives has me annoyed. But it's not a moral thing; it's something tied up with my knee. I go back into the kitchen and get a cold pack out of the freezer. While I ice the knee, I let my thoughts roll where they will. Eventually, I come around to the core of it. Gabe LoPresto and Gary Dellmore

DEAD BROKE IN JARRETT CREEK

don't value their wives. I valued mine and she isn't here anymore. That ties in with my knee in an odd way. I think I had some notion that once the knee was all fixed up, everything else would be fine, too. But that isn't possible. Even with a knee as good as new, Jeanne is gone and there's no recovery from that.

90

CHAPTER 13

I wake up even earlier than usual Friday morning. A cold, spooky fog is hovering close to the ground when I go down to the pasture to see to my cows. The fog makes everything seem a little unreal. Even the sound of my cattle lowing is flat and tamped down.

When I get back to the house, I'm happy to hear Loretta calling out at my screen door. She's brought coffee cake and we sit down at the kitchen table to drink a cup of coffee.

"You'll never guess what's happened."

"Spill it," I say, after I've eaten my first mouthful.

"Gabe LoPresto has taken off with that girl from the bank."

I almost choke on my coffee. "What do you mean, taken off?"

"Apparently the girl didn't show up for work yesterday morning. Everybody figured she didn't know the bank would be open as usual. Then this morning she called and said she was off for a few days with Gabe. Can you imagine calling your work and just saying you won't be in?"

"Did LoPresto tell anybody where he was going?"

"That wasn't in the information I got. I can tell you that everybody is wondering what's going on, though. Are they eloping?"

"That's hardly likely since as far as I know LoPresto is still married."

Loretta looks like she has more to say but thinks better of it. She sips her coffee and looks around with a critical eye. "Samuel, I haven't wanted to say anything, but you could use somebody to come in and clean once a week."

I look around the kitchen. I'm surprised. "I don't think I need anybody. I'm doing fine. You've got higher standards than me, that's all."

"How often do you dust?"

"You've got somebody in mind who needs a job, don't you?"

91

Of course she does. And she says she wants me to let the woman come in one morning a week "because she needs the money."

"I don't like the idea of somebody I don't know coming in here."

"You'll get used to it. She's nice and quiet. She won't bother you."

I tell her I'll think it over.

It seems prudent to change the subject, and I've got the perfect subject. "I met the new woman who's opening the art store downtown."

"Oh, I heard there was going to be a new store. The owner's name is Ellen Forester." Loretta likes to know things, so she trots the name out as if it gives her points. "What does she look like?"

"She's . . ." I pause. What does she look like? "I don't know. She looks good. She's got brown hair and eyes. Seemed friendly."

"Samuel, you could be describing a dog. Is she fat? Thin? Does she have a nice smile? What did she say?"

"You'll see her soon enough. She's having some work done on the space she's rented."

"What kind of work? They just got done renovating that building."

"I don't know. Go down there and ask her. She'll probably be glad somebody is interested."

Her sigh is long-suffering.

"Okay. No, she's not fat," I say. "She's regular size. And she was very nice, all ten words that she said to me."

"Like what?"

"She said she'd like to see my art collection."

She nods. "That makes sense. What kind of art is she going to have in the store?"

"She didn't say, but she mentioned she was also going to have painting workshops."

"Workshops? I don't know who she thinks is going to do that." Then she catches herself being snippy. "But I suppose we'll see. I surely hope she succeeds. Ida Ruth told me she's starting over because she got divorced recently."

"We didn't discuss that," I say. "Listen, I've got to get going." I stand up.

"You didn't tell me what you found out about what happened to poor Gary Dellmore."

"That's going to have to wait for another time."

"All right, then. I guess you've got to keep things under your hat." She gets up and starts toward the door.

"One thing." I stop her, and it seems like what I have to say is momentous. "I got myself a cell phone. You want the number?"

"A cell phone. What do you want with that?"

"Since I'm going to be the law around here, people will expect me to be available."

"I hadn't thought of that. I guess you're right. But now everybody is going to think you're at their beck and call night and day."

I write down the number and she looks at it like it's written in Sanskrit, but she tucks it into the pocket of her skirt.

Bill Odum is already at the police station when I get there and looks relieved to see me. "This came in," he says, thrusting a fax at me before I can even sit down.

It's a preliminary autopsy report from a doctor whose name I don't recognize, affiliated with the hospital in Bobtail. It says the bullet that killed Gary Dellmore was most likely a .45. I point it out to Odum and say, "You got the caliber right. Only problem is half the people in town have a .45 stashed away somewhere."

I tell him to pull up a chair next to my desk, and I fill him in on who I talked to yesterday and what I learned. "So," I wind up, "we know that Dellmore was killed with a .45-caliber weapon, his car is missing, he was playing fast and loose with Jessica Reinhardt down at the office, his daddy was fed up with his behavior, and his wife had every right to be. Plus, Alton Coldwater claims Dellmore had a hand in pushing the city to invest in the water park deal."

Odum grimaces. "Dellmore didn't exactly make himself popular.

93

Makes you wonder why a man who has everything acts that way." He searches my face as if I might have some bright idea I'm not divulging. Suddenly he laughs. "I always got in trouble when I was in police training for making observations like that. They told me if I was so interested in motivation, I ought to study psychology."

"It always seemed to me that a big part of being a cop is knowing what made people tick," I say.

"I like that. It suits me." He rubs his hands together. "How are we going to proceed today?"

"I'd like you to find out more about the outfit that went broke out at the lake. See if they had any hard feelings about the way Dellmore handled the financial end of things. You know how to locate them?"

"I'll ask Marietta Bryant. She must know something, since she's the city administrator."

Oscar Grant doesn't open the Two Dog Bar until ten a.m., but I go around back and find him next to his truck wrestling a keg onto a dolly. I hold the backdoor while he wheels the dolly inside and follow him in, noticing that the floor seems to be tilting more than I remembered.

"Oscar, if this building leans any more, one of these nights it's going to tip right over."

Oscar looks around like he hasn't noticed the state of the building. He moved here and bought the bar from the previous owner a dozen years ago. I know he's divorced and has a daughter, but he's close with his private life. He runs a tight ship, though. He lets people act up just so far before he runs them out of the Two Dog. "I suppose I ought to get some work done on the building. But I have to win the lottery before it comes to that."

"You play the lottery?" He sells lottery tickets and alcohol, and since I rarely see him drink, I suspect he doesn't indulge in gambling much, either.

"No, come to think of it, I guess I don't. So that eliminates the possibility of me winning." He snorts, the closest I've ever seen to him laughing. "You didn't come here to inspect my building. Let me make some coffee and you can tell me what you want."

Coffee in hand, I sit down at the bar. "I want your take on this business with Gary Dellmore. You hear things at the bar. Did you ever hear anybody say they carried a grudge against him, anything like that?"

Oscar takes his time, pouring enough sugar into his cup so that the spoon could stand up on its own, and then stirring while he contemplates my question. "I don't really attract a banking clientele here. But I've been keeping company with a woman who told me something a while back—I don't know if it's of any use, but it did have to do with Dellmore." He frowns and keeps on stirring.

"What did she say?"

"She said Dellmore bragged to her that he was making a lot of money in this water park deal. She didn't get any details because she wasn't particularly interested in Jarrett Creek's water park. But she said he acted like it was a big secret, and she wondered why a banker would need to keep his part of a banking deal secret."

"Who's this woman you're dating and how did she know Dellmore?"

He grins. "I don't know that you'd call it dating. We don't go out on dates and I don't see her that often. She lives over in Bobtail. She's a nurse. She doesn't know Dellmore. She said he was in the hospital having a little procedure done and they got to talking when he was still a little loopy from the anesthesia. She said a lot of people blab all kinds of things when they're coming out of anesthesia. I'm pretty sure she shouldn't have told me. She probably never figured I would have occasion to pass the information on to anybody. So if it's all the same to you, I'd rather nobody knew where you heard it."

"I can't think of a reason anybody would need to know." Or even if the information is relevant.

Now that I know Dellmore was killed with a .45, I have to ask everybody I talk to if they own one, even though I may not get the truth. When I ask Oscar, he reaches under the bar and pulls out a shotgun I've seen him brandish a couple of times. "This 12-gauge is all I need. Makes people nervous when they see a shotgun staring at them."

I'm not due to meet Bill Odum back at headquarters for another hour, so I have time to corner Slate McClusky. I hope I don't run into Angel again, but when I ring the doorbell, there's no answer at all.

I'm turning to leave when a horn toots. Truly Bennett pulls to the curb and climbs out of his pickup, which is even older than mine. Truly and I go way back to when I was chief of police and got him out of some trouble. He is widely respected in the county for his ability to deal with livestock. If there's such a thing as a cow whisperer, it's Truly. Cattlemen often hire him to move their cows to auction or to help buy stock. He's a good judge of cows and seems to know instinctively if there's something wrong with one. When I had to be away for several days for knee surgery, I left Truly in charge of my cows and didn't worry about them for one minute.

"Good to see you, Chief Craddock. What are you up to?"

"I guess you heard they've got me back at work."

"I did hear that. Seems it's all to the good for the rest of us."

After we shake hands he goes around to the back of his pickup and lowers the tailgate. He takes out a ladder and lays it on the sidewalk.

"You heard that Gary Dellmore was murdered?" I say.

"Yes, sir. I didn't know Mr. Dellmore, but then I don't have a lot of use for banks." He continues to work as we talk, pulling out paint cans, brushes, and tarps and setting them on the sidewalk.

"What are you up to?"

"You know I do a little painting on the side when the cattle business is slow, and Mr. McClusky hired me to repaint the east side of his house while they're gone." He points to the house. "The east side always gets a lot stronger sunlight and needs painting a little more often."

"Gone? When are they leaving?"

"Nobody was here when I got here this morning, so I guess they already left."

"Do you know where they were going?"

He scratches his head. "I'm not sure. He hired me last week and said they'd be out of here by today and I should get started."

"Did he say how long he'd be gone?"

"No, sir."

Now why didn't Angel tell me yesterday that she and Slate were leaving today? I don't know whether it's suspicious or if she was simply careless.

Truly grins as I help him with the last of the cans. "Looks like that operation you had turned out okay. You're moving around pretty good."

"Should have done it a lot earlier. Stubborn."

I go next door to find out if anybody knows where the McCluskys have gone. Nobody is home at the big house next door, and the house on the other side has been vacant since Scooter Jefferson died. But across the street Camille Overton is home and invites me in for a cup of coffee. She's a tall, brisk woman with a ready smile. According to Loretta, Camille is a force in the Baptist Church ladies' group.

"Usually I'd take you up on the coffee, Camille, but I'm a little pressed for time. Do you have any idea where Angel and Slate have gone?"

She peers across the street. "I don't have my glasses on. Who is that man in their yard?"

"That's Truly Bennett. He's doing some painting for McClusky."

"Oh, that's all right then. Angel called me last night. She was supposed to come over this morning, but said she and Slate were going out to the resort for a few days. They left early this morning."

"Do you happen to know their phone number out there?"

"Yes, I do. Let me get it for you."

She's back in a few minutes with a slip of paper with two phone numbers on it. She points to one of the numbers. "That second one is Angel's cell phone. She said the phone might not be working out at the resort, and if anything comes up I should try both numbers. I keep an eye on the house when they're not here."

If Slate and Angel decided just last night that they were going to the resort, why did Slate tell Truly last week that they'd be gone? And why didn't Slate call me? If it was too late when he got home last night, he could have called this morning.

I try both numbers Camille gave me for the McCluskys, and no one answers either of them. I don't like it. I decide to drive out to the resort to see if I can catch up with them.

I stop by the station to tell Odum what I'm up to. He jumps up when I walk in. "I was going to call you. I've got a problem. My dad called and asked if there was any way I could help him for a couple of hours. I could come back this afternoon."

"Sure, go on ahead. There's nothing that can't wait. Zeke can be on call if anything comes up."

"I'll be back as soon as I can."

"How did everything go with Marietta?"

"She was out on a real estate appointment, so I didn't get a chance to talk to her. The girl down at the office said she'd have Marietta call me when she got back, but then my dad phoned."

I tell him I'm on my way out to Blanco to see if I can ferret out McClusky.

"Blanco's a long way."

"It is. I may be wasting my time, but it doesn't sit well when somebody tries to avoid me."

There's another reason I want to go out there. I've never seen McClusky's resort. I've always heard it's for people with a lot of money, not the kind of thing people around here can afford—and wouldn't do if they could. When Jarrett Creek folks go hunting, they do it to put meat on the table—and they don't need to go to a fancy resort to do it. I'd like to get a good look at the place.

Before I leave town, I open up the safe to see what kind of weapons the department has on hand. It's actually not a bad assortment and it looks like they've been kept up. Score one for Rodell. I take out a Colt and load it. I haven't used a gun for a while, and it's time I got back into shape with it. Maybe I'll have time to do a little target practice while I'm out in the country. I leave a note on the front door with my new cell phone number on it, telling anybody who comes by that we're all tied up this afternoon and to call me only if it's an emergency.

CHAPTER 14

When I get close to Blanco I start seeing faded signs advertising McClusky's Wild Range Resort. Slate McClusky ought to consider replacing the signs if he plans to keep up the reputation of having a fine resort, but maybe he wants to emphasize the "country" part of "hill country resort." The sign at the turnoff is shot up with bullet holes. It gives me the information that I've got a two-mile drive to my destination. I turn onto a rutted dirt road. I don't know what I was expecting when I headed out to McClusky's resort, but it was certainly something better than what I am seeing. The road is so rutted that it looks like it's gone through at least a couple of seasons with no maintenance. I'm forced to slow way down. At first I'm thinking the reason the road is a mess is that McClusky wants to give people who come here the idea that they're getting a legitimate wild-country experience, but then I notice that the fences are sagging in places. I heard they raise exotic game for sport hunting here—African and Asian antelope and even zebras. It's a good thing they don't keep buffalo, because one of those big creatures could charge right through the fence in a couple of places. But soon I realize I'm not seeing any animals at all.

After being jostled around in my truck for ten minutes, I turn onto a paved driveway, and soon an imposing structure comes into view. The main lodge is what you'd call elegant rustic—or at least it used to be. The huge, two-story rock and wood building surrounded by a wide wooden deck has fallen on the rustic side of things. The dark-green trim on the building is faded and chipped and the deck in need of a new coat of paint. The only thing that doesn't look the worst for wear is a massive rock chimney that suggests there's a castle-sized fireplace.

A weathered sign over the porch says, "The Big House." A sign to the left side of the building points to "Spa" in one direction and "Pool" in the other. Off to the right I glimpse wood cabins scattered among the trees.

Somebody went to a lot of expense on the landscaping in the past. It's now overgrown and weedy. A big flowerbed surrounded by the circular driveway contains a lot of dead stalks. Dead or dying ornamental plants and weeds have taken over the large terra cotta pots on the steps of the Big House entrance.

Slate's Chevy Tahoe is sitting in front of the main house. I'm about to open the door of my truck when a big man with gorilla arms and a worried expression comes from around back and strides over to me. "We're closed."

"I'm looking for Slate and Angel."

"They ain't here."

"That's Slate's SUV."

He pauses for a second, looking at the SUV as if puzzled. "They took the Cadillac." His speech cadence is a little off.

"You mind if I get out and stretch my legs?" I open the door and ease out. I walk around and stretch my arms over my head while he watches as if he thinks I might suddenly dart past him and make a run for the house.

"You know when they plan to be back?"

He scratches his head. "Slate didn't tell me. He said him and Angel were going to get some barbecue."

"My name is Samuel Craddock. I'm the chief of police over in Jarrett Creek, and I need to discuss something with them."

He squints at me and for a minute there's no sign that he recognizes my name, but then a lightbulb goes on. "I remember you. My daddy liked you." His smile and voice are childlike, and suddenly I understand the "something that wasn't quite right" that used to be said about him.

"Yes, I remember your daddy," I say. "He's been gone a long time."

"Yes, he died."

"Where do Slate and Angel usually go to get barbecue?"

"They went into Blanco, and they're going to bring me some back."

"You're Slate's brother, aren't you? Harold is it?"

"Yes, I'm Slate's foreman." He says it proudly.

"Harold, you have cell phone service out here?"

"No. A lot of people who used to come out here said they wished we did."

"Is there a phone in the house?" I nod toward the main building and take a few steps in that direction. "I'd like to call Slate."

"You can't go in there." His voice is suddenly loud.

"Beg pardon?"

"It's under construction and it's dangerous."

"Harold, I don't see any construction tools or vehicles around here, and if it's safe enough for Slate and Angel to go inside, it's safe enough for me to walk in and use the telephone."

"Slate told me not to let anybody inside."

"All right, I'll take your word for it. I'm going over to Blanco and see if I can locate them. What color is the Cadillac?"

"It's whitish."

Blanco isn't a large town and its biggest claim to eating fame is a big barbecue place called the Barbecue Palace. If the McCluskys have gone over to Blanco for lunch, that's likely where I'll find them.

I finally find a parking place in the half-acre lot and walk up to join the people lined up under the huge billboard of Carlton King, owner of the Barbecue Palace, wearing a wide grin and a gaudy crown. The line snakes past big brick pits with sheets of tin lying over them to hold in the smoke. At each pit there's a man stationed who periodically raises the tin and slops barbecue sauce over the grilling meat using long-handled cloth mops. When they lift the lid, the smell wafts out over the crowd and draws murmurs of appreciation. There's a stir of some kind going on up at the head of the line and I hear someone say, "Angel Bright."

I step out of line, walk up to the front, and find Angel holding court with several fans, middle-aged men and women thrusting pieces of paper for Angel to sign. "I can't believe y'all remember me," Angel says. She's dressed in a bright rose-colored shirt with her name spelled out in sequins, so it's no great surprise that they recognized her. Standing off to the side, Slate is favoring the fans with his indulgent smile, the same kind of look you'd have if you owned "best in show" at a county fair.

When I call Slate's name, he turns and I believe his look of surprise is genuine. His smile widens and he grabs my hand and pumps it. "If this doesn't beat everything! What are you doing here?"

Angel glances at me, and her look doesn't convey the welcome that Slate's does. But she recovers quickly. "Hey, nice to see you."

"You with anybody?" Slate says. "Why don't you join us?"

"I actually came out here looking for you," I say.

"For me? How'd you know I was here?"

Before I can speak, understanding dawns in his eyes and his smile falters.

"Your brother told me," I say.

"So you've seen what a mess he's made of my resort." He shakes his head, still smiling. "That's what you get when you leave things in somebody's hands and don't check up on them often enough. He may be my brother, but I can't say he's done a real good job."

"Isn't it terrible?" Angel chimes in. "Poor Slate almost had a heart attack when he got out there a few months ago and saw how Harold had run it into the ground."

Whatever made that resort lose ground didn't happen overnight. The ruin I saw took many months, or even years, of neglect. I'm wondering why poor Harold is taking the heat.

We step inside the cafe and the pungent smell of barbecue makes me put everything else aside for a while. Carlton King himself is behind the counter, looking like he's been sampling his own food a little more than is healthy. His big, booming voice touts the baby back ribs, brisket, chicken, and sausage.

"Well, if it isn't Miss Angel Bright," he booms. "Your order is on the house. These two jokers with you will have to pay for their own food, though." He laughs and Angel gives him her biggest smile. Slate grins and says, "I might know it! My little wife gets a freebie and I have to pay. But I'm going to pay for my friend Craddock, here, too."

Angel orders the chicken, and Slate and I go for the brisket and rib combo. All the plates come with big globs of potato salad. At the end of the line there's a vat of beans and tubs of jalapenos, raw onions, pickles, and three different kinds of barbecue sauce labeled "sweet," "spicy," and "too damn hot to be good for you."

We grab seats at one of the picnic tables set up behind the building. The early morning nip is gone, and the sun is warm and friendly. We have to put up with a couple more people who come over and tell Angel how much they love her music. One man, dressed all in black from boots to hat, hands Angel a card. "I do a little music producing. Why don't you call me if you're interested in a comeback tour."

Slate gets up abruptly. His smile is strained. "Thank you, but Angel isn't interested."

The man tips his finger to his hat. "No offense intended. Sorry, ma'am."

"Not a problem," Slate says. He sits back down, seeming oblivious to the effect the exchange has had on Angel. Her face has gone ashen and she's staring at her plate as if she mistakenly picked up a plate of rattlesnakes. When the man is out of earshot she says, "There was no need for you to be rude."

"Honey, I wasn't the one being rude. If somebody wants to make you an offer, they need to go through channels."

"What channels?" she says, eyes still on her plate.

"Let's don't get into it in front of Samuel. That's for us to work out privately." He turns to me with a smile that doesn't reach his eyes. "Tell me how the investigation is going. Have you figured out who killed that banker yet?"

That banker. As if he didn't know Gary Dellmore's name. We were all at the same meeting and you'd think McClusky had never met him. "Matter of fact, the reason I'm here is that I'm talking with everybody who was at the meeting the night Dellmore was killed. I went by your place this morning and someone told me they thought you'd come out here to your resort. I figured coming out this way to find you would be a clever way to get myself some decent barbecue, too."

"I don't understand why you didn't just call. Surely you could find my cell number."

"I did try. There wasn't any answer."

He snaps his fingers. "That's right. We sometimes have problems with cell coverage out at the resort."

I pick up one of the barbecue ribs and start gnawing on it. Angel is dabbling in her potato salad, leaving the chicken untouched.

Suddenly, the music changes and "I Just Called to Say Remember When," Angel's last big hit, comes blaring out of the big speakers on the roof.

"Listen, Slate, they're playing my music."

"I believe Carlton King has a crush on you," Slate says. He's back to being the indulgent uncle, and Angel is trying to retrieve her cheerful smile. Several people turn to look at her. She nods in time to the music, doing finger waves at people. When the song is over she says quietly, "I'm sick to death of that song."

Slate reaches over swiftly and grabs Angel's wrist. "Just remember the sound of money every time you hear it." He lets go and turns back to me. "Now what is it you came all the way out here to ask me?"

"I wanted to know if you saw or heard anything unusual as you were leaving the meeting the other night."

He gnaws a rib and when he puts it down says, "Like I said at the meeting, I don't remember anything but wanting to get home. I'm sorry you came all the way out here for that."

"It's all right. It's a nice drive." I eat a bite of brisket and then say, "Did you ever have any business dealings with Gary Dellmore?"

The plastic fork Angel has been poking into her potato salad stops moving. I can feel the tension radiating off her.

"I have had some dealings with him," Slate says, "but it didn't amount to much. Couple of small loans. I thought since I lived part-time in Jarrett Creek, I ought to throw some business to the bank there." He shakes his head, his smile rueful. "Can't say I was fond of him. He was something of a know-it-all."

"You own any guns?"

"Of course I do. Hunting rifles, a shotgun, that sort of thing."

"You own a .45-caliber handgun?"

McClusky considers. "No, I don't own any handguns. I'm a rifleman." He grins. "But Angel does, don't you, sugar? She kept one for her protection when she was a celebrity, and with me gone so much, I insist that she keep one in the bedside drawer. Can't have anybody coming in and hurting my girl, here. Why are you asking? You think I had some reason to be mad at Dellmore? He was pretty feisty at that meeting the other night." He laughs.

Angel gets up abruptly. "If you all will excuse me, I'll be right back. I need to powder my nose."

McClusky watches her leave, as do half a dozen other people sitting at tables around us. "Quite a woman," he says and winks at me.

"She had a good career," I say. "She didn't mind giving it up when she married you?"

McClusky shrugs. "I offered her a good bit more stability than the music business. But the real reason she gave it up is because her sweet little voice was slipping. Don't tell her I said so."

Despite McClusky's dewy-eyed smile, his words are biting and I feel like I've had a glimpse behind a curtain that should have stayed closed. I think about that poster I saw announcing a comeback—a comeback I don't remember actually happening. Maybe they had to cancel it because her voice wasn't up to it.

Slate wads up his napkin and throws it onto his plate. "Getting back to the subject, sounds like Dellmore was killed with a .45."

"That's right."

Angel slips back onto the bench across from us. "What are y'all talking about?"

"Maybe you better confiscate my wife's gun and have it tested." He laughs and nods in her direction. "Angel packs a Colt .45. She might have had a grudge against the banker that she's keeping secret from everybody."

Angel gets up from the table again, picks up her barely touched plate and dumps it into a nearby trashcan.

"A .45 is a big gun for a small woman," I say.

"She can handle it if she uses both hands." Angel has come back, and Slate says, "The idea is to have a gun that will stop somebody in his tracks. Didn't I tell you that, honey?"

Angel stares at him but doesn't reply. I get the feeling she's one step short of lashing out at him, though he doesn't seem to notice.

"Yes, I always say you can't ever be too careful," McClusky says.

"Slate, I'd like to go now," Angel says.

"Honey, I don't know if Samuel is done questioning us."

I get up off the bench and pick up my empty plate. "I've got a lot to do. Do you have a number where I can reach you out at the resort since the cell service isn't good out there?"

"Oh, we're not staying there. We always stay at a private condo at the Marriott out in Horseshoe Bay," Slate says. "You can reach us out there on our cell phones."

I'm happy to hit the road and get away from those two. There's something between them that feels off. Maybe they're just having a fight, but it feels like it goes deeper than that. Like for some reason they have begun to dislike each other and it poisons the air around them.

As I pass the turnoff to McClusky's resort on my way home, I have an urge to stop back by and insist that Harold let me go inside. Whatever is bothering the McCluskys extends to their resort as well: something is not right. Where are all the animals? Why did the resort go to seed the way it did? And what's inside the main building that Harold didn't want me to see?

CHAPTER 15

I'm half an hour from home when I hear a strange sound, as if the radio is tuned to a station that's playing some kind of electronic guitar music. Since the radio hasn't worked in some time, I'm especially puzzled. But the sound repeats itself, and I realize it's not coming from the radio but from my pocket. The cell phone. I didn't even notice what kind of sound the phone would make when I was setting it up.

I don't trust myself to drive and talk on the phone at the same time, so I pull over and take the thing out of my pocket and look at it. It's police headquarters calling.

I punch the button to take the call and hold the phone up to my ear, not quite trusting even yet that this contraption will give me the same ability to hear and speak that my home phone does. "This is Samuel Craddock."

"Chief Craddock, thank God, I've been trying to reach you. Where are you?" Bill Odum sounds frantic.

"I'll be back in town soon. What's going on?"

"I got back here an hour ago, and a call came in about a fender bender out at the dam road. Nobody was hurt, but somebody was driving by and said the two guys involved were getting heated up, and he thought we ought to go out there and get it sorted out. So I drove over, and you're never going to believe what happened."

"Don't keep me hanging here, Odum. Tell me."

"Well, sir, one of them was driving Gary Dellmore's car." There's a crackling on the line and I'm not sure I've heard him right.

"Did you say 'driving Dellmore's car'?"

"Yes, sir. A drifter who's been staying out at the lake. He's got some wild tale explaining how he came to be driving it."

"You didn't let him leave with the car, did you?"

"Heck no! I've got him in a holding cell here at the station, and Zeke is out at the dam keeping an eye on the car."

"All right. I'll be there soon."

He sighs. "There is one more thing. You might want to talk to Chief Skinner's wife when you get a chance."

"I went by to see her yesterday. What did she want?"

"She said she needed to talk to you."

"I'll take care of it when I can. It'll take me a half hour to get back to Jarrett Creek. Hold the fort until I get there."

I push my truck pretty hard getting back, and Odum is grinning when I walk in.

"You're sure the car is Dellmore's?" I say first thing.

"Yes, sir, no question. I asked both drivers involved in the accident for their license and registration. The guy driving the Crown Vic tried to make some excuse, but I insisted. Turned out he doesn't have a valid driver's license, and the car was registered to Dellmore. He claimed Dellmore lent it to him. But the story is obviously b.s., so I brought him in. He's in one of the cells."

"And you called Zeke to watch the car?"

"Yes, sir, as soon as I realized what we had, he came out to keep an eye on it."

"Did you mention Gary Dellmore to the driver?"

"No, sir. I just told him he was driving a stolen car. I figured you'd want to start from the beginning."

"You did a good job." I shake his hand.

"I'm really glad I came back in. But I told my dad I'd go back to help him finish up as soon as I could."

"Get on with it, then."

He tells me where the car is located, and I ask if he'll take the dam road on the way out of town and tell Zeke I'll be there as soon as I can.

"Uh, Chief, I could call him on his cell phone."

I start laughing. "You sure he's got one?"

"Yeah, that's how I reached him to begin with." He grins at me. We're both a little giddy. Finding Dellmore's car is a break we needed.

As soon as Odum is out the door, I brew myself a pot of coffee and head into the back where we have the two jail cells, with an extra cup for the prisoner.

"I could sure use that," he says as he snatches it out of my hand. He's a weasel of a guy, in his twenties with ropy arms and longish dishwater-blond hair that doesn't look like it's been washed recently. Neither have his jeans or his jacket, which give off the smell of fish. Most likely he's one of those people who stays out at the lake living on whatever money they can scrounge and supplementing their food with whatever they can catch.

His name is Louis Caton, and he says he's from the Gulf Coast and is just drifting around. "I want to get some living in before I settle down." When I hand him the coffee, he sits down on his cot and leans back against the concrete wall. "Man, I needed this coffee."

I drag a chair in from the office and sit down to question him. "How long have you been staying out at the lake, Louis?"

"Couple months."

"How did you meet Gary Dellmore?"

"Who?"

"The guy whose car you said you borrowed."

"Oh, him. I didn't know his name. I met him and we got to talking and I told him it was hard getting around without a car, and he said he'd be glad to lend me his."

Caton's story is so preposterous that I laugh in spite of myself. Gary Dellmore wouldn't come close to lending his car to anyone, I don't care what the circumstances. And the likelihood that he would meet someone like Louis Caton stretches the imagination even more. "When did this happen?"

He screws his face up like he's trying to remember. "Couple of days ago. I can't remember exactly."

"It's kind of important to know the exact time."

He scratches his scruffy chin. "It must have been Wednesday."

"That's good," I say.

He must hear something in my voice because he puts his coffee cup down on the floor and looks at me warily. "Why is that good?"

"Mr. Dellmore was murdered Tuesday night, so if you saw him Wednesday, that means he woke from the dead."

"No, no, no." Caton jumps to his feet. "That was a mistake. It must have been Monday I saw him. And listen, you've got to believe me. If he's dead, I had nothing to do with that."

I sigh. "Why don't we start over and you tell me how you came by that car. It may be important for a murder investigation. And if you don't get yourself untangled from your story, it might be you that's being investigated."

"Okay, okay." He comes up as close to me as the bars will allow. "I didn't steal the car, okay? I want to say that right out. I did not steal that car. I found it."

I laugh again. "This gets better and better."

"It's true, I really did. It was on the turnout below the dam road."

"On the lake side or the other side?"

"The other side. There's a little park just beyond it."

I know the place. "When was this?"

"Like I said, it was Wednesday, but it was around one o'clock in the morning."

"All right. Now we're talking. Did you hotwire it?"

"I wouldn't know how to do that. The keys were in it."

At that, I get up fast. This sounds more like the truth, and it's a twist I didn't expect. "I'm going to take you there and I want you to show me exactly where you found it. No bullshit. You understand me?"

"As God is my witness."

I call Alvin Raines down at the Texaco station and ask him to meet me at Dellmore's car with a tow truck. "And don't touch the car until I get there."

"My boy is out with the truck and it may be forty-five minutes before he gets back. You'll probably beat me out there. Give me your cell phone number in case I'm held up." I'm starting to see why people like their cell phones.

Before I take Louis Caton out of his cell, I check on the two Jarrett Creek police cars, both small Dodge Chargers, to see what kind of shape they're in. One is low on gas, but the other one has plenty. The fingerprint kit is in the trunk, along with a shotgun, an emergency first-aid kit, a blanket, and half a dozen empty food containers, mostly from the Dairy Queen. I gather those up and dump them in the trash bin at the side of the building.

Although I don't think Caton is much of a flight risk, I keep the handcuffs on him when I lead him out to the car. He complains when he half falls into the backseat. "Man, it's cramped back here. And it smells bad." He wrinkles his nose.

"Sorry it's not up to your standards." And then something occurs to me. "You've never been in the back of a police car before?"

"No, sir, I haven't."

"How did Bill Odum get you over here?"

"He was in a pickup and made me sit in the back, handcuffed to the rail."

"We're not going far. You'll be okay."

On the way over Caton babbles some more, repeating the details of how he found the car. I stop by to tell Zeke the situation. His small SUV is parked behind Dellmore's black Crown Victoria. Seat tilted back, he's lying with his hat over his eyes. His window is rolled down, and as I pull up alongside him, he sits up and resettles his hat back on his head. "Looks like nobody stole the car while I was napping."

"Zeke, I'll be back here in fifteen minutes, and if you don't mind I'd like you to hang out a little longer. I've called to have the car towed."

He looks at his watch. "You know, officially, I'm off duty. Why is this such a big deal?"

"You do know that this is Gary Dellmore's car?"

"I also know you're not likely to get any useful evidence out of it after somebody has been using it for joyriding." He nods to Caton in the backseat. "That the joker who was driving it?"

"It is. I'm taking him down to the scene where he found the car. We won't be long. If you really need to leave, go ahead."

"No, I'll stay here. You're the boss." He settles back in and claps his hat back over his face.

Caton is laughing in the backseat. "This town's got itself quite a police force. Two old geezers and a kid."

He's right, so I keep my mouth shut. I pull over in front of the Crown Vic and get out to take a look at it. It has a crumpled left front fender. I'm grateful Caton was in the fender bender. If it hadn't been called in, we might never have found Dellmore's car. I look inside and it's a mess, with food cartons, wrappers, and beer cans all over the floor and backseat.

Back in the car, I continue driving along the dam road, the lake off to our right. Approaching the park there's no shoulder on either side of the road because of a steep drop-off on the lake side and a swampy creek on the other. When the road opens out I pull off on the shoulder and take Caton out of the backseat and uncuff him. He zips up his light jacket against the stiff breeze that's coming off the lake.

"You say you found the car on this side of the park?" I gesture up ahead where there's a gravel pullout area with a picnic table surrounded by several post oak trees. You can tell from the weeds and leaves that the park isn't used much.

"The car was nosed in right up there." Caton points. "It was parked kind of cockeyed."

I wonder if somebody forced the car off the road. But who was driving the car? Was it Dellmore? If so, why did he leave it here and how did he get back to the American Legion Hall? It's possible that somebody followed him, forced him off the road then drove him to the Hall to kill him. But why go to all that trouble? Why not shoot him here? It's far more deserted here than it is at the Hall.

I can't tell anything from the tire tracks around the car. People use the park as a turnaround when they drive back and forth along the dam road. There are crisscrosses of tire tracks that could be from Dellmore's car or any of a dozen others that pulled off here.

Caton is taking this seriously. He walks a little ahead of me and is looking from side to side to figure out where the car was parked. "Okay, right here," he says. "You see that?" He points to a Coors can in the weeds. "I was walking along here drinking a beer and I threw that can down when I walked over and looked into the car."

"Where were you going?"

"Back to the trailer where I'm staying." He motions in the direction of the trailer camp a half-mile away. "I was at a guy's house back down there." He points to the road that leads back into town. "The guy said he was going to have a couple of girls come over, but they never showed up, so I got tired of waiting and decided to walk back home."

"You said this was one in the morning?"

"Something like that."

"And you've had the car ever since?"

"Yes." His eyes flick to one side. There's something he's not telling me.

I search for a question that will get to what he's hiding. "Was it around here the whole time?"

"Not exactly."

"What does that mean?" I say. "Where was it?"

"I figured as long as I had a car, I might as well make use of it. You know, if somebody's going to leave their car sitting around with the keys in it, they're going to have to expect somebody to use it."

"Where did you take it?"

"Wednesday it sat in front of my place all day because I was sleeping."

Sleeping it off. "You'd had a fair amount to drink the night before?"

"I suppose we did drink a few brews while we were waiting for those girls." He grins. "Wednesday night I went back over to his house, only this time I had the car, so we drove over to A&M to find some girls."

"And did you?"

"Yeah, we did. We had some fun." He grins and raises his eyebrows as if I'm going to congratulate him.

That's where all the trash inside the car came from. Zeke was right, any hope I had of gathering evidence from it is somewhere between slim and none, but I'll still have to go over it in the morning when it's at the service station.

I don't see signs of a struggle—not weeds trampled down or gravel disturbed. I pick up a stick and poke around in nearby clumps of weeds, but I don't see anything that might be of any use. Anything could have happened here. As far as that goes, Louis Caton could have made up the whole thing and he could have come upon Gary Dellmore sitting in the car, killed him, taken the body to where it was found, and then claimed the car for his own. But if it had happened that way, it's unlikely Caton would have hung around here. He seems aimless but not stupid. Besides, the autopsy indicated that Dellmore was killed where he was found.

It's five o'clock by the time I get back to the station, having seen to it that Dellmore's car was towed. I drop Caton off at his trailer, warning him not to leave town.

CHAPTER 16

I t's been a long day, but I need to let Barbara Dellmore know that we found Gary's car. When I phone her house and tell her, she asks me if I'll come over. She sounds shaky. I tell her I'll be right there.

The living room is as dark and gloomy as the last time I was here, with Odum. Barbara jerks open the drapes to the waning daylight. The room has an uncared-for look, as if things landed where they were put a long time ago and nobody has bothered with them since. Barbara looks around the room as if she doesn't recognize it. "Everything looks different without Gary here. I don't know how to describe it."

"Barbara, let's talk for a minute." We sit, but she doesn't really settle into the chair, as if she's hovering a few inches off it. She asks me exactly where her husband's car was found, and when I tell her, she says, "That makes no sense. What was he doing there?" Her voice is shrill.

"I was hoping you might be able to give me some idea."

"You mean why he was driving the dam road at night? No idea at all."

"Do you know if Gary had any friends with a place out at the lake? Anybody who might know what he was up to on the dam road?"

"He never mentioned knowing anybody out there. It's not his kind of people." She gets up. "Do you mind if I make some coffee? Come on in the kitchen." It seems to me like she's already had plenty of coffee.

We sit at counter stools and drink some kind of coffee with a flavor in it that I don't recognize. She says it's hazelnut, like she's proud of it. As far as I'm concerned, infusing coffee with nuts is as unnatural as those genetically modified tomatoes with fish genes in them.

"Did Gary ever mention knowing somebody by the name of Louis Caton?"

She frowns. "No. Who's that?"

"It's the man who was driving his car." I tell her that Caton said he found the car abandoned with the keys in it.

"None of this is making a bit of sense."

"Did Gary have any close friends?"

"We have a few church friends, but no men in particular that he's friendly with. He said he and Slate McClusky went out to eat a few times."

I'm startled by that, after the way McClusky talked as if he hardly knew Gary. And I don't recall the two men being particularly friendly with each other at the meeting. In fact, if I had to swear, I'd say they didn't know each other at all.

"And Gary goes deer hunting with Annalise's husband and some friends of his. They go every year. This year they went after turkey instead of deer. They got two and we had them at Thanksgiving. All of us together at Alan and Clara's house. One big happy family."

"So Gary and his brother-in-law were friendly. Do you get along well with Annalise? Did the four of you socialize?"

Her smile is bitter. "You're wondering about that argument you walked in on Wednesday? We usually do okay, but we never socialized with them except when we were all over at Alan and Clara's house. I don't really care for Annalise, or her husband, for that matter. Pompous and small-minded, both of them. I guess that's one of the consolations I get with Gary gone. I don't have to go over there and listen to Annalise detail every move her kids make."

"You and Gary never wanted kids?"

"No. We agreed on that before we got married. I don't like children. That's not something I tell everyone because people don't like to hear it."

"And Gary was okay with that?"

"More than okay. It's one thing that drew us together. And it's why I don't have many women friends. All they ever talk about is their kids. How can every woman find her children so endlessly fascinating? And Annalise is the worst. She never shuts up about that brat Mikey."

"Tell me about the fight you had with Annalise the day I saw you at the Dellmore's."

She gets up and pours herself another cup of coffee, but I tell her I don't need any. "It had to do with Gary fooling around with other women." Her cheeks flame up and she looks at me with defiance as if I might challenge her version of things. "And of course Annalise and Clara couldn't hear that their precious Gary might be to blame. It had to be my fault."

"I guess that's to be expected."

She shrugs. When she puts her coffee cup to her mouth, her hand is shaking. "Anyway, Annalise had her opinions about why Gary had a wandering eye, and she was only too happy to share them with me."

She tells me pretty much the same story I heard from Alan Dellmore, and ends with saying, "Both of them thought I was robbing the cradle when I married him."

"Seems to me Gary got the best end of the deal."

She laughs, but there's no humor in it. "That's nice of you to say, but the truth is I was pretty old when I met Gary. My daddy thought he was going to have an old maid on his hands. I still think one reason Gary married me was that Daddy offered him a good job in his company." She can't keep her hands still. They move restlessly, clasping and unclasping.

"Were you happy?"

"I thought we were. I suppose I'm not the only woman whose husband developed a roving eye. That happened after my daddy lost his business. Gary couldn't find a job, and I had to go to work to help us make ends meet. Like a lot of men, that bruised his ego."

"What kind of work did you do?" I say.

"I majored in landscape architecture in college, so I went to work as a gardener. Gary thought that was a slap in the face for me to do menial work, but I didn't want to do anything else. I like gardening and if I had to work, I didn't see why I shouldn't get paid for doing what I like to do. You see women spending a lot of time in the garden and they don't expect to be paid. A man would expect to be paid." She flicks her hands as if to shoo her thoughts away. "Don't get me started on that."

"When you went to work—that's when Gary started cheating on you?"

"Not right away, but things went downhill after that. We argued a lot. I guess I was foolish. It never occurred to me that he would cheat on me." She gives me a rueful smile. "Anyway, after Gary had been out of a job for a while, Alan persuaded him to go to work at the bank, and we moved here. But it was never a great match. He and Alan didn't get along."

"What do you mean, they didn't get along?"

She's suddenly angry. "Alan is a wonderful man. Gary was like a teenaged girl, always trying to impress everybody with who he was and what he knew. He never took his responsibilities seriously. More than once Alan warned Gary that it was important to be discreet, that people didn't like hearing their finances aired in public. But Gary said that was old-fashioned. He thought Alan was a fool."

"In what way?"

"Gary said Alan was a dinosaur. He said these days anybody can find out anything about people's finances on the Internet. But the real problem was that Gary didn't value the job. I don't know why, but he felt like it was beneath him or something. He hated working at the bank and he hated this town. He kept saying that sooner or later we were going to move out of here."

"Did you want to move, too?"

"Either way suited me fine. I don't hate it here like Gary did."

"What kept him here?"

"Money. We racked up some debts when he was out of work, but he said as soon as they were paid off, we were leaving."

"Did Alan know Gary wanted out?"

"I don't think he would admit it to himself. He really hoped Gary would change."

I'm surprised that Barbara is spilling all this to me. I don't know her well, but sometimes people will talk to a stranger easier than to a friend.

"I heard that Gary was involved in the deal out at the lake for the water park."

"Oh, yes. He was very proud of that. He thought it was going to be great."

"Did it bother him when the deal went south and the town lost money?"

"It wasn't Gary's way to regret things. He said it wasn't his job to coddle people, and that Alton Coldwater knew it was a risky deal. Gary got his commission on the loan, and that's all he cared about."

Alton Coldwater may have known it was risky, but he was still angry at Dellmore. "Do you know if anybody ever threatened Gary?"

"You mean threatened to kill him? He never told me if they did."

"I don't like asking this, but were any of Gary's affairs serious?"

She stands up abruptly, glaring at me. "What's serious? Do you mean did he ask me for a divorce? Did he tell me the details of his little side activities?" Her face is dead white.

"Did he ever ask for a divorce?"

"We considered splitting a couple of times, but neither of us really wanted to. I'll bet it surprises you that I wanted to stay with him."

I shrug. I don't know why she'd care what my opinion is. "That's your business." She seems reckless, throwing out all this talk. And her anger is free-floating, as if now that her husband is gone she can let it loose.

"We both had our reasons for wanting to stay together. Mine were practical. I like a quiet life. If we had split up, I'd have had to get a job again. I like being at home and working in the garden. The only reason I hired out to do it before was because one of us had to have an income. So if getting to do as I please meant I had to put up with Gary fooling around, then so be it. Let people say what they want to—I was a perfectly good wife to Gary and if he felt like he had to go with other women, that's on him."

"I'm sorry. I know this is hard for you . . ."

She interrupts me as if I hadn't said anything. "And what made Gary stay with me? I think he wanted to be able to play around and use me as a convenient excuse not to get too involved with anybody." She stops as if she's run out of gas. "I guess none of that matters anymore."

"Let me change the subject. Did Gary ever have any dealings with Gabe LoPresto?"

"Dealings? You mean besides flirting with Gabe's girlfriend?"

"What makes you think he did?"

"Cookie Travers and I are friends. At least I think we are. Sometimes I think she takes too much pleasure in telling me every little thing Gary is up to. She told me Gary and Darla had a lot of little private discussions—by that I think she meant they were flirting. She doesn't like Darla. Thinks she's a troublemaker."

"I understand that Gabe LoPresto's company was going to get some of the building business when the water park went in. Did Gary ever mention that?"

"If he did, I don't remember."

I stand up to go. "Can you give me the names of Gary's hunting buddies?"

"You should talk to Annalise. Her husband is the one who knows those men."

"One more thing. Do you keep a gun?"

"I do, but it hasn't been cleaned or fired in so long that it would probably blow up if somebody tried to use it. I'll go get it. I keep it in the utility room." She's back in a few minutes with a shoebox. Inside is a tiny little Smith & Wesson and a box of .22 shells.

"You can put the lid back on that box, and if I were you I'd either get rid of the gun or have somebody clean it and make sure it works."

She follows me to the door, and on the porch she suddenly says, "Samuel? What do you suppose Gary's car was doing out there at the dam?"

"I don't know. But I'll do everything I can to answer that question."

My cat Zelda tells me in no uncertain terms that I've been away too much the last few days and she doesn't appreciate it. It's a good thing she's small, because if she were any bigger, she'd stomp holes in the floor as she storms over to her dish and points out to me that it's empty.

Up the road I hear cars honking at each other and kids yelling. Being Friday night, there's a basketball game. Although football is king, the basketball team is doing well this year and enthusiasm is high. I enjoy watching professional sports on TV, but there's nothing like going to a hometown game with the people you've known your whole life. I had planned to go to the game, but I'm too tired.

Before I can stop my thoughts I'm doubting myself, thinking I might be too old to carry out the duties I've signed on for. But then I remember I was always this tired on the job at the end of the day, even when I was younger. It was one of the reasons Jeanne wanted me to bow out of running for police chief again after I'd put in a dozen years. "You're always on call," she said. "I want to see more of you."

Now she's not here, and I have all the time in the world to stretch myself every which way for the job. I get a beer out of the refrigerator and sit down to watch whatever happens to be on the TV. I don't even have the energy to change channels. I wake up sometime in the night with the half-drunk beer sitting on the floor next to me, and the TV showing an old episode of *River Monsters*.

CHAPTER 17

Alvin Raines moved Dellmore's Crown Vic into the service station garage last night to keep it safe, and this morning he's brought it out into a side parking area and put sawhorses around it so nobody will mess with it. He gives me the keys in a paper bag and tells me he did like I said and only handled them with gloves on.

I pull on latex gloves from our crime scene kit and open up the doors and trunk to have a good look. I won't have time to do the tedious job of fingerprinting. That will have to fall to the Rangers' crime unit.

There are food containers and wrappers from McDonald's and Dairy Queen, and beer cans on the floor of the car. We don't have a McDonald's here in town, but I know they have one over in Bryan-College Station. We do have a Dairy Queen. It's always possible that some of the trash was here before the kids took it joyriding. I can't picture Dellmore eating at the DQ and throwing the wrappers in the back, but I have no way of knowing exactly what happened with the car around the time Dellmore was killed—who rode in the car or what they might have done. All the trash has to be left as is to be dusted for prints and tested for DNA.

In the glove compartment I find some country music CDs: one by Robert Earl Keen, a Ryan Bingham, and a T Bone Burnett. When I come to the fourth one, a familiar face, younger, stares back at me. It's Angel Bright's greatest hits CD. The picture on the front shows Angel on stage, head thrown back, body arched as if she's prepared to be pulled up into the sky.

In addition to the usual road emergency stuff you find in a trunk, Dellmore has some gardening tools and a box of files. I thumb through the files and see that they're job orders for some kind of building project.

The crime unit will need to dust the files for fingerprints, but it's possible they contain evidence pointing to whoever wanted Dellmore dead, so I want to go through them myself before I turn them over. I'll make a note of what's here for Alan Dellmore in case there's urgent business that needs to be taken care of. I move the box to the trunk of the police car. The Rangers' crime team won't be happy with me taking it out of Dellmore's trunk, but I have my own investigation to see to.

I arrange with Raines to have the Crown Victoria locked up in a shed in back of his service station until the crime unit can get to it.

On the way back to the police station I stop by Patty Skinner's house to find out what fresh complaint she called about yesterday.

There's a gleam of triumph in her eye when she answers the door. "Well, lookie who's here. I guess you need some help."

I can't begin to imagine the kind of help she thinks she can give me, but before I can hazard a guess she opens the door wide. "Come on in and lay it out for him."

A feeling of foreboding comes over me. I think I know who "him" is. Sure enough, Rodell Skinner is propped up on the couch in the living room. Patty flings her hand out to present him as if I ought to genuflect. Rodell struggles to sit up and makes an attempt at a smile. His skin is yellow and slack and he's lost a good bit of weight.

"Rodell, I'm glad to see you're back."

"I sincerely doubt that," Patty says.

"Patty, don't be that way," Rodell says. His voice sounds strange. He's always been full of beer and bluster, and now his voice sounds thin, like he's lost his punch. "I need to talk to Samuel, Patty. Will you let us have a moment?"

"I don't know what you have to say to a traitor like him, moving in on your job the minute your back is turned."

"Patty, it's not like that," I say.

"Go on now," Rodell says in that new voice that gives me a bad feeling. "Let us have a few minutes."

As soon as she's gone, Rodell lets himself fall back on the sofa with a groan. "She's trying to be loyal, that's all. She always was loyal." He says it like it's a trait that has less to recommend it than you might think.

"How are you feeling?" Normally I would have said he's looking good, but that's way too big a lie.

"How do you think I'm feeling? I feel a little worse than I look." He gives a short laugh and then coughs. "Patty's got this idea that I'm going to jump up from here and go roust you out of my job. But you can see that's not going to happen."

"What does the doctor say?"

"Says my liver isn't holding up." He snickers and I see the old rascal in him. "Not hard to believe, is it?"

"Rodell, you've given your liver every reason to rebel."

He beckons me closer. "Listen, I've only been home a day, and I'm already going crazy here. I need you to help me."

"What can I do for you?"

"Take me down to the station with you. Patty is a good woman, but I know her, and she's not going to give me a minute's peace."

"I'll be honest, you don't look like you're in any shape to be doing any work."

"If we're being honest here, we might as well say it right out: You're right. The doctor says if I stay off alcohol, I'll last a while, but I'm never going back to work. Not to do real work. But I tell you, Samuel, if I have to stay around here and have Patty hover over me, there's no way in hell I won't get back to drinking." This speech exhausts him and he seems to shrink right in front of me. He closes his eyes.

I'm having an unexpected reaction to all this. Rodell has always irritated me, but as much as I didn't like him doing a bad job as chief of police, I hate seeing him frail and needy. I prefer the bluster to the pleading.

"Rodell?"

He opens his eyes. "Will you do it?"

"Not today. You're in no shape to get up. But I'll tell you what I'd like to do that would be of benefit to both of us. I suppose Patty told you that Gary Dellmore was killed. I'm going to come over here once a day and discuss the case with you. You'll have a chance to think things over and give me advice."

He cackles. "Me giving you advice?"

"It never hurts to have an extra mind working on things."

"Not much of a mind," he mutters.

"Your mind will work fine. It was the alcohol that kept you from being at your best."

"You really think so?"

"I think you'll be surprised." I don't know whether I'm right or not, but Rodell can use the encouragement.

"Samuel, I've got to get out of here, though."

"Look at you, Rodell. You can't even sit up. Wait until you're a little stronger, and then we'll get you down to the station." I stand. "How is all this medical care getting paid for?" Although he looks like an old man, he's several years shy of Medicare.

"That's one thing about having a wife like Patty. She had sense enough to keep good medical coverage over and above the disability the job provided. Patty's trying to find a part-time job, too." He closes his eyes again. "That'll be a blessing." And I know he means more than just having money coming in.

"I'm going to leave you alone now. But I'll come back in the morning and we'll talk things over." Rodell has put himself where he is, but that doesn't make it any less pitiful. Seeing someone take the consequences of abusing their body has never done much to satisfy me.

130

CHAPTER 18

I bring the banker's box containing the files I found in Dellmore's trunk into the station and set them under my desk. I'm curious to know what's in them, but there's no hurry. I won't be able to turn them over to Alan or Cookie until Monday morning. The light on the telephone is blinking with five messages, and I take care of those first. Three of the calls are things that can be put off: Tools are missing from a construction site, an abandoned house has been vandalized, and someone is playing music too loud. The fourth one needs a follow-up.

"Mrs. Witz, is your car missing?"

"No, it's right out front."

"What makes you think somebody was riding around in it?"

There's a long pause. "I know I sound crazy, but when I got in it to go to the store this morning, I was pretty sure somebody else had driven it."

"When was the last time you drove it?"

"I go to the store once a week, every Thursday. That's when the Qwik Mart puts things on sale."

I'm patient with her. She admits the seat hadn't been moved and as far as she could tell it had the same amount of gas in it. "But my mamma always told me I've got second sight, and I had this strange feeling that somebody had been in it. Maybe it had a different smell. Something."

I tell her to call me if anything like that happens again.

The fifth call is more worrisome. A woman living out in the area where I was looking at property with Marietta Bryant yesterday has called to say that her teenage daughter seems to have run away from home. She sounds a little hysterical. It's probably a teenager who got mad at her folks and is off sulking somewhere, but there's always a chance it's something worse. It needs to be handled right now. I don't see a duty roster anywhere, so I call Zeke and tell him about the missing girl. "When are you scheduled to come in?"

"Not until this afternoon, but I'll come in right now. You've got your hands full with the Dellmore thing. I'll go talk to the missing girl's mamma right away. Gives me an excuse to get out of cleaning the gutters."

I re-record the message on the machine to give out my cell phone number and then sit back to plan what to do next to investigate Dellmore's death. I feel like a rusty wheel that's not able to move as smoothly as when it's oiled. But there's a method to be followed, and I'll get there. I start by trying to think of a motive. The motives that pop to mind right away where Dellmore is concerned are sex and money—motives don't get any more basic than that.

I'm not entirely convinced of Barbara's explanation for why she stayed with Gary when she knew he'd had multiple affairs. Maybe I was too quick to dismiss Loretta's suggestion that she'd had enough and killed Dellmore. But if she did decide she'd had enough, why now? Is there something going on that made her suddenly decide she'd be better off with him dead? Maybe he asked for a divorce, and this time he meant it. It's hard for me to imagine that Dellmore seriously considered Jessica Reinhardt as a possible replacement for Barbara. Was he seeing someone else?

I don't for a minute suspect Jessica of killing Dellmore, even if he disappointed fantasies she might have had about him. But if Rusty Reinhardt knew that Dellmore had actually gone to Jessica's house, he might have been angry enough to confront Dellmore. Jim Krueger said he overheard Rusty asking Gary if he could talk to him after the meeting. Maybe the confrontation got out of hand. And it's always possible that if I dig deeper into it, I may find other boyfriends or husbands or fathers angry at Dellmore.

The phone interrupts my thinking. It's Barbara Dellmore. "I got a call from the funeral home. The medical examiner released Gary's body yesterday afternoon, and nobody bothered to call and tell me."

"That's not the first time someone told me that. I guess they think it's up to the funeral home to let the family know. Anyway, I'm sure you and his folks are relieved. Do you know when you're going to have the funeral?"

"It's not going to be a public affair. We want it private, with just a few friends. I'm calling because it would be nice to have a law enforcement person there."

"I'm glad to be there, Barbara, but what do you mean it would be nice to have the law there?"

"In case anybody shows up uninvited. Anyway, it's Monday afternoon at the Episcopal Church at two o'clock. Can you be there?"

"Of course I will." I don't mind going, but I wonder who she thinks will show up that she didn't invite.

Still considering possible motives for Dellmore's murder, I turn my attention to money—always a complicated matter. Maybe Dellmore meddled in somebody's business that he shouldn't have. Or maybe somebody was involved in illegal transactions, and he found out and threatened to expose them. I'll need to ask Cookie Travers what kind of banking matters Dellmore was currently working on.

Then there's his involvement with the water park out at the lake. Alton Coldwater claimed that Dellmore was partly to blame for that fiasco. And according to Oscar Grant, Dellmore bragged about making a secret killing on the deal. It seems straightforward—Dellmore put together the loan and probably got a commission. What else could he have done that he needed to keep secret? I could ask Alan Dellmore, but I decide to consult Cookie first. She's been Alan's loyal right-hand man for a long time, and if she can answer my questions it will mean I can spare Dellmore having to dredge up what may have been shady business practices on his son's part.

The door opens and Truly Bennett pokes his head inside.

"Come on in," I say, rising.

Bennett steps inside, cringing as if he's expecting to be hit. In his fifties, Bennett grew up at a time when daily life could be hard for men of color, especially in small towns. For Bennett there's the extra history of the time he spent in jail for a crime he didn't commit. He has his old straw hat in his hands, and it looks like he's going to tear it apart if I don't settle him down.

"What's up, Truly? You look worried."

"Chief Craddock, I had to come around and see you because something happened over at Mr. McClusky's place, and I don't want to get blamed for something I didn't do."

"Sit down here. Let me get you a cup of coffee." I set the coffee in front of him, but he's still working on the hat. "What happened?"

"Somebody broke into Mr. McClusky's house last night."

"Uh-oh. Tell me about it."

"You know I've been over there painting. This morning I planned to start early, but my truck had a dead battery. I had to wait for somebody to give me a jump. So I only got there twenty minutes ago. I went around back to pick up some brushes I cleaned last night, and I saw that the backdoor was open a little bit. I thought maybe Mr. McClusky or Ms. Bright had come home, so I called out, but nobody answered. And then I saw that the little window next to the door was broken. I knew then that somebody must have broken in. I went around and rang the front doorbell and called out some more in case they hadn't heard me, but nobody was home. I came down here because I don't want anybody thinking I did that."

"Settle down. Nobody's going to accuse you of anything. I'll go over there with you to check it out right now. I'll call McClusky and tell him what's going on in case he wants to come back."

"And if you don't mind, would you ask him if he wants me to keep on working?"

"I'll do that. You go on back to the house, and I'll be right behind you as soon as I call him."

I call the cell phone numbers I have for both Slate and Angel, but both numbers go to the answering machine. I leave a message on Slate's phone. And then I call the Marriott out at Horseshoe Bay to see if I can leave him a message there.

"We don't have anybody here by that name," the desk clerk tells me. "Could it be under another name?"

I give them Angel Bright's name.

"You mean that country singer?" the clerk says.

"That's the one. Her husband told me they were staying there."

"No, sir, I would have remembered that. She was one of my mamma's favorite singers. I would have wanted to get her autograph. She hasn't been here."

CHAPTER 19

Before I can get out the door, the phone rings again. I forgot how much of a slave you are to the telephone when you're in law enforcement. I start to let it go, but they'll just call me on the cell phone, so I might as well handle it now.

"Mr. Craddock, this is Camille Overton. I talked to you yesterday when you were looking for the McCluskys?"

"That's right. I found them. I appreciate your help. What can I do for you?"

"I'm calling because somebody broke into my house last night. That man who's working across the street worries me. He showed up again this morning and I don't like the look of him."

"I'm coming over there right now. Sit tight."

Five minutes later I knock on Camille's door and she opens it so fast, I suspect she was standing by the door waiting for me. She's wearing glasses that make her eyes look large, and there's no mistaking the alarm in them. "I'm so glad you came. I'm a nervous wreck." She glances around me to where Truly Bennett's truck is parked on the street, with Truly sitting in it. I've told him to wait until I talk to Mrs. Overton before we look at McClusky's house. "I just don't like having that man here."

"Mrs. Overton, I've known Truly Bennett for thirty years. He's absolutely trustworthy. I can guarantee he didn't break in to your house."

She looks over again at Bennett's truck. "If you say so. I guess if he was the one who broke in, he wouldn't have come back here brazen as you please." She opens the door wider. "Come on in and I'll tell you what happened." She leads me into the kitchen and points to the door that leads to the backyard.

"I was out playing bridge last night, and when I got home, this backdoor was wide open. There was a draft coming through the whole house."

"What time was this?"

"I got home around ten o'clock. I can tell you I surely didn't leave the door open like that, though. It was cold outside and I wouldn't have left it open anyway, even if it wasn't cold. It like to've scared me to death when I saw it."

"You didn't call down to the station, though."

"No, I didn't want to bother you. And I wanted somebody to come right over so I phoned Mary Rusk next door—that's where I was playing bridge—and she sent Paul over to check it out. He went through the house to make sure nobody was hiding in any of the rooms. He said he thought maybe the wind blew the door open. I said I didn't think the wind was that strong last night, and besides the door was locked."

"Was anything missing?"

"Not as far as I can tell. But Paul said I should call you this morning and let you know. He said police like to keep track of things like that."

"He's right." I open the door and take a look at the handle and lock on both sides. It's a round knob with a simple push lock, and no dead-bolt. I see a few scratches on the lock, but not enough to indicate the door was jimmied. "Are you sure this door was locked?"

There's a chilly breeze coming from the open door and she holds her sweater tighter around her. She looks at the lock as if it could tell her something. "It's possible I didn't lock it. Sometimes I go outside and don't bother to lock it during the day, but usually I'm careful if I go out at night." She shakes her head with a rueful look. "I was only going next door and was running a little late. I may have forgotten to check it."

"I have to tell you that Truly Bennett came to my office this morning and said he found the McClusky's house broken into when he came to work. I was coming up here to check on the house when you called."

She shivers and closes the backdoor and locks it. "Oh, my gosh, somebody is going around the neighborhood breaking in. You know, I have to tell you that a week or so ago I came home and had the strangest feeling that somebody had been here, but nothing was out of place, so I thought I was being foolish."

"This could be kids going around trying unlocked doors and looking around inside, so be sure you lock up when you leave. And if anything else happens, you call me. It's no bother. One more thing. Why don't you go through the house again after I leave and make sure nothing is missing. I'll be across the street. Come and tell me if you find anything that doesn't look right."

"I'll do that. And I thank you for coming out so fast."

At the McClusky's, Truly shows me the lock and the broken window. The lock has more serious damage to it than Camille's lock, but this door has a deadbolt. "It looks to me like somebody tried to jimmy it," Bennett says, "and when they couldn't get it open they broke the window, reached in, and unlocked it."

"Looks like that to me, too," I say. I'm always surprised people don't realize that having a window right next to the door makes it easy to break the window and get to the lock.

"I don't like this one bit," Bennett says. "Did you talk to Mr. McClusky?" Bennett's shoulders are hunched up and he still looks nervous. Given Camille's immediate reaction of suspecting him of the break-in, I understand how he'd be anxious.

"I couldn't reach him. I'm going to go inside and check things out. You can come with me if you want."

"No, sir, I'd prefer to stay out here if it's all the same."

The backdoor opens into a laundry room, which leads to the kitchen. A cup has been left in the kitchen sink, but otherwise everything is orderly. My first thought is for the Remington that I took note of the first time I was here, and I go on through to the living room. It's still in place, and when I walk through the rest of the house, it doesn't look to me like anything was disturbed. It's a big, sprawling place with three bedrooms and bathrooms, an office, a TV room, and the living room I was in before. Of course I wouldn't know if something small was stolen, like jewelry, or if the intruder found money kept around the house, but there are no open drawers or closet doors.

Outside, Bennett has put himself to work watering plants. He turns off the hose and wipes his hands on his pants as he walks over to me. "How is it inside?"

"Nothing seems to be disturbed. But the McCluskys will have to look through things to make sure nothing was taken. Can you repair the broken window?"

Bennett hesitates. "I'd rather have somebody else do that."

"A white man," I say dryly.

That brings a shy grin to his face. "Maybe that would be best."

"Until somebody does that, it would be good if you go on with your painting and keep an eye on the place. I expect Mr. McClusky would be grateful."

"I surely will do that." He shakes my hand.

I'm concerned that I still haven't heard from McClusky, so I call and leave another message. It could be that he's back out at his resort today where there's no coverage.

I call down to Gabe LoPresto's construction business and they tell me they'll send somebody out this afternoon to replace the broken window.

As soon as I get to my truck, my cell phone starts its clamor. It sounds angry, although I know that's impossible.

"Craddock?" It's Slate McClusky's voice. "I've been trying to reach you. Where have you been? Never mind, we're almost home.

I got your message about the break-in. Can you meet us there in twenty minutes?"

I swing by my house to grab some lunch, and there's a note sticking on my door. "Mr. Craddock, I stopped by on the off chance you might be home. Everyone seems to know about your art collection, and I'm dying to see it. Can you call me when you can spare some time to show me around? Ellen Forester."

"Samuel! You've been making yourself scarce around here." I turn at the sound of Loretta's voice, the note in my hand making me feel guilty for some reason.

"Come in. I've just got ten minutes to grab a bite to eat."

"Ten minutes! It's hardly worth the effort of me walking down here in this cold weather." But she scoots up the steps. She always moves briskly, which I envied when my knee was bunged up. But now that it's over the worst of the healing, I'm pretty sure there'll come I time when I can match her again.

I make us a quick cup of coffee. Loretta says she's already had lunch. I throw a couple pieces of roast beef between two pieces of bread slathered with mayonnaise.

"How are you getting along?" she says, looking at the rough sandwich with distaste.

"Being back on the job is taking some getting used to. But guess who's offered to give me a little help?"

"Who?"

"Rodell." I tell her I visited Rodell and he wanted to do something useful, although I don't tell her the part where he said he'd go crazy if he didn't get away from Patty for a while.

She snorts. "Help you? With what?"

"Figuring out who killed Gary Dellmore. If he really has cut out the drinking, he'll have a little more on the ball. I never thought he was stupid."

"Maybe not, but he's never going to give up drinking. You mark my word. I've known Rodell since he was a little boy. I used to babysit for him and his sister, and he never had a bit of control over himself. That mother of his didn't know the word 'no.'"

"The shape he's in, I don't think he's going to be out buying beer anytime soon."

"I'm surprised Oscar Grant stays in business with Rodell not drinking down at the Two Dog," she says. Loretta isn't above having a little glass of wine or a cocktail, but she has no patience for people who overindulge, including, if she is to be believed, her late husband. I never saw him drink much, but her standard of overindulging is more stringent than mine.

"What did Gary's wife have to say for herself?" Loretta says.

"You know good and well I'm not going to answer that."

"I wondered if she's as pleased as she seems to be that Gary is gone." Her voice has that false innocent tone that tells me she's got a tidbit of gossip to tell me.

"What do you mean?"

"Apparently she went into Bobtail yesterday and bought all new dishes."

"How did you happen to come by that bit of information?"

"You're not the only one who hears things." Her tone is lofty. I'm reminded of my cat Zelda, when she's managed to kill a mouse.

"I don't think you can read a lot into that. She might be the kind of person who makes herself feel better by going shopping." I wouldn't know a thing about that—I'm only repeating something Jeanne told me.

"Still, it doesn't look good." She waits for me to say more, and when I don't, she says, "Not to change the subject, but I saw some woman come up to your door earlier. She left you a note?"

No sense in holding out on Loretta. It would make me look guilty of some vague crime. "Yes, it's that woman who's opening the art store. She wants to see my art collection and came by in case I was home."

"That makes sense," she says, but I can tell she doesn't like it. Trying to read behind all this subtlety tires me out more than trying to investigate a murder.

I'm trying to figure out how to wiggle out of saying any more when I'm startled by my cell phone ringing. When I reach into my shirt pocket and pull it out, I realize I've already gotten used to it. "Craddock."

It's Zeke Dibble. "Chief, I wanted you to know the missing girl was a false alarm. She called her mother and said she'd gone over to a friend's house after cheerleader practice and forgot the time."

I'm relieved that's one thing out of the way. As I hang up it occurs to me that it's good to have Dibble at the station to field all those little things that we get called for every single day.

I stand up and drain the last of my coffee. "I've got to get going. I'm supposed to be meeting the McCluskys at their place."

"What for?"

"Somebody broke into their house last night. They were out of town and I called them so they could come back to see if anything is missing."

I can tell Loretta's not happy with being whisked out of my house, so I suggest we go out to eat next week. "I'll take you to that new Italian place in Bobtail."

"That would be fun. Martha Jenkins said she didn't think it was very good, but she's particular about what she eats."

I have to give Loretta credit. She likes to experiment with new dishes when we go out. I'm more in line with Martha Jenkins. Give me a good steak and I'm satisfied.

When I drive up, Slate McClusky is listening to Truly Bennett, his head cocked to one side, smiling, eyes on the ground near Bennett's feet. He starts to nod, and when I park at the curb, I see him clap his hand on Bennett's arm in a friendly gesture. Angel is nowhere to be seen.

McClusky turns to me as I get close. "Bennett here was explaining to me how he found the backdoor open and went down to the station to alert you." I've never seen McClusky dressed the way he is now. His jeans look like they've been dragged through the dirt, and there's stubble on his chin. His eyes are sunken in as if he could use a good night's sleep. But he's still got that benign smile plastered on his face.

"I was hoping Angel would come with you so she could see if anything is missing."

"She's already inside. She was worried that somebody might've stolen her jewelry."

"I didn't see anything disturbed when I looked around, but I wouldn't have known what to look for."

Angel comes out the backdoor, looking flustered. "There's nothing missing as far as I can tell, but I feel so violated that somebody has been in here. What do you suppose they wanted? Oh, wait! My gold records." She runs back inside and we follow her and find her standing in front of them.

"At least they didn't take these. They're about the last valuable thing I own."

"Honey, now settle down. You're talking crazy." McClusky tries to pat her shoulder, but she shies away.

He turns to me. "Do you take fingerprints when you have a break-in?"

"No, I'd be surprised if whoever did this has prints on file. I'd guess we're looking at kids poking around for the hell of it."

"Kids!" Angel says. "How did they get in here?"

"You saw the broken window at the backdoor? It's never a good idea to have a window next to a door lock."

She stares at me. "My God, I never thought of that. Criminals are so sneaky."

"I'm glad I was able to get hold of you two," I say. "I tried several times this morning. And I called the Marriott, too. They said you weren't there."

"The Marriott?" She frowns. "Did Slate say we were staying at the Marriott? I'm so sorry. That's where we usually stay, but Slate had some business to take care of and we needed to talk to a title company, so we stayed in Marble Falls."

"For future reference, where do you stay there?"

"At a little Holiday Inn over there. It's not the greatest place, but it's convenient."

She shoots a glance at McClusky, and for some reason I get the feeling she's not telling the truth. Why would she lie? Why would it matter where they were last night?

CHAPTER 20

I don't have many occasions to dress up, but Jenny roped me into escorting her to a formal affair in Bryan tonight to honor a judge who is retiring. "I have to put in an appearance, and I hate to walk in by myself," she said when she invited me. "So I want you to figure out if you've got something decent to wear and go with me." This was a month ago and I put it out of my mind, convinced the time would never really get here. But it has, and tonight is the night.

After I talk to the McCluskys, I head home and go through my closet to find something to wear that won't disgrace Jenny. She laid down the law when she invited me. "If you need me to go with you to buy something, then I'll do it. I don't want to. But I want even less to have an escort who looks like he's picked through the ragbag for his clothes."

I have a more or less respectable suit that I wear to funerals around town, but in the back of my closet is a fine suit I haven't worn in a long time. Jeanne picked it out for me when we went to a big museum event in Houston before she got sick. I put my foot down and refused to buy a tuxedo, but she said a good suit would do as well. She said it was "classic." She teased me, saying, "In case you don't know, that means it's always more or less in style." Not that I would know the difference, but now I'm glad I have it. I don't want to embarrass Jenny in front of her peers.

I also have a decent collection of ties and shirts because at Christmas my nephew Tom and his wife Vicki supply me with those basics. So when I show up at Jenny's door at five-thirty, she says, "I didn't need to worry. You clean up pretty good."

Jenny usually wears boxy pants suits and doesn't bother with much makeup. Tonight she has gone all out. She has on a green dress in soft material that looks good on her and she's wearing strappy little shoes that don't look like something you'd want to wear if you have any hiking to do.

"I know it," she says when I tell her that. "But I don't get to dress up very often, so here I am." She's blushing. We long ago established that she isn't on the lookout for a man, but I can imagine some younger man in her office being surprised tonight at this pretty woman who has been right under his nose.

The retirement party is held at a newly renovated hotel. It's a lavish affair with an abundant buffet and a full bar. I stop to talk to a couple of people I know from Bobtail, and Jenny goes off to mingle. I'm surprised to see Alan and Clara Dellmore here, with Gary not even buried yet. When I go over to greet them, I can see that they're here in body only.

"Samuel, I'm glad to see a friendly face. Do you know the judge?" Alan says.

"Only by reputation. I'm here with my next-door neighbor, Jenny Sandstone. It's good that you came out."

Clara manages a smile. "We've known Judge Crocker since he was fresh out of law school and we felt like we had to come."

I have questions I want to ask them, but this is neither the time nor the place, so we discuss the judge and his career. For Clara, it's tough holding up her side of the conversation, but Alan seems like his usual self. He goes off to get another cocktail, and no sooner am I alone with Clara when she says, "Samuel, do you mind talking shop for a minute?"

"We can discuss anything you want. What's on your mind?"

"It's a little delicate, but I'm tired of being coddled and I need to know the answer."

"I'll do my best."

"Gary's wife—you know Barbara?"

I nod.

"She said that Gary had had several affairs. Do you know whether that's true? I know he had flirtations, but I guess I thought it was harmless. I'm sorry to pin you down, but every time I ask anyone else, they say something vague and put me off."

"Clara, will it do you any good to know the answer?"

She blinks a few times as if she hadn't thought about why she was asking the question. "I guess I want the answer to be no."

"The fact is, it seems like Gary had an eye for women, but I don't know why that should matter to you now. Do you?"

"Not really. Barbara and Annalise got into an argument when Barbara was at the house last Wednesday, and she told Annalise that Gary had had several affairs. She said that's probably what got him killed." Her voices rises as if she's going to start crying.

"Sometimes people say things in the heat of an argument that they don't really mean. You'd be better off putting the whole thing out of your mind. No good will come from dwelling on it."

She nods and keeps her eyes on her glass. Whatever is in it, she hasn't touched it.

Alan comes back with the judge in tow and introduces me. The judge is amused that Jarrett Creek is having to rely on volunteer efforts to keep services going because we're out of money. I don't see the humor in it, but I go along. At least it's something to keep Alan and Clara's mind off their son's death for a while.

When Jenny joins us, Judge Crocker greets her warmly. He has a reputation for being a tough judge, and I expect there are some people who will be glad to see the last of him, but he seems popular with the attorneys who have come to send him off. As soon as the Dellmores walk away, Crocker turns to me, his expression suddenly grim. "That's a bad business about the Dellmore boy. I heard you were in charge now, with that drunk Rodell Skinner out of the picture."

"I am in charge for the time being, while money's tight." I feel uncomfortable with the judge's potshot at Rodell.

"How is the investigation going?" he says.

"I can't tell you I'm going to be able to solve this thing, but I'm going to give it my best shot."

He gives me a close look. "I remember you had a fine reputation when you were chief before, and I believe you're up to the job—a lot more than Rodell Skinner is."

"Rodell has offered me some help, and I think he can put his mind to it now that he's not drinking."

Jenny gives me a sidelong look of disbelief. I don't know why I feel obliged to defend Rodell, but what goes on in our small town is our problem and I don't need somebody from Bobtail gossiping about our incorrigible lawman, even if the one doing the gossiping is a judge.

Jenny goes off to get another glass of wine for both of us and Jack Daniels for Crocker. When she walks away he says, "I don't want to press you, but what line of thinking are you pursuing in the case?"

I put him off with some vague idea about somebody being upset by a financial deal and then tell him we found Gary Dellmore's car."

"Where was it?"

I tell him about Caton "borrowing" the car after he found it abandoned out on the dam road. "I don't have a clue why the car was out there, when Gary was shot at the American Legion Hall."

"Well, it's early times. How's Barbara holding up?"

"She's doing okay. The funeral is Monday. It's always good for the family to get that over with."

The judge gets a frisky look in his eye. "I remember her when she was a youngster. Good-looking. And a fine figure."

"How did you know her?"

"I was a friend of her daddy's. I had my law practice here in Bryan before they tapped me to be a county judge."

"I never knew Barbara's daddy."

"Mike Johnson was a good man." He lowers his voice and leans in closer. "It was a damn shame what Gary Dellmore did to him."

"What did he do?"

"When Gary married Barbara, Mike hired him to be his financial man. Gary made some bad business decisions, and the next thing you know Mike was bankrupt. I think that's what killed him. And his wife died not six months later."

Jenny shows up with our drinks, which cheers up the judge considerably. He may have a low opinion of Rodell Skinner for his drinking, but Crocker is putting away a fair amount himself.

"Who was this fellow you said showed up driving Dellmore's car?" the judge asks. "Has he got a record?"

"No, he doesn't. I think he's just a kid who's drifting around."

Crocker narrows his eyes. "Too much of that element around here these days for my taste. You get some drifter like that coming in, and next thing you know you've got breaking and entering, and then somebody gets killed."

Jenny says, "Samuel, on the way over here you told me that you had a couple of places broken into this week. Could it be this drifter who did it?"

I describe the two break-ins. "Nothing was missing. One of them was Slate McClusky's place. He's got a houseful of goods. If whoever broke in had been somebody like this kid, he probably would have taken something—money or something he could hock."

"You say this was at Slate McClusky's place?" Crocker asks.

"You know him?"

He nods, knitting his brow. "I'm not sure what I heard recently, but it was something to do with Slate having some financial troubles." He shakes a finger to indicate that he's thinking it through. "I know what it was. I know this old boy that used to go out to hunt at that resort and he said the past couple of years it's been closed. He said somebody told him McClusky was trying to sell it. Apparently he lost some money and needs cash."

"Maybe he got tired of taking care of all those animals and then having them get shot," Jenny says.

The judge laughs. "Jenny, I'm going to miss you. You're never afraid to let people know where you stand."

"I don't see the point of raising those beautiful animals inside a fenced area and having people come out there and shoot them. That's not hunting. There's no sport to it. If you're going to hunt, go out and hunt in the free range."

Somebody comes up and pulls Crocker away from us, and shortly afterward Jenny tells me she can't take one more second of standing in her shoes, and we make a break for it.

The weather has eased up some, and although it's still cold, the night is clear and fine. We're halfway home when I tell Jenny that I'm puzzling over why Gary Dellmore wanted the loan he was putting together for the water park kept secret, as if he was doing something underhanded. "I'm going to talk to Cookie Travers at the bank first thing Monday, but I wondered if you had any ideas."

"First thing that comes to mind is maybe he got a kickback from the company for arranging the loan with his bank. If the company didn't have good credit and couldn't get a loan anywhere else, they might have paid him off."

"You're talking about a finder's fee. That's illegal?"

"You're damn right it is. The banker making the loan gets a commission, but he can't take money on both ends. It gets complicated, and there are some exceptions, but that's the bottom line. I dealt with a case like that a few years back and the banker didn't go to jail, but he got probation and had to pay a big fine."

"I wonder if that's what he was up to. And how that water park group decided to go to him for the loan."

"Like I said, maybe they couldn't get one anywhere else. You think this has to do with why he was murdered?"

"I'm not far enough along to say one way or the other, but anytime you get people sliding around the law with money, there's likely to be trouble."

"Especially since Jarrett Creek lost out on the deal. You'd think Dellmore would have studied the water park deal to find out if it was too risky for the town to take on."

CHAPTER 21

Loretta drops by after church the next morning and demands a detailed description of the party. I tell her all the details I can remember and make up a few, like what the women were wearing. I don't mention how pretty Jenny looked.

When Loretta leaves, I call Marietta Bryant at home. Her husband says she's gone to the office and is showing property this afternoon. At Grange Realty Dale Waller answers the phone and says Marietta should be in soon. I ask him to keep her there until I've had a chance to talk to her.

Giving her time to get to the office, I make one more call. I'm not a bit surprised when the Holiday Inn in Marble Falls tells me they have no record of Angel Bright or Slate McClusky staying there last week. There's definitely something odd going on with those two, but their lies are transparent, as if they aren't used to having to cover up their activities.

I get down to the real estate office right after Marietta arrives. "I'm trying to find out more about the people who were involved in that water park deal. You said you handled the deal and I'd like to find out who actually bought the property."

"Hold on, let me pull the file." She goes to a file cabinet at the back of the room and brings back a fat folder, which she lays on her desk and leafs through. "Here's the contract. There were two men, Pete Fontaine and Larry Kestler. They work for 'Liberty Water Unlimited' out of Houston. It's a big outfit that owns several water parks, not just in Texas. They've got them in Louisiana and Arkansas, too."

The front door opens and Bill Odum walks in with his young wife, Sissy. "Hey there, Samuel," Odum says. "What are you doing here?"

"Since you didn't get a chance to talk to Marietta, I thought I'd follow through on that. You two fixin' to buy a house?"

"We can't afford anything just yet, but we wanted to start getting some idea of what's available."

Sissy, a pale, blue-eyed girl with hair the color of maize, beams at her husband and I feel a twinge of nostalgia, thinking how nice it is for a young couple to be setting out on the road to building their lives. Jeanne and I walked into this very office years ago, when we decided to settle down in Jarrett Creek. I still remember the sense of the future sprawling out in front of us.

Marietta walks out the door with the Odums. Dale Waller says he's on his way, too. "I'll set the lock so all you have to do is close the door behind you when you leave."

Suddenly Marietta comes back inside. "I wanted to tell you something. It's in the strictest confidence, but I thought you ought to know that Slate McClusky called me yesterday and he wants to put his house on the market."

"He say where they're going?"

"No." She pauses. "And he's selling it rock bottom." She smiles. "You have any interest in buying? It's got all the modern conveniences."

"I'm sure it does, but I expect the backyard wouldn't suit my cows all that well."

Left alone I look through the file Marietta left for me and find a plat map of the property the water park was supposed to be built on. I manage to figure out their copy machine and make a copy of the map and the contract with the buyers' names on it.

I head out to the lake with a copy of the plat map and a drawing I copied from Marietta's file to help me locate the lot where the water park was supposed to be. It's a big piece of land north of one of the marinas. There's a road that leads to the marina, but I have to leave my truck there and walk a ways until I get to the wooden stakes bearing faded blue plastic flags that marked the boundaries of the property.

I didn't pay much attention to the water park at the time it was proposed. I thought it sounded like a perfectly good idea, but I was still in deep mourning for my wife and had no interest in the details.

I walk around the lot to give myself a sense of the area they had in mind. Even after all these months, you can still see that some preliminary work was done—the land was bulldozed and a couple of trees felled. The land is raw and choppy-looking. The grass has grown back sparsely, but most of it is bare clay.

It would have been a fine thing for the economy around here if the plan had worked, but I have questions that I wonder if Coldwater and the city council took into account when they were considering it. I've seen pictures of water parks, and they look like elaborate contraptions with a lot of water involved. Where was the water going to come from? This is a fair-sized lake, but in Texas we're always subject to drought. If the water to run the park rides was to come from here, what would they have done when we had water rationing, as has happened a few times since the lake was built?

It seems to me the liability would be high, too, with the danger of kids drowning or being hurt on the slides. So between insurance, water, and the need for lots of alert employees to make sure no one got into trouble in the water, they'd have a pretty high overhead. That means they'd have to charge high prices for tickets.

The question is, why would the state okay a permit, given those constraints? People around here come to the lake because they can have a cheap vacation. The state has kept it that way. There are nice little state-maintained areas at various places around the lake where people can camp out in tents or hook up their RVs. I wonder if those people would be willing, or even able, to pay the price to bring their kids to a fancy water park.

If an unsophisticated bystander like me can figure out the limitations, how come those who were supposed to study the pros and cons didn't figure it out? There must have been some heavy persuading going on. I wonder if that's where Gary Dellmore's participation came in. I hate to bother Rusty Reinhardt again, but I need to find out what kind of state involvement there was in the deal and who their liaison was.

I walk down to the water's edge and I'm looking out over the lake when I hear a familiar voice behind me. "Yo, Chief, what are you doing out here?"

I turn and say, "How are you doing, Louis? You fixing to do a little fishing?"

"Yeah. Gotta eat." He scratches his head. It looks like Louis Caton is wearing the same clothes he was wearing when he was sitting in jail, and that he hasn't had an opportunity to clean them up. He's carrying a fishing rod and a tackle box that looks like they might be somebody's cast-offs. But he looks as cheerful as he did before. I guess there's something to be said for being young and not beholden to anybody, even if it means you sometimes don't have enough to eat.

He's shifting from one foot to another, like he's got something on his mind. "I wanted to thank you," he says.

"For what?"

"For not arresting me when I was driving a stolen car."

I smile. "Louis, I'd say you should count your blessings that you happened to commit a crime in a town that can't afford to put you up in jail. But if you want me to arrest you so you can get a square meal, just say so."

He grins. "No, sir, if it gets that bad, I'll go on home. My mamma would be glad to see me anyway."

I laugh. "What possessed you to take the car in the first place? You don't have any criminal record and you don't seem like much of a criminal, otherwise you would have taken off for parts unknown with that car and we never would have seen it again."

He turns on that lazy grin again. "I'd had a few beers and I was tired of walking. When I saw that it was still there when I was walking home, I thought, 'Hell, if somebody is going to just leave it there unattended, I might as well use it.'"

I laugh and he continues to talk, telling me that it was nice to have a car for a few days. "Mine is down at the cabin I'm staying in. It needs a battery and I can't afford to buy one."

I'm only half-listening. Something Caton said earlier tickles my thoughts. I hold up my hand. "Wait a minute. You said the car was still there. What do you mean 'still there'?"

"I mean it was parked there when I was walking to my friend's place earlier in the evening, and it was still in the same place when I came back by." A little worry line appears between his eyes. "I thought I told you that."

"If you did, the information didn't stick." My heart has started to pump a little faster. "What time did you pass it the first time?"

He squints out over the lake. "Had to be before nine o'clock. I was at my friend's place by nine."

The meeting we had that night didn't let out until nine thirty. Gary Dellmore's car was sitting in the parking lot when I left, so it couldn't have been on the dam road. "You're sure it was the same car?"

"What?" He's half-smiling, searching my face for a clue to what I'm after. "Why would it be a different car?"

"Give it some thought. Same car?"

He blinks at me a few times. "Damn! I don't know. It was pretty dark out and the car was dark-colored, that's all I can tell you. I assumed it was the same car."

"Was it facing the same direction the second time you came by?"

He chews on his lip while he considers it. He begins to shake his head. "You know, it could have been a different car. I couldn't swear to it either way."

I think I've just had my first break investigating Gary Dellmore's death. "One more question," I ask. "Did you see anybody walking along the road?"

He hesitates and then shakes his head. "No, it would be unusual to see somebody walking along there and I think I would have remembered it. Sorry, I wish I could help you out with that."

"Doesn't matter." I clap him on the shoulder and nod out toward the lake. "I hope you catch something today."

"So do I." He grins and ambles away.

My impulse is to give him some money for a decent meal, but he's told me he has a family to fall back on. He's on an experiment with himself to see how far down he has to go before he's had enough. Who am I to disturb that?

I walk back to my truck, turning over in my mind what I've learned from Louis Caton. Whoever killed Gary Dellmore didn't do it on the spur of the moment. He left his car up in that rarely used park on the dam road and walked the mile to the American Legion Hall to lie in wait for Dellmore. After he shot Dellmore, he drove his Crown Vic back up to where he'd left his own car. Then he left Dellmore's car and took off in his own. I'm thinking "he," but it could just as easily have been "she." It's a small thing, but at least now I have an idea of how it could have been done. And I know this was no argument gone wrong; it was premeditated murder.

I'm not back at the house ten minutes when I hear a knock at the front door. "Mr. Craddock?"

Ellen Forester is standing on my porch. She's dressed in jeans and a jazzy black-and-white blouse with a black jacket. I can't help thinking of Loretta asking me what Ellen looked like, and I realize I should have said that she's pretty and has a nice figure.

I open the screen door. "So you found your way to my place."

"I hope I'm not disturbing you. I was over at my shop getting some of the art unpacked and I needed a break, so I thought I'd see if you'd mind showing me your collection. I didn't have your number or I would've called."

"Come on in. I just put some coffee on." She's wearing running shoes and looks fit enough so that I suspect she uses the shoes as they were intended.

As she enters the living room her eyes widen. She's looking right at the Diebenkorn on the far wall facing her. The Neri sculpture is next to it. I see the duo through her eyes, and they look complete together, like a couple of old married people. "Oh, my." Her voice is almost worshipful.

"Come on back to the kitchen and we'll get coffee first."

She trails me into the kitchen.

"You left me a note. Sorry I haven't had a chance to get back to you."

She looks a little panicky standing in the kitchen. "Are you sure I'm not disturbing you?" I wonder what makes her so timid. I'm pretty easygoing, and yet every time she looks at me, she seems jumpy.

I gesture to the kitchen table. "Not a bit. Sit down. When the coffee's ready we'll take a tour around the house."

She pulls out a chair and sits at the table. "Several people have told me you've got a great art collection and that I should see it, but I had no idea."

I smile. "They're making conversation. Most people haven't seen my art, and most of those who have don't have a clue what they're seeing."

She laughs and sounds like she means it. "I got that impression. People could tell me you had a wonderful collection, but they couldn't tell me what was in it."

I pour us some coffee and say, "Let's go take a look."

I lead her to the hallway, where I've hung the paintings I feel least connected with. First is the Hans Hoffmann that I liked so much when we first bought it, but now it looks gaudy to me. When Jeanne and I got married, she had a few pieces that her mother gave her, and those are here, too.

"I love this Calder," Ellen says, clasping her hands to her chest. "It's so exuberant."

"The colors are nice," I say, although that's the best I can come up with. Calder doesn't do a thing for me—and it didn't for Jeanne either. She felt we had to hang it somewhere out of loyalty to her mother, but as she said, that didn't mean we had to like it.

I tell Ellen how Jeanne persuaded me to graduate from blue-bonnets and cactus to abstract art by dragging me to art galleries in Fort Worth, Houston, and Austin. "One day we were in a gallery in Houston and I spotted this." I point to a piece and tell her it's the first picture Jeanne and I ever bought together, a small but lively abstract that reminds me of Kandinsky. "The artist never became famous, but I still like the picture."

We wander through the house, me pointing out my old and new favorites, everything from my beloved Wolf Kahn to the work of a young boy whose career is just being launched and whose grandmother was a good friend of mine. I find Ellen easy to talk to. She makes comments that are smart, but not pedantic.

"We have to organize an event here," she says. She's standing in front of the Bischoff that Jeanne's mother willed to us. "It's not right for people not to be able to see these things."

"Maybe so," I say.

"Don't you agree?" she says. "I get so mad when I read that some rich collector has bought a masterpiece and plans to hide it away in a vault so no one ever gets to see it."

"My collection isn't in that league."

"I'm not going to let you off the hook," she says. "You have some wonderful pieces that should be seen." She moves back to the Wolf Kahn. "This one right here is my favorite." And then she laughs. "But if I came back tomorrow, I'd probably choose a different one."

She doesn't know she's chosen my favorite and for some reason I don't tell her so.

"My wife Jeanne and I used to host tours. But I haven't felt much like it on my own. Maybe sometime I'll be ready to have another tour."

"You won't be on your own," she says briskly. "You'll have me." She turns and sees the look on my face and claps her hand over her mouth. "Oh, I've let myself get bossy, haven't I? My best friend tells me that happens when I get carried away talking about art." She sets her coffee cup down on a table and moves toward the door as if she wants to escape.

"Wait a minute. You don't have to go—I'm not going to bite you. Yes, you were a little bossy, I'll grant you that. But it's for a good cause. I'm not quite ready yet, that's all. Give me a little time. Besides, you haven't even moved into your new place yet."

She looks more upset than I think my words deserve. "You're being nice. I hope when you see my art you won't think it's silly."

"No, it takes all kinds of art to make people happy. Now let me calm you down a little bit by taking you to see what I spend the rest of my time on. That is, until I got hooked into being chief of police."

I escort her out the back door, and we head down to the pasture so I can find out what my cows think of the new art dealer.

CHAPTER 22

"They're back." Loretta can only mean Gabe LoPresto and Darla Rodriguez.

We're sitting at the kitchen table. It has turned cold overnight again, and Loretta is bundled up like she's off for a ski trip. We're all wondering if this winter is ever going to let go of its grip.

"Don't you want to know where they were?"

I want to say I don't care, but it would be mean to steal Loretta's thunder. "Okay, I give up. Where were they?"

"They went off to some fancy resort in Galveston to celebrate Darla's birthday."

I take a bite of Loretta's coffee cake. It's my favorite of all the baked goods that she makes. "That was a nice thing to do."

Loretta smirks. "I don't know how nice it was. The way Darla's mother tells it, Darla shamed Gabe into taking her away for a long weekend. Apparently he got her a diamond necklace and she didn't think it was enough of a birthday present, so he agreed to take her to Galveston for a few days to make up for it."

"So they're back and pretty pleased with themselves?" I'm trying to think of something to say, because the subject of Gabe LoPresto's affair has ceased to interest me. I've got too much else on my mind.

"At least one of them is."

I set my coffee cup down. "Loretta, tell me what's going on."

She slaps her hand down on the table, her eyes sparkling. "They had a big fight and they broke it off. The question no one seems to know the answer to is which one of them wanted out. Either way, he's out the money not only for the necklace but for the trip, too. Serves him right."

163

I can't help laughing. "I suppose he'll be walking around with his tail between his legs for a while."

"I guess. But I'll bet we haven't heard the last of it. He'll try to get her back, and no telling how long she'll keep him on the leash."

"Like you said, serves him right."

Suddenly her laughter dies away and she says, "I saw that new woman's car down here yesterday. Tell me what she's like."

"Ellen's nice." I'm still trying to absorb what Ellen said when I took her down to see my cows yesterday.

"That's telling me a lot. Did she like your art?"

"She did. She said she probably wouldn't have much of that kind of art in her gallery. She doesn't think it would sell very well around here."

"She's right." Loretta has never pretended to like my taste in art— or any art at all, as far as I can tell. She's more of knick-knack kind of person. "What else did she say?"

I sigh. "She's a vegetarian." I blurt it out, still trying to get over that awkward exchange. When I took her down to see the cows, she acted really funny and finally asked me if I eat meat. I told her of course I did, that you couldn't get any better beef than raising it yourself. And she told me she didn't eat meat.

"A vegetarian. I swear, who would have guessed it?" I might just as well have told Loretta that Ellen Forester keeps monkeys in her house. "Nona Peterson told everybody she had decided to be a vegetarian. Somebody asked her if she was going to be a Buddhist, and she said no, she thought you could be a vegetarian even if you were a Christian."

"We didn't get into the religious side of things," I say.

"A vegetarian. Well, that's interesting." She takes a sip of coffee. "When does she plan to open her store?"

"She was hoping to get things ready before Christmas, but construction took a lot longer than she thought it would. She said it should be done pretty soon."

"Does she have a family?"

"I didn't ask."

"Of course you didn't, being a man."

I'm in the office by eight thirty. For once I had trouble getting to sleep last night. I started thinking about the files I removed from Gary Dellmore's trunk. I intended to get to them this weekend, but the time got away from me. I pull the box out from under my desk and set it on top.

To save money, I turned off the heat in the police station last night, and this morning it's colder inside than it is outside, which is saying something. After cranking up the thermostat, I sit down with a cup of extra-strong coffee, put on a pair of latex gloves, and get to work.

If Dellmore hadn't been murdered, I wouldn't have thought a thing about him carrying files around in his trunk, although I suspect it's a violation of good banking practice. But since he was murdered I need to check if anything he was working on at the time might have led to his death. At the least I need to see if there's anything in the files that Cookie Travers or Alan Dellmore ought to be handling.

The file folders aren't labeled, and they don't have anything to do with loans. The first one contains blueprints. I set that file aside. The next one contains lists of building specifications. So maybe someone was planning on building a structure and the bank had to approve a building loan. But in the third file I find something that makes me take notice. It's got two brochures in it—from McClusky's hunting resort. The brochures are flashy, with pictures of exotic animals labeled Yak, Axis Deer, Mexican White Deer, Whitetail Bucks, Fallow Deer, Texas Eland, and Aoudad Sheep. And there's a picture of a herd of zebras. I don't know why I don't have a problem with somebody hunting all these exotic African animals, but I draw the line at zebra. It's like hunting a horse. How could anyone find sport in that?

There are other folders containing information about the McClusky resort—an outdated prospectus, annual reports, expense sheets dating back several years, and more building specifications. Tucked at the back of the banker's box that holds the folders is a *Texas Amusement* magazine.

If it hadn't been for the McClusky resort brochures, I might not have taken a closer look at the blueprints and expense sheets. But when I open one of the blueprints and orient myself to it, I realize it's a blueprint of the main house at the McClusky resort. Now what in the world was Gary Dellmore doing with this?

Maybe McClusky was telling the truth and there is a big renovation project being prepared. But either way, it's clear that McClusky and Dellmore knew each other better than McClusky said. It looks like maybe Dellmore was planning to get McClusky a loan to renovate his place. There are no other financial statements in the files, though, so I can't tell how far they got with the deal.

Before I put the *Texas Amusement* magazine back in the box, I notice it's an issue dedicated to water parks. I thumb through it. It's full of pictures of water slides and river floats, chutes that look like vertical roller coasters that drop their little cars with people in them straight down into a pool of water. There are tide pools and swimming pools. I glance at a couple of articles, glowing reports on the health benefits of water parks or the great investment they make. They do look like a lot of fun. I see how people would've been seduced by the idea of something like this out at the lake.

But toward the back I run across an article titled "Has the Water Park Wave Crested?" I decide to read it, wondering if Dellmore had seen it. It describes the water park craze and how it enjoyed a time of popularity. But then it says that water parks are expensive to run and many of them have closed down. The liability insurance alone is staggering. Construction costs; maintenance costs; and city, county, and state taxes make up another big chunk. According to the article, the parks also have to hire more employees than most types of amusement parks, which means they have to charge a lot—just as I thought. Did Gary Dellmore read this article?

At the end of the article, I spot the name of Jarrett Creek in a little box at the side, listing it as one water park that was being planned. The end of the article says that Liberty Water Unlimited was particularly hard hit when one of their big moneymakers in Texas had to shut down because of code violations. And then I come to the part that makes my mouth drop open. A spokesman for Liberty Water Unlimited, one of the principals of the company, says, "We continue to believe that water parks are good, wholesome family fun and will strive to make our parks the best in the country." The spokesman? Slate McClusky.

When Bill Odum comes in, I tell him about my conversation with Louis Caton over the weekend. "When he told me Dellmore's car had been sitting there when he was walking to his friend's house, I knew it couldn't be Dellmore's car. Had to be one that looked like the Crown Vic." I tell him my theory that the killer parked there, walked to the American Legion Hall to confront Dellmore and then drove his car back and exchanged it for his own.

Odum nods. "So we're looking for somebody who drove a car like Dellmore's."

"Looks like it," I say.

I then describe to him the contents of the files and magazine article I found in Dellmore's trunk. "I'm closer to thinking this water park failure had something to do with Dellmore getting killed."

He frowns. "If it was somebody from that water park outfit who killed him, the car we're looking for isn't from around here."

"You're right. I don't think we should concentrate on the car. It could be anywhere. But at least now we know somebody planned the murder."

"What do we do next?"

"First let's take care of these calls," I say, punching the message machine. Carrie Landau called at six a.m., frantic, saying her car is missing. "I heard Gary Dellmore's car was gone. Maybe we've got a car theft ring." But an hour later she called back to say she remembered that she'd left it at a friend's house. There's one other call from an elderly man complaining that his neighbor is letting his grass get too long. Odum is grinning, listening to these sad tales.

I laugh. "We file those under 'Not enough to keep them busy.'"

I tell Odum I'm going to Gary Dellmore's funeral this afternoon. I give him the name and phone numbers of the two men who were involved in the water park deal. "I'd like you to set up a meeting with them and with Alton Coldwater Wednesday morning. Tell them it's police business and we'd rather not have to come interview them in Houston."

I want to take what I found this morning in Dellmore's files to Cookie Travers and ask her if she knew anything about Gary's involvement in the water park, but first I want to get more information. I put in a call to my brother-in-law, DeWitt Simms. He's my wife's brother, and he and I have always gotten along well.

I figure he'll be out playing golf, but I'll talk to his wife Lucille and ask her to have him call me. At the same time I can find out how she's doing. She suffers from anxiety that makes it hard for her to leave the house sometimes. But it's DeWitt who answers the phone. He doesn't sound like his usual hearty self, but he perks up when he hears my voice. "Tell me you're coming out here to see us. I think Lucille could use some cheering up."

"What's going on? You don't sound any too chipper yourself."

"We've had a little rough patch. I had a bad cold and Lucille has had some problems with her vertigo. And you know that really throws her for a loop."

I know that means DeWitt is stuck in the house and can't get out on the golf course. "How long have you had to stay in with her?"

"It's just a few days. I don't mind a bit. She'll be okay before too long. But I think a visit from you would cheer her up."

"I'll see what I can do." I tell him I've become temporary chief of police while the money issues get sorted out in town and that I'm dealing with a murder.

"Life has taken an interesting turn for you," DeWitt says. "I'm glad. Jeanne would be happy you're staying busy."

"Yes, and I have a problem I hope you might be able to help me with, but it sounds like it would be hard for you to get away right now."

"Now don't be too hasty. Why don't you tell me what's up and I'll see what I can figure out."

I tell him that Slate McClusky said he'd be staying at the Marriott and wasn't there when I phoned. "I drove out to his resort and I was surprised to find it in pretty poor condition. Do you think anybody you play golf with might know McClusky or know something about his financial situation?"

"That resort is pretty well-known around here. I didn't realize it had fallen on hard times. Let me see if I can't line up a game with a couple of boys I play golf with who also hunt, and see if I can scare up some information from them."

"I don't want you to leave Lucille if you're not comfortable."

"Lucille's best friend has been after me to let her come over and spend some time with her while I'm out of the house so they can have some girl talk. I think Lucille is feeling good enough that I can leave her with Betsy."

My next call is to Rusty Reinhardt. He's still huffy after our last exchange, but I tell him I've got some questions about the water park deal. "I wonder if I can get a look at the files about that park."

"Fine with me. The files are in the city office. It's shut down, so I'll have to meet you with the key, and I can't get there until the afternoon."

I've got the funeral this afternoon. "Maybe you can answer something for me. When you and Marietta were looking through the deal on the park, did you ever see any permits from the state or any documents the state might have provided?"

"I'm going to put you on hold for a minute. I've got a vendor here I have to take care of."

It takes several minutes. When he comes back he says, "I'm trying to think, but I never saw anything like that. You know, Marietta and I have been so concerned with the town's finances, I didn't pay any attention to the park. That's old business."

"I'd like to come and get the key from you. I need that information as soon as possible."

"I'll tell you what. I have to run over to Bobtail to pick up some stuff. How about if I drop it off there on my way out of town? I'll be there in a half hour, forty-five minutes." He tells me where to locate the files in the office.

That gives me time to go over to the café for an early lunch and, if I'm honest with myself, to see if Gabe LoPresto has decided to show his face or if he's off pouting. But he's there, looking more satisfied than he ought to. Everyone at the table around him looks like they've got feathers on their faces. They may be LoPresto's friends, but they aren't above gloating a little at the fact that his affair with Darla Rodriguez has come to a bad end.

Remembering my confrontation with Sandy LoPresto, I'm almost embarrassed to be seen with him, but Harley Lundsford waves me over to the table. "Come on and sit down. Gabe has quite a tale to tell, and some of it may even be true."

"I don't know what makes you say that," LoPresto says. There's a whole lot of bluster in his voice. "I'm telling it like it is."

I'm glad to find out I don't have to act like I don't know what's happened. After I tell Lurleen that I'm having whatever's on special today, I say, "Gabe, I hope you've come back to the land of reality."

He snorts with laughter, although if I read him right, he has to work at it. "Not a minute too soon! That little gal was bad business."

"How so?"

"I believe she thought I was a wealthier man than I turned out to be, and when she realized I wasn't ready to turn over the bank account, she decided she could do better elsewhere."

"We better tell Slate McClusky to look out," Lundsford says.

Everybody laughs except LoPresto. "He can take care of himself. If anything, he's part of the problem. All I wanted was a little fun. But she's after somebody to set her up." He tries to give his words a light touch, but I can tell he's feeling put upon.

"Listen, Gabe," I say, "you're better off without her."

We don't mind needling him a little, but I notice that nobody asks for particulars, like what LoPresto plans to do now. If I'm any judge of his wife, it won't be long before he's back with her. I wouldn't imagine all will be forgiven anytime soon—he'll have to pay his piper—but eventually it will work itself out.

Reinhardt has left the key as promised and I walk over to the city offices, which are just a block away. During the financial crisis the office is only open Tuesday and Thursday mornings. When I go in, I find Reinhardt's desk covered with spreadsheets and file folders pertaining to the city's finances. I'd rather be a prison guard than have to deal with this mess.

I locate the water park files where Reinhardt said they would be. There's a whole drawer dedicated to them. I riffle through them and don't see one for state permits or the like. I find files for studies and blueprints and contracts. I open the contracts and locate the one between Liberty Water Parks and the City of Jarrett Creek. It's huge. In the table of contents I find the part pertaining to the permits and licenses.

I wish Jenny were here to point me to the pertinent sections. I have to wade through a good bit of legalese before I come to the part I'm looking for. It says all permits and licenses with the state will be obtained by Liberty Water Parks and that the City of Jarrett Creek will receive copies of all such permits. If those permits ever got here, they've been filed somewhere else.

I remind myself that as much interest as I have in the busted water park deal, the only reason I need to concern myself with it is if it has anything to do with Gary Dellmore's death. If I find shady dealings, and it looks like I might, that will be for the mayor to sort out with lawyers and accountants.

I hurry home with barely enough time to get dressed for Dellmore's funeral. I don't know why Barbara wanted me there, but I said I'd do it. I'm putting on my tie when I remember something LoPresto said at lunch. I wonder what he meant when he said that McClusky was part of his problem with Darla Rodriguez. I'll have to ask him next time I see him.

CHAPTER 23

There are only thirty or so people at the funeral service for Gary Dellmore. It's mostly relatives, but a couple of board members from the bank are there, along with Cookie Travers. Barbara insists that Cookie sit with her and the family. The person who seems most upset is Annalise, Gary's sister. She cries pretty much nonstop. I'm glad she's finally letting herself grieve. When I was at the Dellmore's the other day, she was under awfully tight control. Her husband doesn't seem particularly supportive and barely hides his boredom at the proceedings.

It's hard to figure out why I was invited—or was it commanded?—to attend the service. Barbara and Cookie keep an eye on the door leading to the chapel. Every time it opens, they tense. But each time they see who's at the door, they relax.

I can't tell that there's much difference between the Episcopal Church and the Catholic Church. They're both small congregations, but they don't skimp on the ornate trappings. I'm not one for church to begin with, and the incense and robes and gold paraphernalia set with jewels make me feel smothered.

After the service we're all invited to refreshments, set up in a small room off the kitchen, consisting of coffee, delicate sandwiches, and cake. It's a subdued and elegant affair that seems strangely foreign from the way things are usually done in Jarrett Creek.

By the time the service and reception are over, it's clear that whoever Barbara thought was going to show up hasn't made an appearance. I'm going to have to find out who she was worried about.

I'm home by five o'clock. I don't know if it's the tension of the funeral or having to readjust my days to being a working man, but I'm tired. Yesterday, showing my art collection to Ellen Forester, I remembered how much I enjoy looking at it. For a while after Jeanne died, the paintings were a double-edged pastime—the good and bad side of being reminded of Jeanne—where we were when we bought a piece, the discussions we had before we decided, and sometimes even the arguments. But gradually I've come to enjoy the art for itself again. There were a couple of pieces that particularly caught my eye when I was showing them to Ellen. I walk into the hallway and study the Kandinsky lookalike. It sometimes seems too busy to me, but right now it looks like a puzzle being unraveled. Maybe solving the puzzle will rub off on me.

I've been going strong all day, but I still have a long evening ahead of me. I stow away a good meal and am headed out the door a little after six o'clock when the phone rings.

"I had the best afternoon I've had in a long time," DeWitt says. "And I got some information for you."

"You already had that golf game?"

"Yes, sir, you didn't have to ask twice. I was ready to get out of here and I think it did Lucille a world of good to spend the afternoon with her girlfriend. I was starting to get on her nerves."

DeWitt has always been good to Lucille, always pretending that her affliction is a minor discomfort instead of a debilitating disease. It's typical that he says it's him getting on her nerves, when probably it's the other way around.

"I imagine it was good to get out on the golf course."

"I really enjoyed myself. And I picked up a thing or two you might be interested in."

I want to go back out to McClusky's resort anyway, so I arrange with DeWitt to have lunch with him tomorrow. "I'll come by and pick you up so I can visit with Lucille first."

"She would love that."

Angel Bright pulls her Cadillac into the driveway long after dark. It's the same size as Dellmore's Crown Victoria, but it's a light color, so it wouldn't be mistaken for Dellmore's.

The McCluskys told me yesterday that they were going to be home tonight. I've tried to reach them several times today to tell them I need to ask them some more questions, but as usual I haven't heard back.

Angel is not happy to see me. "Samuel, I'm sorry, if you're looking for Slate, he stayed out at the resort."

"I can talk to you," I say.

"I'm awful tired. I hope it won't take long."

"No, just a couple of questions. I can always drive out to see Slate tomorrow if you don't know the answers."

Her eyes flick away and back. "I don't know if he'll be around tomorrow. We've got some financial things he's having to take care of."

"Oh, right. The things in Marble Falls. Taking care of all those financial deals seems to keep you two pretty busy."

Her laugh is false and tinkly. "The financial deals are Slate's thing. I don't get involved in that."

She leads me through the house into the kitchen, but I don't get the same sense of warmth from her that I did the first time I was here. Marietta Bryant told me they're going to put the house on the market, and it already has taken on an impersonal feel, as if they've moved out mentally.

Angel takes a beer out of the refrigerator and offers me one, but I decline. In the harsh kitchen light, she looks a little ragged. Her hair is tucked back behind her ears, exposing her face, which looks drawn and tired. She doesn't sit down and doesn't offer me a seat.

"Now what can I do for you?"

"How friendly were Slate and Gary Dellmore?"

She puts a hand on the kitchen counter. "That's a funny question. Like Slate told you, he didn't know Gary well at all."

"Barbara Dellmore told me that Gary said he went out to eat with Slate a few times."

"Maybe they did. I don't know. Even if they did, that doesn't mean they were friends. It was probably business." She's pulled a strand of hair over her shoulder and is twirling it around her finger. She looks trapped. There's something about Gary and Slate that she doesn't want to admit. Maybe it's a habit with Angel to be on guard when she answers questions, but this is not the first time I've thought she was lying to me.

"Slate had a lot to do with that water park deal out at the lake, which means he and Dellmore would have had some dealings."

She looks startled. "That's not really true," she says. "Slate was a backer, but he didn't do any of the hands-on dealings with Gary. That was Pete Fontaine and Larry Kestler. Slate was more in the way of a silent partner." She moves quickly to a kitchen drawer and opens it. "I've got Pete and Larry's numbers here somewhere." The drawer is a mess and she scrabbles around in it until she finds a business card. "Here you go." She thrusts it at me. Wanting to get rid of me. "You should call them. They can probably tell you everything you need to know."

"I'm wondering why you and Slate didn't mention being involved with the deal out at the water park."

She shoves her hands into her back pockets, then takes them out again and grabs her beer. "I can't tell you that. It doesn't seem that important to me. Like I said, Slate's the one who does money stuff. You know everybody thinks we're moneybags, but when that deal went bad it was just as hard on us as everyone else. As far as I know we just put up money for it."

Having read the article, I know that's not true. But maybe she doesn't know the particulars. I'll give her the benefit of the doubt for the time being.

"I guess if there's no way to get in touch with Slate, I'll leave you and try to find him tomorrow." I step toward the backdoor. The look of relief on her face is laughable. I turn back to her. "One more thing. Slate said you have a Colt .45. Do you still have it?"

She looks startled. "I suppose I do. It should be in the drawer by my bed. Why?"

"Do you mind showing it to me?"

"Let me get it."

She's back quickly. "Here it is." She's holding it by the handle and thrusts it at me like she's handing over a dead rat.

I use my handkerchief to take it from her. The safety is on. I take out the magazine. "There's a bullet missing. Do you know when it was last fired?"

"I don't know why any bullets would be missing. Slate usually keeps it loaded." She's staring at the open gun.

"This is his gun, not yours, isn't it?"

She glares at me. "I don't know what difference it makes. Slate said having a gun would scare off somebody if they broke in. He showed me how to pull this thing back and fire it if I had to." She points to the body of the gun.

"Have you ever fired it?"

"Once or twice Slate took me out to do some target shooting. Why are you asking me all these questions about Slate and Gary and the gun?" She takes a swig of her beer and wipes her mouth.

"I'd like your permission to take this Colt with me."

"To have it tested to find out if it was used to kill Gary." Her voice is flat.

"If that's all right."

"Do I have a choice?"

"You can make me get a warrant for it."

"Oh, go ahead." She waves her hand in an attempt to seem blasé, but her hand is shaking.

CHAPTER 24

As soon as I get to the station the next morning I track down Luke Schoppe, the Texas Ranger who came out the day Dellmore's body was found. He tells me he's in his car on the way to Waco. "How can I help you?"

I tell him I'm officially the chief now.

"Good. How are you doing on the investigation?"

"Moving along. I want to find out where you're keeping the shell casing found at the scene of the Dellmore murder. I've got a gun I'd like to have ballistics tests done on."

He grunts. "It's been awhile since you were on the job. I expect you don't know that we've got a big backup in ballistics testing."

"How big?"

"Months. Could even be a year."

I thank him and hang up. That's a blow.

When Odum comes in, I take out the bag with Slate McClusky's gun in it and lay it on the desk.

"What have you got there? Looks like a Colt."

"Belongs to Slate McClusky. I'd planned to see if we could get a ballistics match between the shell casing we found near Dellmore's body and the one this gun would produce."

"You think McClusky could have killed Dellmore?"

I describe to him the connection between Dellmore and McClusky with regard to the water park deal. "We need to eliminate McClusky's gun, but we've got a problem." I tell him what Schoppe said about the time it would take to do ballistics tests.

"Yeah, we heard in training that the labs were backed up. They told us over a year. Maybe they've speeded things up if Schoppe said it would take months instead of years."

"Still a long time."

"I can do a test and at least find out if we should eliminate the gun," he says.

"How are you going to do that?"

"There's a crude way to do a fairly accurate ballistics test. It wouldn't be official, but at least we could get some information." He's fidgeting like a kid in grade school.

I laugh. "You have your own little ballistics testing lab?"

"Naw. At the academy we had this instructor who was sort of a loose cannon, you might say. He didn't have a lot of patience for how slow things get done in law enforcement, so he showed us a way to test ballistics. He told us you can't get a good enough match to stand up in court, but you can use it to eliminate a gun."

"How long will it take?"

"Not long. Couple of days. I'll have to get the spent casing. Can you get me authorized to borrow it?"

"What you're going to do won't damage the casing, will it, in case we need to have the ballistics tested officially?"

"No, sir, all I'd need it for is a comparison under a microscope. I can go over to Bobtail Junior College and they'll let me use a microscope in the science lab."

I call Schoppe again and tell him I'd like to have the bullet casing on loan.

"What are you planning to do with it? I like to keep evidence on hand."

"One of the deputies here says he can do an approximation of a ballistics test so we can rule out the gun."

He laughs. "He knows the cotton batting trick?"

"He didn't tell me what he's doing, but he seems to think he can work with it."

"All right. You know I normally would have left the casing with you, but hearing what kind of mess your department was in, I figured I'd better stash it over at police headquarters in Bryan. Can your deputy pick it up from there?"

"He can go over there right now."

"I'll notify the duty officer to get it out of storage for him."

When I hang up, Odum hops to his feet, eager to get on the road to Bryan.

"Whoa!" I say. "Were you able to set up the meeting Wednesday morning with those two fellows from Houston and Alton Coldwater?"

"Yes, sir. They said they'd get on the road early."

"Good. And Coldwater?"

"He'll be here, too."

I tell Odum I'll be out most of the day, and that he can reach me on my cell phone if anything comes up.

On my way out of town, I have two stops to make. First I swing by to see if Slate has made a surprise appearance at his house. I've left messages this morning and as usual got no return call. If I were inclined to take it personally, I might think he was avoiding me.

Truly is just arriving when I get to the McCluskys. He says he hasn't seen either of them. "I've got to paint the wood around that window that got replaced. And then finish up with a last coat of the outside paint, and then I'm done." His tone implies it can't be too soon to suit him.

I tell him if the McCluskys do happen to come home, to ask Slate to call me. I'm not holding my breath.

I promised to keep Rodell Skinner in the loop, and he's my next stop. Although he's still lying on the couch, his face has a little less yellow in it today.

I apologize for not getting to him yesterday. "I guess I don't have to tell you that being down to me plus two part-timers, I don't have enough time in the day."

He gets an eager gleam in his eye. "That's where I think I can help you out."

"You're looking a lot better. It won't be any time before you're down there shoving me aside."

As quick as his eyes lit up, they grow dark again. "Don't patronize me," he snaps.

I laugh. "Now, that's the old Rodell showing through."

He's mollified, and I tell him about the break-in at the McCluskys' and Camille Overton's."

"It would sound like kids to me, too, but I don't know about them breaking a window. If they went that far, I think they'd take something."

"You might be right. But who else would break in? And why?"

He shakes his head. "You got me."

I describe the party for Judge Crocker Saturday night. He tells me that he knows for a fact that the judge is a drinker and that he keeps a flask on him at all times. I don't say it takes one to know one, but I think it.

"Here's the biggest thing that happened this weekend." I tell him that my conversation with Louis Caton led me to understand that whoever killed Gary Dellmore must have left a car at the park, then driven Gary's car there and swapped them back.

"You need to find out who's got a car that looks like Dellmore's," he says.

"I know it. The problem is so many cars look alike these days."

"Too bad it wasn't one of those Hummers," he says. "Then you'd have a limited field."

I tell him I attended Gary Dellmore's service yesterday afternoon.

"I didn't know you were big friends with Alan Dellmore," he says. There's a hint of resentment in his voice. I imagine being laid up, he's feeling left out of a lot of things these days. That was the one thing that would make my wife Jeanne fretful when she was too sick to go out—feeling like she was out of the social loop.

"I'm not particular friends of the Dellmores, but I don't think they invited me to be social. I'm still not sure exactly why they wanted me there, but they seemed afraid that somebody would show up that they didn't want at the funeral."

"Somebody Dellmore was cattin' around with, I expect."

"Doesn't seem likely to me. Seems like anybody like that would want to steer clear of the family."

"Unless it's somebody who likes to cause trouble. Like that Darla Rodriguez. Stirring things up with Gabe wasn't the first time she was slipping around with somebody, the way I heard it."

Rodell has heard the news that they're back in town and have split up. I tell him that at the café LoPresto acted like it was his idea to break it off.

Rodell grins. "Gabe's always going to make it sound like he got the good end of the stick. But he's a good old boy." He lies back, closes his eyes, and sighs. "I guess I don't have the energy I thought I did."

"You're looking better than you did last time I was here. I'll check with you tomorrow."

He opens his eyes again. "I appreciate your coming."

As I get up to leave I say, "Has James Harley been by to see you?" They were thick as thieves when Skinner was chief and James Harley Krueger was his right-hand man.

For some reason Rodell's expression turns shifty at the mention of James Harley's name. "He dropped by."

"Has he found a job?"

"He's working over in Bobtail."

"Doing what?"

He licks his lips. "He's working for an old boy I know over there." I wait. "He's doing bartending."

My heart sinks. If Rodell is looking guilty, it probably means he's arranged with James Harley to supply him with booze. He might as well be signing his death warrant. I had visions of Rodell coming down to the station and being able to do a little of this and that, but if he starts drinking again, that's never going to happen.

The thirty minutes I spend with my sister-in-law Lucille is tedious, not only because I'm impatient to find out what DeWitt has to say, but also because I've never really taken to Lucille. Jeanne insisted that Lucille's problems are real and that she can't help herself, but I have often had the distinct feeling when I'm with her that she finds it convenient to languish and have everyone fuss over her. It's most likely mean-spirited on my part and is most certainly unkind. If karma is a real thing, I can expect something unfriendly in my future.

I'm glad to get out of the overly warm, scented house. DeWitt and I go to a café close by in case Lucille needs him to come back fast. It's a slick place light-years away from the grungy Town Café, but I like Town Café better. This one is too shiny for my taste. We order club sandwiches and get down to business.

"You were right about McClusky," DeWitt says. "That resort did get shut down a good while back. The two fellows I golfed with yesterday said they used to go out to the hunting lodge every year for antelope. And then a couple years ago they got a notice that the lodge was going to be closed for renovations. They said they didn't see what needed renovating—it was always top of the line. But the letter said McClusky was going to take it from a good four-star facility to a five-star. And that's the last they heard of it."

"Here's what I don't understand," I say. "I drove out there and it was a rundown mess. I didn't see any animals anywhere or any sign of activity. McClusky's brother is out there taking care of the place, such as it is. He said I couldn't go inside because there was construction going on. But I saw no sign of any construction. I have a feeling something is going on there, but what?"

"One of the men I talked to said he wondered if something happened with the animals. He heard some of them were sick, but he didn't know the details. Another one of the men said he heard McClusky was having some financial problems. Of course, a lot of people have in the last few years, so I don't know what that amounts to."

I tell him I appreciate him looking into it for me.

"I don't know that I gave you a lot. I hope it wasn't a wild goose chase for you to come out here, but it was good to see you."

We don't spend long over lunch. I can tell DeWitt is anxious to get back to Lucille and I'm anxious to get on my way. On the way back out to Jarrett Creek, I'm planning to stop by McClusky's place. I need to get inside the "Big House" and find out what Harold didn't want me to see.

This time when I drive up, though, the gate to the McClusky resort is chained and locked with a new padlock that means business. I get out of my truck and look up close, but I don't see a way to signal to anyone inside that there's someone wanting in. Apparently, if you aren't expected, you aren't getting in. As rundown as some of the fencing looked the first time I was here, the fencing around the gate is solid. Now I know McClusky is hiding something here.

Back out on the main road, I drive a few miles in each direction in case there's a second entrance that isn't advertised, but there's nothing but fence as far as I can see. And still no sign of any animals. I have no reason to believe anything bad happened to the stock he kept, but the whole thing gives me an uneasy feeling. I try calling McClusky once more, but the call goes straight to his messages.

Then I have an idea. I drive east back in the direction of Jarrett Creek, pausing when I see billboards facing the other direction. Before too long I see one for the resort. The next chance I get, I turn around and approach the billboard. Sure enough, there's a telephone number on the sign. I pull over and dial it. A message comes on that deepens the mystery.

"This is the McClusky resort. The resort is closed for renovation. For information regarding the new facility, please contact Gary Dellmore of Citizens Bank." I dial the phone number given in the message and am told it has been disconnected. I sit and stare at the phone for several seconds as if it could tell me what I need to know. Meanwhile, traffic whizzes by on my left as if demons are chasing the drivers.

Driving home I have plenty of time to mull over what DeWitt told me, and the answer to what may have happened to the animals stocked out at the resort comes to me. A few years back every cattleman in the state was chilled at an especially widespread outbreak of foot-and-mouth disease. When I thought of the exotic animals stocked at the resort, the fact that they were cloven-hoofed animals slipped past me—I was thinking more of their exotic hides. Of course they would be vulnerable to the disease—maybe even more than domestic animals. If McClusky had an outbreak, the entire herd would have been quarantined until such time that it was determined that the soil no longer harbored the disease.

I spend the rest of the time worrying about whether I've inadvertently exposed my herd to the disease by being on the resort property. I think back and realize I did no more than walk on the pavement when I was confronted by Harold. Next time I go, I'll be sure to disinfect my boots afterward—or maybe even wear old ones that I can throw out.

When I get home, I call Jenny and have a long talk with her about what I found in the contracts so I'll be prepared for the meeting tomorrow morning. She scolds me for not bringing them home so she could look over them.

"Jenny," I say, "you're a lawyer. If you got your hooks into those contracts, I'd have to postpone the meeting until next July."

CHAPTER 25

Alton Coldwater is the first of our visitors to arrive at the station the next morning, but he only has a few blocks to drive—the other two are coming from Houston. I've got the coffee on and some of Loretta's cinnamon rolls laid out on a paper plate on my desk where I'm seated. Coldwater plunks himself down in one of the three chairs facing me. If you were to go by his jovial manner, you wouldn't think he had a care in the world—much less that he was the target of scorn in town. He snatches up one of the cinnamon rolls and attacks it with gusto.

Bill Odum arrives a few minutes later. He's supposed to work this afternoon, but since he did the setup for the meeting, he wanted to be here. He brings a folding chair out of the closet and sits down against the wall, away from the three chairs I set up for our visitors. He's got good instincts, knowing to keep himself apart from the main attraction and to be an observer.

"Alton, I'm glad you're here early," I say, "I want to ask you a couple of questions before those other fellows get here."

"Ask me anything." He's got a mouthful of cinnamon roll, and the words come out mushy.

"Whose idea was it to build a water park out at the lake?"

"You know, Samuel, that's a good question. It wasn't my idea, but it seemed like a good one."

I wait while he sips some coffee to wash down the rest of the roll. I can't tell if he's considering the answer to the question or stalling, but his attention seems completely focused on eating and drinking.

Finally he sits back and pats his belly. "Seems to me Slate McClusky came to me with the idea. He said he had an interest in water parks in other towns and they were doing pretty well."

187

"I only recently heard that McClusky was involved in it. Did he want his part kept secret?"

"He said he'd like to be a silent partner. He said that since he only lived here part of the time people might think he was trying to come in and ram the idea down our throats."

Which is, more or less, the way it happened. "Am I right that there never was a vote on the project or much discussion of it? The first thing I heard was that the land had been bought and plans were in place."

Coldwater passes his tongue around his teeth to clean out the remnants of the roll. "City Council voted for it. I guess they didn't think it was necessary to have it on the ballot." There's a challenge in his voice.

The door opens and two men in suits step into the room. Coldwater gets up and shakes hands with them, eyeing them the way he might look at disgraced relatives, although they don't seem to notice. He introduces them to Odum and me. Pete Fontaine, a slight-built man pushing fifty, steps up eagerly to shake hands. He tells me he's happy they had the time to come in. Larry Kestler is younger, maybe forty, with a substantial head of hair and the thick body of an ex-football player. He flicks wary eyes around the room, as if looking for a backdoor exit.

After they get settled, I say, "Bill explained to you that we're investigating the murder of Gary Dellmore. I'm trying to piece together what his interest was in the water park you fellows were planning to build here in Jarrett Creek."

"I was sorry to hear that Dellmore had been killed," Fontaine says. "We didn't have much in the way of dealings with him, but he seemed like a nice fellow."

"Can you give me a general idea how a deal like this water park works? Does a city come to you with a proposal, or do you do a search for sites?"

The two men look at each other. Coldwater has slipped himself another sweet roll and is concentrating on it. Fontaine answers again.

"It can go either way. Sometimes we put out feelers and sometimes people come to us. That's what happened at our park in Beaumont."

Kestler shoots him a warning look, and I know why. The Beaumont water park is one of the parks that's in trouble. Of course they think a rube like me couldn't possibly have that information. But getting the information was as easy as looking at a magazine article. Which is why I wonder how come no one else knew there were problems.

"Which was the case for the Jarrett Creek plans? Did Coldwater here come to you, or did you go to him?"

Coldwater takes his time working over his latest bite of roll, no doubt hoping someone else will fill the void. Fontaine obliges. "I don't remember. That would be somewhere in my files, I guess. Mr. Coldwater here would be the best person to answer your question."

Coldwater wipes his mouth with a paper napkin. "It's no secret. Dellmore came to me and said you fellows had come up with an interesting proposal and I ought to take a look at it. Slate McClusky had already told me he thought a water park would succeed here."

"Anybody ever do any studies about how it would work here in Jarrett Creek?"

"That's not our department," Kessler says. I don't believe him. Their names were sprinkled through the documents in the files I saw.

"How about you Coldwater? You ever get any studies?"

"We saw some. I don't recall if it was specific to us or to small towns in general."

"And at the time the city was having financial problems and you were looking for a way to make a good investment that would bring in some money," I say.

Coldwater grasps at my suggestion. "That's exactly it. We were having real problems. You know, with the economy going bad, we were in trouble. Lot of towns had the same problem. I thought this water park thing would be a boon. It's too damn bad it didn't work out."

"When you talked to Dellmore, did he happen to mention there was lot of risk involved in a deal like this?"

"Now hold on a minute," Fontaine says, ignoring Kestler's narrowed eyes. "Our water parks are no more risky than any other amusement-type venture."

"Maybe this was a tad riskier," I say. "One other question. What kind of permits did the state give you? Who paid for them?"

Coldwater swallows. "It was up to the water park builders to get that."

"You should have gotten some copies. Did you ever get any?"

"I can't make out what you're getting at here," Kestler says. "Like Pete said, this is not our department. We just arranged to get the land and then passed it on to another group for implementation."

"Coldwater, did you ever have any dealings with anyone but these two men?"

"No, but I only met with them a couple of times. After that, Dellmore took over. He was sort of the go-between."

"Can anybody tell me if Dellmore got a kickback from your company for putting together a loan on this deal?"

Kestler hasn't taken his eyes off me. "I don't have any particulars, but that's illegal," he says. "Our company wouldn't do anything like that."

"Even if you were having trouble getting a loan for the park?"

"Again, we didn't have anything to do with that part of it."

"How many parks does your outfit own?"

"We've got ten water parks. Six in Texas, two in Louisiana, and a couple in Arkansas," Kestler says.

"How many of them are making money?"

"They're doing okay." He looks at Fontaine, who is staring out the window.

"How many of them have closed in the last three years?"

"I don't know what that has to do with Gary Dellmore. You said this was an inquiry into his death, not an attempt to place blame for a business venture that your mayor here went into with his eyes wide open."

Coldwater glares at him.

"I believe this does have something to do with Dellmore's death. You fellows put together a deal you never had any intention of following through on, and I think that got Dellmore into trouble with somebody."

Kestler gets up abruptly. "We're done here. I don't need to sit here and listen to wild accusations."

"Wild accusations? Maybe you'd be interested in this." I open the *Texas Amusement* magazine to the article about water parks and push it over to them. "According to this, some of your parks were going under at the time you were trying to sell one to Jarrett Creek. I believe a judge would be interested to know that Gary Dellmore knew the parks were in trouble before he pushed this loan through."

"This has nothing to do with us. It's on the banker."

"The contracts have your names all over them. And you knew the water park was not going to be built."

Kestler sits back down. "We're the front men for a big backer," he says.

Fontaine shuffles in his chair and coughs once, the only sound in the room for several seconds.

"So who's the big honcho? Or are you willing to let him hang you out here on your own?"

Coldwater looks puzzled and the other two men exchange glances.

"Looks to me like sort of a Ponzi scheme, you gathering money for a new park here in Jarrett Creek and using the money to shore up the ones that aren't doing so well. Was Dellmore aware of this? I know Slate McClusky must've been."

Fontaine gets up fast, almost overturning his chair. "I didn't come here to be accused of being a crook. I thought we were helping you out.

If you're complaining about the way this was handled, I suggest you take it up with McClusky and . . ."

"And Dellmore? He's not around to defend himself, which seems convenient."

Now Kestler gets to his feet again. "We didn't have anything to do with that. Like we said, we barely met Dellmore. I believe I'd look to your mayor here for answers about Dellmore." They start toward the door.

"If I were you," I say, "I'd be consulting with your lawyer, because I'm pretty sure there's going to be legal action coming your way."

"You can't touch us," Kestler says.

"I wouldn't be too sure of that."

They slam the door behind them.

While this has been going on, Alton Coldwater has risen to his feet and started to ease toward the door as if he'd like to slink out right behind them. "Sit down, Alton," I say. "We have a little more to discuss."

When I hold his feet to the fire, Coldwater doesn't hold out long. He's all too willing to tell us that Slate McClusky handled all the dealings with Gary Dellmore. "Like I told you, McClusky wanted his name kept out of it."

To hear Coldwater talk, he was an innocent small-town mayor, hoodwinked by big city slickers. We'll see how that holds up when the time comes for the courts to try to wrangle some of the town's money back from this outfit, but for now he's pointed the finger at McClusky. That doesn't mean McClusky is guilty of killing Dellmore, but it brings up a lot of questions about what the two of them were up to, and why McClusky pretended he had nothing to do with Dellmore.

CHAPTER 26

Cookie Travers says she's swamped trying to straighten out matters Gary Dellmore left behind, but she'll make time for me on her lunch break. While I sit in the lobby to wait, I notice that Darla Rodriguez has come back to work. I mention that to Cookie when we sit down to talk.

"She has. But if I have my way, it won't be long before she's looking for a job." We're sitting in a small, empty conference room with no windows, off the room where the safety deposit boxes are kept. Cookie has spread a napkin on the table and brought out sliced tomatoes and deviled eggs in plastic containers. Diet food. She offers me some, but I tell her I've already eaten.

"Darla seems to have brought Gabe down a notch or two, and that can't be a bad thing," I say. We both laugh. "Why do you want to fire her?"

Cookie takes her time answering. "I don't trust her. Ever since she started up this thing with Gabe LoPresto, I've thought she was playing with him. I just don't understand why. I suppose that's really not enough reason to fire somebody. And now that Gary's gone, maybe she'll straighten up."

"What do you mean?"

"She and Gary were thick as thieves. She was always in his office or they'd be whispering off in a corner. I got the impression they were up to something, but I don't know what. And then she took up with Gabe." She throws her hands up. "It's a mystery to me."

"I know you're pinched for time," I say. "The reason I'm here is that I want to ask you about some of Gary's bank business."

"I'll help if I can. What do you need?"

"I found some files in the trunk of Gary's car, and in going through them to see if they might give me some idea of what he was working on—anything that might have gotten him killed—I ran across something troubling. It looks like Gary might've been involved in some shady dealings having to do with the water park that was supposed to be built."

She puts the tomato container down and goes still. "What kind of shady dealings?"

"Gary might've done more than arrange the loan. He might have conspired with someone to have the city put up money for the park even though he knew Liberty Water Park was in financial trouble."

"Oh, my Lord. If Alan heard that, it would kill him."

"How much did Alan know about this water park deal? I imagine there's going to be a lawsuit against the company. I talked to Jenny Sandstone last night. She thinks that if Alan didn't know what Gary was up to, we can keep him out of the legal proceedings personally. But I need some assurance that it was done without his knowledge. I'll talk to him, too, of course, but I wanted to get your take on it first."

Her eyes are smoldering. "Alan would never do anything like that. He'll be humiliated when he finds this out." Her voice is like steel. "You know, the only reason Alan hired Gary is because he felt sorry for him after his father-in-law's business failed."

"Speaking of that," I say, "I heard a fairly reliable rumor that Gary had something to do with the failure."

Cookie draws a breath like she's about to speak, but then she hesitates. Finally she says, "Barbara is a friend of mine and I don't know how much she knows, so I wouldn't want it noised around . . . oh, never mind. I know you'll keep what I say confidential." She lowers her voice as if the walls have ears. "Gary pushed Mike Johnson into expanding his business at a time when money was tight. Alan told me at the time that he wished Gary would stop playing around with Mike's business, but nobody could ever tell Gary anything. He was always cocky; always thought he knew better than anybody else. He went ahead with the expansion and they got overextended and the business went under." Her voice is trembling.

Like Cookie, I wonder how much of this Barbara knew. She's sharp, and it's hard for me to believe that somewhere along the line she didn't find out that Gary had a hand in her father's failure. She had more than enough reasons to be furious with Gary. I'm wondering how far she could be pushed before she'd had enough.

I also wonder how much money Gary made from putting together those loans for his father-in-law's business. "Did Citizens Bank loan the money to Mike Johnson?"

Cookie nods.

"That was before Gary worked here, so who arranged the loans?"

"I was supposed to handle them, but Gary went over my head to Alan." She picks up the lids and snaps them sharply onto the plastic containers. Then she looks me straight in the eye. "But don't even suggest to me that Alan knew those loans were too much for Mike. Gary was in charge of the whole thing from Mike's end, and I wouldn't be one bit surprised if he cooked up false numbers to make sure Alan gave him the loan. And that fits with him making loans to Jarrett Creek under false pretenses." I wouldn't want to be on Cookie's bad side right now.

"Cookie, is it possible to find out whether Gary got a kickback from the water park company for arranging the loan?"

"You mean besides the commission?"

"Yes."

Cookie considers the question. "The only way I know of is to find out from the company, or I guess from Gary's bank account. You know as well as I do that getting his bank records is going to take time."

"I understand. Did you ever discuss the park deal with Gary?"

"No occasion to. Would've saved everybody a lot of trouble if I'd been involved." She looks like she's going to cry.

"Gary's not the only person who may have benefited from the phony water park project."

"Who else?" She bites her lower lip.

"Slate McClusky had a lot of involvement in it."

"Slate? Wait a minute. How did that happen?"

"Apparently he has a big interest in the water park outfit. He may be the owner of it, for all I know. I'll try to find that out. But whatever his position in the company is, he told Coldwater and the two front men on the deal that he wanted to keep his investment quiet. He thought people in Jarrett Creek wouldn't want him butting in since he lives out of town most of the time."

"That's ridiculous. Slate's daddy was from here, and Slate has had his place here for a long time. That makes him part of the community."

"I agree. I think his real reason for keeping quiet is that he never had any intention of building a water park here. I think he was counting on getting money from Jarrett Creek to shore up his parks in other cities."

Cookie shakes her head. "Like I said, I'll swear on a stack of Bibles that Alan had no knowledge of this."

"One more thing. I don't know if you can legally tell me the answer to this. Do you know anything about Slate McClusky's other business dealings?"

She shakes her head. "This gets worse and worse. Look, even if I did know anything about Slate's finances, I couldn't divulge details. But I don't. He doesn't keep his money here and doesn't have any personal loans with us." Interesting. Angel said Slate did have some small loans here. Of the two, I'd be inclined to believe Cookie.

Cookie tucks the remnants of her lunch in the bag, folds up the napkin, and then puts a couple of fingers to her lips, frowning. "I wonder if one reason Gary got involved with Slate's outfit was to try to lure his business here? If I thought that, at least I'd think a little better of him."

As I'm walking out, I notice Jessica Reinhardt is in the teller area. She didn't quit after all. Before I turn away, Darla Rodriguez walks over to her and bends her head close, and the two women giggle. In that moment I understand why Cookie said she doesn't trust Darla. There is something furtive about Darla Rodriguez. It may be time for me to have a heart-to-heart talk with Gabe LoPresto.

Rusty Reinhardt is still reluctant to meet with me after I wounded his pride by questioning his daughter's behavior. I tell him the subject is the water park and not his daughter. "I found some things in the city's files that I think we ought to discuss." He says he'll come down to the station right away.

When he walks in, his greeting is curt. "I think we've done everything we can to put that water park fiasco to bed," he says right off, "but I'm willing to listen to what you have to say."

"Did you ever consider a lawsuit against Slate McClusky?"

He frowns. "What does McClusky have to do with it?"

"You might be surprised." I get him to sit down and give him details of the conversations I've had in the past few hours pointing the finger at McClusky and Dellmore.

He slaps his hand on my desk. "That snake."

"Which one?"

"McClusky. We all knew that Dellmore was up to no good. But a snake hides in the grass, and that's exactly what Slate McClusky did. He hid behind that big old smile he always has plastered across his face."

"Bottom line is both men conspired to cheat the town."

Reinhardt slumps back in his chair and pulls at his mustache. "If that doesn't beat everything. I was willing to go along with the idea that Coldwater and the city council made a mistake, but being scammed? It never occurred to me. What's the point of living in a place if you can't trust your neighbors to do right by you?"

"You can find greed anywhere," I say.

"Do you think Coldwater knew the details?"

"I think he knew something wasn't right, but he was desperate to shore up the town's finances, so he didn't look as closely at the deal as he should have. For example, he didn't insist on getting copies of permits the water park company should have obtained from the state."

"I didn't have much use for Coldwater before I became mayor, but I've sort of figured out that he was doing his level best to find a way to fix things. But he should've had more sense than that." Gloom settles over Reinhardt. He folds his hands over his belly, and his eyes have a faraway look.

"Anything else bothering you?" I ask. I'm hoping he'll come out and tell me that he had a talk with Gary Dellmore after the meeting the night he was killed so I don't have to bring it up.

"Yesterday Marietta and I took some time going over the city's bills, trying to figure out how we were going to settle up. It's a mess."

"There may be something to be done." I tell him that Jenny Sandstone suggested the city sue the water park outfit. "I expect they're on the verge of bankruptcy themselves, and we won't get a lot out of them, but maybe enough to help with the bills."

He nods. "We'll see. Marietta is sharp. She thinks if we pay a little toward each bill and write a letter explaining our predicament, we can get creditors to cut us some slack until we get money from property taxes."

"My guess is that once Alan Dellmore finds out what Gary was up to, he's going to do what he can to ease the loan payments."

"That would be a big help."

Since it's clear that Rusty isn't going to bring it up on his own, it's up to me. "Rusty, there's one more thing I need to talk to you about." I tell him that someone overheard him arranging to meet with Gary Dellmore after the meeting last Tuesday night.

"I don't know what that has to do with anything," he says.

"How could you not know? You might have been the last person to see Dellmore alive. What did you want to talk to him about?"

"No big secret. I told Dellmore to leave my daughter alone."

"What did he say to that?"

Fire flashes in his eyes. "Son of a gun told me she was a grown woman and could make her own decisions."

"How did you first find out Dellmore was pursuing your daughter? Did she tell you?"

"No, in fact when I heard it and mentioned it to her she said it wasn't anything I should be concerned with. My wife heard it from somebody down at the bank."

"How did you and Dellmore leave it?"

Reinhardt frowns at me. "If you're asking me did I leave him dead on the ground, I can't tell you I didn't want to. But he was alive when I left him. I told him if I heard he'd messed around with her anymore, I was going to take a whip to him."

He gets up, picks up his hat and claps it on his head. "I don't think we have any more to discuss."

"There is one thing," I say.

He turns around, too polite to walk out on me. "Make it quick. I have to get back to the store."

"That night, when you had the discussion with Dellmore, where did you talk to him?"

He looks at me like he thinks I've gone off a rail. "We went around the west side of the building to have a private discussion, since everybody was getting into their cars on the other side. Why?"

"I want you to think hard, remember exact details. Did you hear or see anything that would make you think someone was out there in the trees?"

He moves back toward my desk. "You think somebody was out there?"

"If you didn't kill him—and I'm willing to go along with you when you say you didn't—then somebody was out there waiting for Dellmore."

He stares at me and slowly shakes his head. "I wish I could help you, but I was pretty riled up and didn't pay any attention to my surroundings."

"Where was Dellmore when you left him?"

"He was standing there by the side of the building where we'd been talking. By the time I got to my car, everyone else was gone, and his car was the only one left parked out there."

"So his car was there."

"Yes." He shakes a finger. "I remember something else. As I was driving away, something made me look back, and the American Legion Hall had gone dark. I figured he had gone inside, turned out the lights, and was locking up."

"Did you see any cars parked out on the street near the entrance or anybody walking along there?" It would have been hard for someone to park there without being noticed, since the street has a deep dropout into a culvert for a block.

"Not that I recall." A ghost passes across his face. He must be picturing someone waiting out there in the dark for Gary Dellmore.

CHAPTER 27

Bill Odum and I are mostly quiet on the drive out to the McClusky resort. Odum talks a little about his mother and how she fusses over his dad and drives everybody a little crazy, including his wife.

We stop by Cooper's Barbecue in Spicewood for supper and make short work of ribs and sausage with all the trimmings. I get them to fill up my thermos and they tell me it's on the house. And then we're back on the road.

A half hour later we stop at the entrance to the resort to check on the gate. It's still closed and locked. I've tried calling McClusky several times and gotten no answer. Even if he isn't out here, something tells me there's information here that will solve this puzzle. McClusky doesn't want me to see something inside the main building. Is he running guns or drugs? Has he kidnapped somebody and is holding them hostage? Is he hiding fugitives? Everything I think of seems too outlandish. I've brought Odum along to help me snoop around and find out some answers.

The main road is narrow along here, and we have to drive several hundred feet before we find a spot wide enough to leave the squad car. We've just started walking back along the road toward the gate when a light-colored car slows down and turns into the driveway. We're far enough away that whoever it is probably hasn't seen us. We step off into the shadow of some trees next to the fence and wait. After a time I hear the clank of the chain on the gate. The gate squeaks as it swings open, and then the chain clanks again, when the gate is locked back up.

"Who could that be?" Odum says.

"Let's go find out."

As we approach the entrance, I'm wondering if I can climb over that fence. Before I had my knee surgery, I would have said forget it, but every day the knee seems stronger and more willing to do what needs to be done. Walking along the verge, our soft shoes crunch on the gravel. I don't wear tennis shoes often, preferring my boots to any other kind of footwear, but I figured it'd be easier to stay quiet wearing soft-soled shoes. I told Odum to wear shoes he'd be willing to throw out once we're done here. I haven't verified if McClusky's place was hit with foot-and-mouth disease, but I'm not prepared to take a chance either way.

The fence is meant to keep out cars, but it turns out not to be particularly hard for a person to climb across it. I hook my foot onto an iron bar across the middle and hoist myself up and over, more pleased than I should be at not having to ask for a hand.

"They don't have a dog, do they?" Odum asks. He sounds nervous. It's not good for a lawman to be scared of dogs. I'll have to tell him so.

"I didn't see one when I was out here." I'm hoping they don't have a dog. Both Odum and I are armed, and if we had to, we could take down a dog, but I'd prefer not to have to go that way.

He squares up to me, hands on his hips. "You sure this is a good idea? We're breaking the law, trespassing. If we get shot, it's on us."

"Then we have to make sure we don't get shot. I told you that you didn't have to come. You can go on back to the car and I won't think any the worse of you. But something's going on out here and I want to know what it is." He's right, of course. We are trespassing, but I don't know any other way to find out what I want to know. McClusky is avoiding me, and there's no way I'd get a warrant to come in here and search the place—I don't have anything to go on but my gut feeling that he's hiding something.

It takes us twenty minutes to walk up to the resort, staying to the side of the rutted road and then the pavement. It looks spooky in the dark. There's not much moon to speak of, and the main building looms up like some kind of haunted castle. The light-colored car we saw coming in is parked next to Slate's SUV and Angel's Cadillac.

Odum and I decided in advance to check out some of the surrounding cabins first. Those might tell us what we need to know, and we could avoid trying to navigate the porch without alerting anybody to our presence.

I motion for Odum to go down to the farthest cabin. There are no lights on in any of them, but we've each brought a penlight.

I ease along until I find one with the curtains open. First I peer inside, but it's pitch-black, so I can't see anything. I shine my light inside and am so startled that I jump back and almost drop the flashlight. Eyes were staring back at me. My heart bangs in my chest. I wait, but I don't hear any movement inside so I shine the light in again. I laugh silently. There must be twenty or thirty stuffed animal heads stacked in the room, some of them turned to face me, their eyes glittering in the light.

On high alert from that encounter, I move to the next cabin. The curtains are closed, so I ease around to the back and find one window with curtains parted enough for me to shine my light into it. This room is full of armchairs piled high, all of them upholstered in plaid fabric.

I step back and think. Maybe Slate's brother was telling the truth. Maybe they are doing renovations and all the furniture has been moved out here in preparation for the work to be done.

I hear Odum moving and I hiss to alert him that I'm there. He comes over and we confer. It turns out he's seen a cabin full of beach umbrellas and lounge chairs. We creep along the back of the cabins to the one closest to the main lodge and move along the side of it until we can peer around to see the front door.

I'm eyeing the car sitting in front of the lodge, wondering who drove it out here and how we're going to get a look inside the lodge, when the front door swings open. Silhouetted in the light from inside, Darla Rodriguez steps onto the porch. She says, "You're going to have to find someone else to do your dirty work. I'm done."

I can't hear the reply from inside.

"It's not my fault Gary's dead. And without him, it's not going to work anyway."

Slate McClusky appears in the doorway. He reaches out and catches Darla's arm. "Come on, now. Don't be that way. We can find some way to work it out."

"I can't stand another minute of Gabe LoPresto," she whines. "And I think he's smarter than you and Gary thought he was."

"Darla, I'm going to give you a little time to get your thinking straight so you'll realize it's in your best interest to help me." He puts his arm around her shoulders and steers her down the steps.

"But Slate, I don't know how it's going to work without Gary." She sounds close to tears.

"You don't give yourself enough credit. I'm sure you'll be able to get LoPresto on board. You've done the biggest part of the job. I hate for you to quit now."

She puts her hands to her face, shaking her head. "Oh, all right. But we've got to think of some way to sweeten the deal. As it is now, he's not going to buy."

She unlocks her car and he gives her shoulders a squeeze. "I'm counting on you, honey. And remember, you're going to make a lot of money on this deal. And if you quit now . . ."

Her voice is harsh. "I sure better make some money. That puny diamond necklace he gave me isn't worth nearly enough for all I've had to go through."

We wait for a while after Slate goes back inside. The whole time I'm wondering where Angel is. Her car is here. More than ever I want to get a look inside that lodge. I thought when Slate and Angel lied to me about where they were staying, they just didn't want me to know the name of the motel. I hadn't expected to find them here. It seemed like it was going to be easy—I would either knock on the door and find Harold here and talk my way inside, or no one would be here and I would shine a light inside to get the lay of the place.

I suppose we could just walk up, bang on the door, and ask to come inside. But I can't think of an excuse for why we climbed over the fence to get onto the property. And if we sneak up there and for some reason McClusky catches us, he would be within his rights to shoot us for trespassing, just as Odum said.

We scout around back to see if there's a window we can get to more easily than walking onto the wide front porch. Also, I'd like to see if there's a light on anywhere else, since I don't know if Harold is inside the big house or if he has quarters elsewhere.

We make our way through the trees that line one side of the property and into the back area. In the back I see the spa buildings, totally dark, at the end of a long path that leads past a fenced-in structure I imagine is a swimming pool. We walk over to look. The pool is white concrete that gleams, even in this low light. It's empty. At the end of the other path are a couple of small buildings. One of them has a light on. I'm going to bet that's where Harold stays.

The porch extends all the way around from front to back. One way or another, I'm going to have to walk up onto it. At least one piece of luck is with me—the curtains are open enough that I can peek inside. Light spills out onto the porch.

"I'm going to go up there and take a look," I whisper. "I want you down here with your gun out in case anybody comes out and decides to shoot me."

Odum takes his Colt out of its holster, and when he nods to me that he's ready I start up the steps. It's slow going, testing each footstep to make sure none of the stairs creak. A couple of them groan a bit, but I doubt it's loud enough to alarm anyone. I'm grateful once again that there isn't a dog around. By now he'd have started up a racket.

I make straight for the nearest window, hoping I only need one glimpse. I peer into a huge room that extends from the front to the back. Elegant wooden staircases leading up to the second floor flank the room, one on each end. The sight takes me a minute to process. In the middle of the room a fire is blazing in the massive fireplace. There are two big armchairs in front of the fireplace, each with a small end table. Aside from that the room is almost bare.

Across the room from the fireplace, up against one wall, is what puzzles and interests me most. Two foldout beds are set up, complete with bedding, as if two people are sleeping here. I don't see Slate or Angel, but as I watch, Angel comes down the stairs closest to me, dressed in a sweat suit. She's carrying a towel and a toiletry bag. She walks to one of the beds and sets the bag down on a little stand next to it. Slate follows her, in a bathrobe.

"Jesus, it's cold up there," he says. I'm surprised I can hear him with the windows closed up tight, but there is no furniture in the room to muffle the sound and it echoes off the walls.

"You don't have to tell me." Angel's voice is surly. "I don't know how much longer I can put up with this."

"You'll put up with it as long as I say we have to," Slate says. "Unless you've suddenly come up with the money for the Ritz-Carlton."

"I can sleep back at the house."

"Not much longer you can't."

I ease to one side of the window and stand there a few minutes longer listening to hear if they say anything of importance, but it's only the last bits of conversation before two people go to bed. "At least that fireplace keeps it warm," Slate says. He goes over and adjusts the screen and then he slumps down into one of the armchairs. "I'm going to sit here a little longer."

I move down the porch steps, and Odum and I take off walking down the driveway. I've seen what I came to see, and it's not like anything I thought. I've seen two people who are flat broke, making do. From what I heard Darla say, she's been talked into trying to get Gabe LoPresto to buy the place. LoPresto acts like a buffoon most of the time, which must have led them to believe he'd be an easy mark.

They've found out different. But what this has to do with Gary Dellmore's death is a connection I have yet to make.

McClusky has always had the reputation of being the richest man in town. I don't know what took him down, but it's pretty clear that his empire has toppled. He's doing everything he can to scrabble together something of the remains.

Desperate men will take desperate measures. I'd be tempted to think that desperation might have led McClusky to kill Gary Dellmore, but from what I overheard Darla say, without Dellmore the scheme they've hatched up is in trouble. Now I need to find out more about the scheme. And for that I'll be talking to Gabe LoPresto.

CHAPTER 28

Thursday morning Loretta seems to sense that I'm in no mood for a chat. She hands off a fresh slab of coffee cake and says she's not going to stay. "Now don't work too hard. You're not getting any younger."

"I don't need you to remind me of that. My bones are doing a fine job of keeping me informed."

But the fact is, although I'm tired from the late-night activity, I also feel alert and ready to roll. I'm pretty sure that by finding out the magnitude of McClusky's financial problems I'm closer to finding out what led to Gary Dellmore's murder. The only bad part is that the dire straits the McCluskys are in makes me doubt that the town will be able to get back any of the money put up for the fraudulent water park project. It looks like McClusky has lost whatever money he had.

As soon as Loretta leaves, I call Bill Odum. When he picks up, there's a lot of noise in the background. "Hold on," he hollers into the phone.

He comes on the line again, and the sound is muffled in the background. "We're finishing up shredding the crop from last fall. What's up?"

I ask him when he'll be able to do the testing on the bullet casings. "I know we were out late last night, but I wondered if you'd have any time today."

He groans. "This shredding operation is going to take the rest of the day. I'll spend some time testing the casing this evening, and tomorrow I'll get over to the college to take a look at the markings under the microscope. I'll call you as soon as I know anything."

I stop by the café on the way to the station for some eggs and coffee.

Alton Coldwater is getting out of his car as I drive up, so I invite him to have breakfast with me.

After we order, I say, "Alton, who was it who decided to get a loan from Dellmore's bank for that water park? Seems to me those guys from Houston would have had their own bank connections."

Coldwater looks gloomy, as if yesterday's meeting brought back to him all the trouble that had happened on his watch. "Let me try to remember exactly how it happened."

Our breakfast comes, and we fall quiet and start eating. After a minute, Coldwater says, "I believe if I'm not mistaken Fontaine and Kestler said they liked to get local banks involved when they could. And they said somebody had suggested they talk to Dellmore. Now I figure it was probably McClusky who did that. I introduced them to Dellmore, and they took it from there."

"Who came up with the idea that it would be a good thing to put city money into it?"

"That's easy. That was Dellmore." He wipes his face with his napkin and then puts his hands on his thighs, as if girding himself. "But like I said, McClusky had already primed the pump. I can't put all the blame on those two, though, even if they are crooks. I thought it was a good chance to take care of our financial problems. Nobody needed to push me. I should've been more careful." He looks like he's eaten a sour plum. It's a hard admission for him to make.

"Did anybody try to talk you out of it?"

"Oh sure, a couple of people on the city council. I thought it was the same old thing, though—there's always people who are against progress. I hate to admit they were right."

Back at the station, I start making phone calls and within an hour have more information than I ever wanted about Slate McClusky's slide from prosperity into desperation. He is the sole owner of the water park business, and it's on the verge of bankruptcy. He had to walk away from his multimillion-dollar house in Vail, and if I read between the vague lines the real estate broker in Dallas told me, McClusky is behind on payments on his house in Dallas, too. The place in Jarrett Creek is being spruced up to put on the market, which is why Slate and Angel are camping out at the resort.

Thinking about the resort, I need to make one more call, this time to the Texas Animal Health Commission. What I find out confirms everything I'd heard. Of all the things that have happened to McClusky, finding out that he did have an outbreak of foot-and-mouth at the resort and that it's quarantined hits me the hardest. It's a piece of bad luck, pure simple. That kind of thing could strike anyone.

Adding everything up, I understand why McClusky is trying desperately to unload the resort onto Gabe LoPresto.

But why was Gary Dellmore helping him to get LoPresto to buy it? Dellmore went to a lot of trouble to set LoPresto up with Darla Rodriguez's help. What did McClusky promise the two of them if they succeeded? Or, was it what he promised he wouldn't do: tell anybody about the kickback he must have given Dellmore. One way or another, this will all come out. What I have to figure out is what it has to do with Dellmore's murder.

LoPresto's office manager gives me the address of the job he's working on today. As I turn the corner, I recognize the place. The house is one I've always liked. It used to be an elegant home, a fine two-story brown shingle with a nice wide porch. When the elderly woman who owned it died, her sons got into a big squabble, and neither wanted the other to have the benefit of money from the sale of it. The result was that the house went vacant without upkeep for twenty years until it was a mess. Finally one of the brothers died and the other one sold it a couple of months ago.

As I approach the house, a small car darts away from the curb and barely misses me. Startled, the driver glances toward me and I see that it's Ellen Forester—but she doesn't look the way I've seen her before. Her expression is as bleak as anything I've ever seen. Her eyes are as dark as coal. She's gone before I have a chance to react.

Gabe LoPresto is standing in the front yard talking to a man I don't recognize. He's a burly guy, shorter than LoPresto but with several pounds of muscle to his side of things. He's almost bald, with a bulldog face that exudes menace. He has his hands on his hips and his chin thrust out. LoPresto is gesturing toward the house, clearly exasperated. I climb out of the car and stand by it for a few seconds to give my presence a chance to register, but they're too deep in their argument to pay attention to me.

"Mrs. Forester hired me to do this job, and I don't see where you come into it," LoPresto says.

"And I'm telling you she's my wife and I can halt the work on this if I please."

"I'm afraid I have to disagree. Mrs. Forester said you two are divorced and this is her project and you don't have anything to do with."

The man balls his fists. "Like hell! She can't just walk away from me. And if you keep working on this house, you may find yourself wishing you hadn't."

Two workers pulling shingles off the roof have stopped working and are watching the altercation.

I move toward the two men. I don't like the implied threat in the man's words, but I've never known LoPresto to back down, and now is no exception. "You get the hell off this property. Don't come around making threats to me."

"Who's going to back you up when—"

"I am, for one," I say.

"Who are you?" The man looks me up and down. He's used to getting his way.

"I'm the chief of police." I don't generally find it necessary to wear a badge, but I pull it out of my pants pocket and display it.

"You look a little past your prime to be strutting around like you're going to be of any use to anybody."

LoPresto comes out with short, sharp "Ha!"

Startled, the guy turns his attention back to LoPresto.

"I believe you'll find Chief Craddock equal to whatever nonsense you want to dole out."

"Mr. LoPresto is prone to exaggeration," I say, taking a few steps closer. "But unless you want to spend a little time thinking it over in our little jail—which is sufficient but not real comfortable—I'd suggest you do as he says and get off this property." I don't know why, but the look on Ellen Forester's face as she sped away from here makes me want to punch this man.

Maybe he sees a little of that on my face. He pulls his chin back ever so slightly.

"I didn't catch your name," I say.

"You go to hell," he says, and considers that enough of an exit strategy that he stalks off to a big black four-by-four truck. He gets in, starts the engine and revs it up, all the while looking back at us. Finally he pulls slowly away from the curb. There's more menace in that slow move than there would've been had he peeled out. It comes to me now that if Ellen had to put up with him, I understand why she's jumpy around men.

LoPresto looks up at the guys on the roof and gestures for them to go back to work.

"What was that all about?" I say.

"I don't know if you heard that a woman has come to town to start a new business."

"I met Ellen Forester."

He raises his eyebrows. "You already got your eye on her?"

"Gabe, I just met the woman; I didn't ask her to go to the motel with me."

He shrugs. "You could do worse. Anyway, she came along at the right time to buy old Mrs. Ellison's place here. I don't know any details, but Ellen said she inherited some money and decided to relocate—without her husband. She and I were going over the plans this morning, and the ex-husband came wheeling up here and started threatening her and threatening to shut me down." He looks over at the house. "Be a shame for anything to happen to this house."

"Like what?"

"Her ex said he was going to send somebody out to take a bull-dozer to it. She told me he has a business with contracts to the highway department, so I guess he could do it if he took a mind to."

"Are you planning to take any security measures?"

He puts his hand on his hips. "I may have to hire a security guard at night. Maybe get a restraining order. I don't know what I'm going to do. This is a fine thing to come home to. Well . . ." He tears his gaze away from the house and looks at me "What can I do for you?"

"I need to have a serious talk with you, Gabe."

"If it's anything to do with Darla, don't bother to say one word you'll regret. She called me first thing this morning and told me she'd made a big mistake and wants to get back together."

"I'm not surprised."

LoPresto grins. "You figured she'd see the error of her ways?"

"Not exactly. I need a bit of your time. You free right now?"

"It's that urgent?"

"It is."

"Hold on and I'll be right with you." He walks over to the house and hollers instructions up to the guys working there. When he comes back, he says, "Let's go inside. I have a table set up there with a couple of chairs."

"Inside" is speaking loosely. The house has been stripped down to the studs. We walk up temporary steps into the living room. There's still a mustiness to it, overlaid by the smell of fresh wood where some of the studs have been replaced.

"Place needs a lot of work," I say.

"Stripping it down was the hard part. Once I pull a crew off another job that's winding up, things will speed up here."

We sit down in two plastic chairs Gabe has set up next to a plastic table with plans laid out on it. With the place open to the air and no sun inside, there's a heavy chill. Gabe turns on a space heater facing the table. "Now, what's on your mind?" he says.

In public LoPresto plays the fool, slapping people's backs and making smart-aleck remarks. But he's professional here at the job site.

"Couple of questions. At the café yesterday, you said Darla thought you had more money than you do. Can you tell me what you meant by that?"

He splays his hands out on the table. "I think I may have made more out of it than there was. She was being presumptuous and I think she knows it. Like I said, Darla called me this morning to make up."

"Presumptuous about what?"

He pulls his hands back and lays them on the arms of the chair. "She was talking about wanting to get me involved with a place that needs some heavy renovation."

I nod. "Go on."

"Only problem is, she thought I should buy the place and do the renovations on spec. I told her that's not the way it works, and that I couldn't afford to buy a place that big anyway."

"She was talking about Slate McClusky's resort."

He had been looking off into the distance, and his head whips back toward me. "How do you know about it?"

"It came to my attention while I was investigating Gary Dellmore's death."

"Wait a minute. What does this have to do with Dellmore? As far as I know, Gary Dellmore had nothing to do with this. Darla is a friend of Angel Bright's, and she said Angel is sick and tired of Slate running the resort and wants somebody to buy it and fix it up."

"Did you ever go out there to look at it?"

"Naw, this just came up while we were in Galveston this weekend. Poor little gal thought it was a great idea. She brought it to me like it was a present she was giving me. She was damn disappointed when I told her it wouldn't work. That's when she got all riled up and said she didn't want to see me anymore. She had her feelings hurt, that's all."

"Gabe, I hate to tell you, but no, that's not all."

He goes still. Usually he starts blustering when things don't go his way, but either something in my voice warned him that I'm dead serious, or deep down he knows he's kidding himself.

"I wish I could sugarcoat this, but getting you to buy McClusky's resort is a scheme cooked up by Darla, Gary Dellmore, and McClusky himself."

I expected LoPresto to explode with anger or protest that I must be wrong, but he nods a couple of times, his expression blank. When he speaks, his voice is hollow. "I guess you wouldn't say that unless you were pretty sure of your facts."

"That's right."

He nods a few more times. "Well, I've been a fool, haven't it?"

"You fell for a pretty girl who was trying to pull the wool over your eyes, but you're not the first man that ever happened to. The important thing is that you didn't get sucked into buying the property."

A tic twitches in his eye. He rakes his hand hard across his mouth then slams it down on the table. "I don't understand why they thought I would buy a game resort. I'm a contractor!"

"McClusky was desperate and was looking for anybody who might be gullible enough to buy him out. The other two were just plain greedy. I suspect they thought you were just like them—that you would be excited at the chance to buy into a big project. Dellmore seems to have had a habit of letting his ideas outrun his good sense."

LoPresto gets up, walks to the frame, and leans against a wall stud, staring out into the yard. "That makes two of us."

216

"No, it doesn't. You may have gone overboard with the girl, but you've got better business sense than they gave you credit for. And it's a good thing, too. They figured if they roped you in, you wouldn't go to the trouble to find out the biggest problem with the place."

He walks back over to me and sits. "What's that?"

"The property is under quarantine—they got hit with foot-and-mouth disease, so there can't be hoofed animals out there until they test the soil and lift the quarantine. Without all those exotic animals, hunters don't have any interest in going there. If you had bought the place, you'd have been sunk."

He laughs bitterly. "They're right. I wouldn't have thought to ask. I guess I'm lucky I couldn't afford to buy the resort."

Before he can say anything more, one of the men who was working on the roof comes into the room. "Gabe, we're all done up there. Can we take lunch?"

LoPresto looks at his watch. "I didn't realize it was so late. Sure. I may not be here when you get back. You know to get started pulling the plumbing in that back bedroom, right?"

The guy gives him a thumbs-up. When he leaves, LoPresto stares after him and then inclines his head in my direction. "How did you get this information about Darla?"

I tell him how it started, with finding files in the trunk of Dellmore's car and the more I looked into it, the more suspicious I became. "McClusky's finances are in a mess. He needs somebody to take that resort off his hands, and he and Dellmore hooked up with Darla to try to rope you into it."

He's chewing his lip vigorously. I don't want to hear the next question I know is coming. "You figure it was all plotted out from the start? That's why she came after me in the first place?"

"Gabe, it's possible that after she took up with you, Dellmore and McClusky saw the opportunity to have her talk up the resort to you."

He nods, drumming his fingers again. "But you don't think so."

"What difference does it make? Either way, you can't trust her."

LoPresto puts his head in his hands. His voice is muffled. "It's possible that she's coming back to me because she told McClusky I'm not interested and he sent her packing."

I let the silence stretch out so he can get a sense of how desperate he sounds. Finally I say, "No, Gabe, that's not the way it is."

He turns his head aside and glares at me. "You seem pretty sure of yourself. With Dellmore dead, I don't see what she gets out of it now." He gets up and paces to look out at the wintery backyard again.

"I don't know exactly what she gets out of it either, but I do know that she and McClusky are still planning for you to buy the place."

"Oh, no. No, no, no." He turns back to me, shaking his head. "That doesn't make sense to me. She doesn't even like McClusky. She told me one reason Angel had taken up with Gary Dellmore is that McClusky is a mean son of a bitch underneath all that smiling glad-handing he does. In fact, she said she hoped I'd buy the resort for Angel's sake because Angel hates the place. She wouldn't do it for McClusky."

I'm hardly listening. All I can think about is Angel and Gary Dellmore. I remember that CD in Dellmore's car. Why didn't I see it before? I don't even have to ask if LoPresto has any evidence of it. It makes total sense. It explains all kinds of little things.

I get up from the table. "Gabe, I'm going to ask you a favor. Pretend everything is fine with Darla. Put off seeing her, whatever, but don't tell her what I told you, at least for a few days."

Except where Darla Rodriguez is concerned, Gabe has always been sharp mentally. "Until you wrap up this investigation into Dellmore's death?"

I nod.

"You think this deal has anything to do with that?"

"I'm not going to take any odds just yet, but I'll find out before too long."

LoPresto stoops down, picks up a bent nail from the floor, and hurls it outside. "I hope to God you find out one of them killed Dell-more and they spend the rest of their sorry lives in jail."

"You can count on one thing, Gabe. McClusky is in deep trouble financially, and now it looks like he and Dellmore committed fraud on the water park deal. One way or another, McClusky is in deep shit. I trust you'll keep all that under your hat for now."

He gives a sharp, bitter laugh. "You can count on that. I'm already going to be the laughingstock here in town because I got in so deep with that little bitch. No need to tell everybody the worst of it."

CHAPTER 29

There's only one place I can think of that I want to be right now. If I go inside my house, I'm likely to get waylaid by Loretta. If I go to the station, somebody's going to walk in and need something.

I don't want to read too much into it, but my cows seem surprised to see me in the middle of the day. Usually they come up close and mill around me when I come down to the pasture first thing in the morning, but now, at midday, they raise their heads and stare at me. Some of them continue to chew, looking at me with a hint of speculation. I lean on the fence and stare back, sorting out what I know.

McClusky and Dellmore put together a deal to have the town invest in a water park. It looks like money from the loan was supposed to help McClusky shore up his slipping finances. Unfortunately, his financial problems came along when everybody else was in trouble. There's no need for me to worry about the particulars, but the end result is that McClusky is as broke as Jarrett Creek. In the middle of it somehow Angel hooked up with Gary Dellmore. I should have seen that in the way she talked about Dellmore, the way she lingered on his name. And in the way she and Slate could barely stand to look at each other at the barbecue place—the way he spoke of her to me in a disparaging way.

Did McClusky kill Dellmore because he was having an affair with Angel? It sounds plausible, but I have a strong core of doubt. Dellmore was running the scheme to get Gabe LoPresto to buy McClusky out. I don't know what he was going to get out of it, but with him gone, McClusky is sunk. I'm not ready to think that McClusky was so blind with jealousy that he killed Dellmore because he was having an affair with Angel.

That brings me back to the women in the mix. I need to talk to Angel as soon as I can get hold of her and find out how far the affair had gone with Dellmore. Were they serious? Was Dellmore planning to divorce his wife? And I need to talk to Barbara Dellmore again, to find out if she knew Angel and Gary were having an affair. She had every reason to want to be rid of a husband who couldn't keep his hands off other women. Not to mention that her husband had ruined her father financially. Angel may have been the last straw.

I put in a call to Angel, and to my surprise she answers, so I know she's not out at the resort. "Who is this?"

"Angel, it's Samuel Craddock. Where are you?"

It takes several seconds for her to answer, her voice cold. "I'm on my way to Jarrett Creek. But I don't have time for you. I've got business to take care of."

"Is Slate with you?"

"No."

"I need to talk to you. I'll meet you at your place and I don't want you trying to avoid me."

She reluctantly agrees to meet me at her house at three-thirty. I have time to make a stop before I meet her there.

Although Cookie assured me that Alan Dellmore did not know his son was involved in fraud, I have to ask Alan directly. And if I'm convinced he didn't know, I want to warn him of what his son was up to. Clara answers the door and tells me that Dellmore has gone to the bank for a couple of hours but should be back soon. She insists that I come in for a cup of coffee, and we go into the living room where a fire is blazing in the stone fireplace. "If you don't mind, I'd like to sit in here. I can't seem to get warm."

She comes back with coffee and we sit next to the fireplace. "Alan has taken this so hard because of the fight they had before Gary died. I keep telling him that people have fights all the time—it's part of life."

"Did they have frequent arguments?"

"It seemed like they fought more and more lately." She smiles a little, like she's thinking of something private. She seems to be in such a reverie that I hate to break in.

"Clara, at the funeral Barbara and Cookie were watching for someone they thought might be coming to the service. They seemed worried. Do you know what they thought might happen?"

Clara closes her eyes and leans back against the chair. "Not exactly. I wish Gary had been a better husband to Barbara." She opens her eyes again and there's a spark in them. "Not that it's all his fault. Annalise is right. Barbara is a cold fish."

I'm surprised to hear Clara use such a term and in such a cold voice. She's always a lady, always gracious. "Everybody's marriage is different. And it can change people."

I know it changed Barbara. As a young woman, Barbara was pretty, with a beautiful figure, but when did I last see her smiling?

"I remember your wife," Clara says. "Marriage changed you, you know."

A pang of sadness arches through me. "For the better."

"That's right. You were a bit bitter in your youth, what with your mother and all. Some people aren't cut out to be parents, and your mother was one of them."

It stuns me to hear Clara talk like this. She's several years older than me and she must have been old enough to know something of what went on in my family. Between my daddy's drinking and my mamma's rage, there was plenty for people to gossip about.

This is as intimate a talk as I've had with anyone for a long time. I couldn't even imagine such a talk with this woman a month ago. The death of her son has put her in a pensive mood.

"So you don't know why Barbara wanted me to be there at the funeral?" I say.

"They didn't tell me exactly. But I suspect they were afraid that some woman would show up where she wasn't wanted. And I think I know who it was."

Did Clara know that Gary was having an affair with Angel? Maybe Barbara told her. "They really thought she would show up?"

"From what I've heard about Darla Rodriguez, she'd do anything," she said.

"Darla? I'm confused."

"She was after Gary. It's as simple as that. I don't care that she was carrying on with Gabe LoPresto. The one she really wanted was Gary."

"Where did you hear that?"

"Cookie told me. She should know; she works with both of them."

There's a sound at the front door, and Clara's face relaxes subtly. She puts a finger to her lips and whispers, "He doesn't like me to talk about this."

Alan Dellmore kisses Clara and shakes hands with me. "Samuel, I suppose you're here in connection with your investigation. Any news?"

"Not yet. I have a couple of banking questions I wanted to pass by you."

Clara gets to her feet. "I'm going to make you some lunch, Alan. Samuel, can I fix you something, too?"

"I already had a bite to eat, but thank you."

Dellmore watches his wife cross the room, and as soon as she's gone, he says, "She's doing okay, don't you think?"

"Coping. That's the best you can do right now."

Dellmore takes off his glasses and pinches the bridge of his nose. "I keep waiting to wake up and feel better, but until I know exactly who killed Gary and why, I won't be able to move forward."

"Alan, I had a talk with Cookie yesterday and I need to verify a couple of things."

"If Cookie told you something, it's going to be correct."

"The problem is, she may not know the truth. This has to do with the water park project."

"Yes. What a nightmare. But Cookie would know everything I know."

"Were you aware that the company contracted to do the park was in financial trouble?"

If it's possible for Dellmore to get any paler, he does. "No. But I assume you're asking because you thought Gary knew. Is that right?"

"It looks like he and Slate McClusky conspired to get the water park deal through."

"McClusky? What did he have to do with it? Gary told me McClusky was just a backer."

I shake my head. "Liberty Water Park is his company."

Alan closes his eyes and rubs a hand over his forehead. "I don't understand. What did Gary stand to gain from this?" But even as he says it, his mouth drops open and I see understanding in his eyes. "They gave him a kickback. Is that it?"

"That's what I'm assuming. It looks like they paid him off so he wouldn't look too closely at the financial state of the company. Even the slightest investigation would have shown Gary that they were having financial problems and that they wouldn't be able to go through with the project, no matter how good a loan they got. So it's likely they bought him off to keep him quiet."

Dellmore looks off into space. "Who told you this?"

"I had a couple of sources."

He nods. "You're not telling."

"Does it matter?"

"Only if they aren't telling the truth."

"Right now the important thing is that it sounds like you were never a party to it."

"No, I wasn't. I tried to give Gary freedom to do business in the

DEAD BROKE IN JARRETT CREEK

way he thought best. After all, at some point, he'd be taking over the bank. At least that was true until recently."

"Had that changed?"

"I was beginning to realize that he was the wrong person for the job."

"Did you ever suggest to Gary that you might not choose him to run the bank?"

"It wouldn't be up to me anyway—it would be a board decision. Not that they wouldn't have listened to me, but I had to admit to myself that I was less and less inclined to push the board in his direction." He sighs. "A few months ago Gary and I fought about it. I suggested to him that it might be prudent for him to take it seriously, that the board had traditional ways of doing things and they may not name him to head the bank if they felt he didn't have the bank's best interest at heart."

"He wouldn't listen?"

Dellmore's shoulders sag. "Gary said he didn't plan to be a banker his whole life and he was working on a way to get into a different line of business. I never thought he was serious—I thought he was just being spiteful." Dellmore has become agitated, but suddenly reality descends on him again. "Of course, this is all moot now."

"Do you know what kind of business he meant?"

"No. Like I said, I thought he was just blowing off steam."

"Your daughter doesn't have any interest in the banking business?"

"Not at all. She'll inherit my interest in the bank now, but she always made it clear that she wanted to be a wife and mother. And quite frankly, old-fashioned as I am, that was fine with me."

I remember how broken up Annalise was at the service yesterday. "Gary and Annalise were close?"

"We were lucky. They got along well. Gary liked her husband, too."

I see no need to divulge the details concerning how Darla Rodriguez, the McCluskys, and Gary Dellmore planned to hook Gabe LoPresto into buying McClusky's resort. That will all come out eventually, and Alan and Clara will have to deal with the knowledge that their son was a crook, pure and simple.

I know now that Clara isn't as fragile as she seems, and that she has a philosophy that will hold her up, although after our talk I wish I could spare her.

I'm getting used to the sound my cell phone makes when it goes off, so I reach for it easily in my jacket pocket. "Craddock."

"Chief, it's Bill Odum. I've got some news for you."

"What news?" I'm driving to meet Angel at her place.

"After I talked to you this morning, I told my dad we needed that ballistics test. He called somebody to come help out, and we finished early so I could get the test done. I just finished up here at the college."

I hear the smile in his voice. "And?"

"Like I said, it won't stand up in court, but as far as I can tell, we've got a match on the gun."

"I'm going to be talking to Slate, but I wanted to get your version of this apart from him."

I'm standing in the living room with Angel, who has her arms crossed and is glaring at me. Camping out doesn't suit her. Her eyes are bloodshot and her skin is pale, almost waxy. She's dressed as usual in a Western shirt and tight jeans, but the shirt is buttoned all the way up and she's wearing a sweater. The room is cold, as if they can't even afford to keep the heat on. "What is it you want from me exactly?"

"You told me Slate didn't know Gary Dellmore, but that wasn't true. He had a lot of business dealings with Dellmore—including the water park deal."

"I also told you that doesn't mean they were friends. It was business."

"Was it just business between you and Dellmore, too?"

"I hardly knew Gary either." She looks at me with a steady gaze. It isn't true that liars won't meet your eyes.

"Come on, Angel. You were having an affair with him. How long had that been going on?"

She tries to laugh, but it comes out hollow. "Where did you hear that?"

"From a reliable source. Did it start before or after the water park deal?"

When she speaks her voice is coarser. "What are you, the morals police? It's nobody's business if I saw Gary."

"It is if your husband found out and shot him."

"That would never happen." She paces to the window. With her back to me, she says, "Slate had a use for Gary. Trust me, as long as Slate can use somebody, he'll get everything he can out of them. Anyway, I hope to God it wasn't him that killed Gary."

"Why is that?"

She wheels and takes a step toward me, a look of fierce hatred on her face. "Because if he did, I'll have to kill him. Gary was the only thing keeping me going."

"How long had you two been carrying on?"

Her eyes are blazing. "You make it sound like a cheap affair. But it wasn't cheap. Gary treated me like I was valuable. He really loved me." Almost exactly the same words Jessica Reinhardt used. Too bad Dellmore couldn't have bottled that ability to make women feel special—everybody except his wife.

"Was he going to divorce his wife? Were you going to leave Slate?"

She whimpers, hugging her arms to her chest. "We were considering it. We knew it was going to make a big mess. We thought we had all the time in the world."

"Had he told his wife?"

She wipes her eyes with the back of her sleeve. "Of course not! We were waiting for the right time before we told anybody."

"Whose idea was it to try to get LoPresto to buy your resort?"

"That's something you have to take up with Slate."

As I drive home, I remember that Barbara said Gary stayed with her so he had an excuse not to get too involved with anyone. Had Dellmore finally found someone he wanted to leave Barbara for? Did he tell Barbara he wanted a divorce? Or was Angel Bright indulging in wishful thinking? And was she telling the truth that her husband wouldn't care if she was having an affair?

CHAPTER 30

Normally I would have called the Texas Rangers or the highway patrol to go out to the resort with me, but I want to get out there tonight, and they would've wanted to wait. Despite the fact that I warned Angel not to contact Slate and she promised she wouldn't, by tomorrow morning she might've had second thoughts. She might have driven out to the resort to tell him I was onto him, and he might have disappeared. Zeke Dibble and I leave right after sundown. I bring sandwiches so we don't have to stop to eat. I know Bill Odum would like to have been part of this, but I think Dibble is the better choice to come with me due to his experience.

I never had much occasion to talk to Dibble. The few times I've been around him, he seems happy just to be a backup, but I notice a subtle change in his voice tonight, more authority in it, like he's remembering what it's like to be a practicing lawman. I asked him if he was coming armed and he seemed surprised by the question. "Of course I am. I've got a Luger. That's what they used in the Houston PD before I left, and they let me buy the one I carried because they were phasing them out."

"Do you carry it all the time?"

"In my glove compartment. I do some target shooting once a month. I like to stay sharp."

I'm glad I thought to bring bolt cutters, because the gate is still chained up. I cut the chain, open the gate, and drive through. It's dark when I park the patrol car halfway up the road to the resort. Although it's a moonless night like last night, I don't feel the same sense of unease I did then.

There are two vehicles parked in front of the resort—Slate's SUV

231

and an old Ford pickup. I expect the pickup belongs to Harold. I didn't see any sign of him last night when Odum and I were out here, but he may have been parked in the back. I don't like the odds of two geezers like Dibble and me having to face two younger, stronger men, but it won't be the first time I've had to work with bad odds. If words fail to do the job, Dibble and I have our guns and the element of surprise on our side.

I've worn my boots this time, and so has Dibble. No sneaking across the deck. Before I can knock, the door swings open. Harold McClusky stands in the doorway, holding a cup of coffee in his hand.

"How did you get past the gate?"

"Is Slate here?"

"What do you want?"

"I need to discuss my business with him in person."

"Harold, bring him in."

"There's two of them."

"Then bring both of them in." There's a touch of impatience to Slate's voice, and I hear him walk toward the door.

I step into the room.

"What can I do for you?" Slate tries for a smile, but his eyes follow my gaze around the bare room. He's dressed in jeans and a sweatshirt, and his hair is sticking out as if he's been running his hands through it.

I open my jacket so he can see my gun in the chest holster. I never was much for wearing a gun out in the open, but some show of force seemed appropriate tonight. "I'm here to talk to you about a couple of things. I had a good conversation with Angel this afternoon and I have a clearer understanding of what you and Dellmore were up to."

Slate laughs. "I don't know what she told you, but there's nothing for you to see here. We're gearing up for renovations so we can get this place going again."

"Slate, you can't keep your financial situation secret forever. You've got no intention of renovating this place, because you don't have the money to do it."

"That's not true," Harold chimes in, sounding panicky. "Slate, tell him what you're going to do." Harold turns puzzled eyes at Slate, and all of a sudden I realize he's been kept completely in the dark. He turns back to me. "Slate's getting the hunting resort going again."

"Where are the animals?" Dibble says.

Harold looks confused and again turns to Slate. "I thought nobody was supposed to know what happened to the animals."

"They got sick, didn't they?" I say, directing my question to Slate. "That variation of foot-and-mouth that ran through a while back. Is that what happened?"

"Look, can we . . ." He glances toward his brother.

Harold looks wildly between Slate and me and blurts out, "We had to put some of the animals to sleep."

"And the others?" I ask Slate.

He looks down at the floor. "We had to send them off to a quarantine facility."

"Cost you a lot of money, I'll bet. That, along with the water park business going off, you were scrabbling for money."

"Slate, what is he talking about?" Harold says.

Slate throws his hands out in appeal "We've had some problems, it's true. Like Harold said, we had issues with the animals that had to be resolved. We have a certain length of time before we can bring animals back in, to make sure it's safe for them. Now why don't we come over here and sit down and have a drink and I'll tell you the details." Dibble and I follow him to the two armchairs, which he indicates we should sit in while he pulls up a stool from the side of the fireplace.

Dibble and I say we don't need a drink. Slate refills his glass with bourbon. Harold paces around with his arms folded while Slate spins a fine fantasy of his plans to spruce up the resort and then restock the animals. "You're right. I've had some financial setbacks. But nothing I can't work with. This resort has always been a big moneymaker. Once it gets going again, I'll be back on my feet."

I nod as if I believe him. "Is that why you were trying to sell it to Gabe LoPresto?"

McClusky's leg starts to jiggle. His ever-ready smile is long gone, replaced with a wooden look as if the smile is the only expression he has practiced enough to use freely.

"Here's what I don't understand," I say. I see Dibble tense up, ready if there's a problem. "Gary Dellmore was helping you try to rope LoPresto in. What happened that made you think you'd be better off with him dead?"

Slate looks from me to Dibble, shaking his head. "You've got the wrong idea. Not only did I not have any reason to kill Gary, but him being gone has created a lot of problems for me."

"I thought maybe it was a jealousy thing."

"Jealousy?" He laughs low and mean. "What do I have to be jealous about? Angel can do what she wants to."

Harold stares at him. "Angel is nice to me."

Slate looks down into his drink, lips set in a grim line.

"Slate," I say, "I wonder if you have a job you might want Harold to take care of."

Slate looks at his brother for a second and I see him falter. "Yes, let me . . . uh, Harold, you remember we were going to take some of those animal heads over to Blanco and sell them to that antique place?"

"Yes, I remember."

"I'd like you to carry some of them out to your truck right now. We can take them over to Blanco first thing in the morning."

"Tonight?" Harold peers at the window. It's pitch-dark and he sounds fearful.

"I guess you're right, it's too dark right now. But why don't you go get things set up for it? You know, in the spa we've got some blankets. I'll turn on the power out there, and you can turn on the lights and gather up a bunch of blankets so we can wrap up those heads first thing in the morning."

"I can do that."

McClusky goes to his foldout bed and brings his brother a flashlight he has beside the bed. As soon as Harold is gone, McClusky says, "I need to go down in the basement and turn on that power."

"I'll have to go with you," I say.

"Suit yourself."

I follow him down to a big basement that's stacked with tables and chairs and kitchen implements. He goes straight to a bank of switches, peers at them, and flips a few on. "That should do it." He turns back to me, and for a second I tense, seeing in his eyes that he's weighing how to get past me and out the door.

"McClusky, let me ask you something. You've got all this furniture stacked in the cabins and down here. What are you doing with it?"

"Auction company is coming next week to take it all off my hands. I'll get pennies on the dollar. Maybe enough to pay the mortgage here a couple more months. I don't know what I'm going to do about Harold. It's going to break his heart."

I tense, waiting for him to do something to throw me off or get away, but the calculation in his eyes dies when he mentions his brother. Dibble is waiting for us at the top of the stairs, and we return to our seats by the fireplace.

My mind is working furiously. McClusky is right—he's worse off with Gary Dellmore gone. His source of funding with the bank is gone, and he was counting on Gary's smooth talk to persuade Darla to rope in Gabe LoPresto. Not that LoPresto would have been roped in anyway, but McClusky doesn't know that. So he doesn't have much motive that I can see for killing Dellmore.

But there's still the fact that McClusky's gun was used to commit the murder. If neither he nor Angel killed Gary, who else had access to the gun? And then I think about the neighborhood break-ins. Suppose the break-in at Camille Overton's house was a cover-up to hide the fact that the real target was the McClusky house? What if someone broke in to steal the gun, and the second break-in—the one where the window was broken—was to put it back after it was used to kill Dellmore? There are still details to be ironed out, but if that theory is true, it means someone is framing the McCluskys for Gary Dellmore's murder.

"Slate, I'm willing for now to go along with you when you say you didn't kill Dellmore, but you're not off the hook. I found out you never had any intention of following through with building a water park in Jarrett Creek. You defrauded the town. You had a Ponzi scheme going, getting money from the town so you could put the money into your parks that were already failing."

"I swear to you, that's not true. I had every intention of building that park. It's just . . ." He stops and stares into the fireplace. "I couldn't seem to buy a break. Everything went to hell all at the same time. I intended to put the money from the Jarrett Creek loan into a couple of places that were going under. And then once they were back in business, I was going to start the Jarrett Creek one." He runs his hands through his hair. "And that's when that damned foot-and-mouth thing happened. What a piece of bad luck! I was already forced to stop having people out here because I didn't have the money to maintain the resort, but I couldn't stop taking care of the animals . . ."

"You were scrambling."

He stands up suddenly. "Bottom line is, you can't prove I did anything wrong."

Dibble and I get up. "It's not up to me to prove it. That's what lawyers are for. I think you better get yourself a good one sooner rather than later."

CHAPTER 31

Gary Dellmore was killed ten days ago, and I'm starting over from the beginning in my investigation. It looks like someone was trying to frame the McCluskys. That means whoever killed Dellmore had something against the McCluskys as well. The McCluskys weren't just a convenient target—someone went to a lot of trouble to frame them.

Barbara Dellmore fits that scenario better than anyone I can think of. On the way to talk with her, I stop by to see Camille Overton. I've been wondering how somebody managed to get into the McClusky house to steal the gun in the first place. I think I know how it was done.

I drive up as Camille is walking out the front door. The wind is whipping up today and clouds are moving in. She's bundled up and carrying an umbrella.

"Let's go back inside," she says, when I tell her I need to talk to her. "I'm already tired of the cold weather and winter's not even half over." She shivers. "Now what can I do for you?"

"Do you keep a spare key for the McCluskys?"

"Oh yes, all of us keep each other's keys in case someone locks themselves out. Mary next door has mine."

"Where do you keep it?"

"On a pegboard in the utility room. I'll show you."

We go through the kitchen into a room with a washer/dryer and utility sink. Jenny and I have the same arrangement, though I keep hers a little better hidden. Putting them in plain sight on a pegboard isn't much in the way of security.

"My goodness, I don't know what to tell you. It's not here." She points to a nail on the board, tagged "Angel." "I don't know where it could have gotten to."

Whoever planned to steal the McClusky's gun got the spare key from right here—may have even been invited into Camille's house and seen the key at the time, or even took it then. It could be anybody.

When I drive up to Barbara Dellmore's house, she's climbing out of her Toyota. She reaches into the backseat and takes out a sack of groceries, then walks toward me, looking flustered. The slacks and sweater she's dressed in are a lot more flattering than her gardening clothes. She's done something to her hair, too, and it looks better.

"Have you made any headway?" Her voice holds a note of belligerence.

"No, I wish I had better news. But I do have a couple more questions."

"More questions?" She looks annoyed. "I don't know what more I can tell you, but come on in."

I take the groceries from her and we go into the kitchen. There's nowhere to set the groceries down. The counters are covered with dishes, and the cabinet doors are standing open.

"You going somewhere?"

She takes the sack from me, sets it on the kitchen table, and starts putting food into the refrigerator. "I have to sell the house eventually, but right now I'm reorganizing. Ever since Gary died, I can't stand not to be busy. It's not a good time of year for gardening, so I have to think of other projects. I woke up at four-thirty this morning and decided to clean out the cabinets and get rid of dishes I don't use anymore."

She folds the grocery sacks, looks around, and says, "I was going to offer you coffee, but I don't think that's possible. You want a soft drink?"

"No, let's sit down."

"I'm going to get some tea anyway. She puts the kettle on. Through all of this I see what she meant when she said she has trouble being still.

For the first time it occurs to me that despite the front she puts on, she is grieving her husband's death.

She sits down with her cup of tea. "What did you want to ask?"

"At the funeral service the other day I got the feeling that you and Cookie Travers were watching for somebody. Do you mind telling me what was going on?"

She blows on her tea and then takes a sip. "I guess it doesn't make any difference now if I tell you this. Gary was having an affair with Angel Bright. I was afraid she'd try to come to the funeral."

"What made you think she might show up?"

"I wasn't really so concerned, but Cookie was worried. She said Angel sometimes came down to the bank, and anybody with eyes could see something was going on between her and Gary. She thought Angel was capable of anything."

"Gary had told you he was seeing Angel?"

Barbara gets up, rummages around in the cabinets, and comes back with a sugar bowl and spoon. She stirs sugar into her tea and takes another sip. The whole time, she's been keeping her face averted from me. Now she looks at me head-on, and her eyes are full of pain. "He told me a few days before he died. He said she was hot to get married."

"Did he ask you for a divorce?"

She looks startled. "No, of course not. The only time he ever admitted an affair was when he was ready to call it quits. He actually told me he thought Angel was acting a little crazy. Too possessive and demanding."

What must it have been like for this woman to hear again and again that her husband had slept with other women? How could her pride have allowed her to stay with him, time and again? Maybe she really loved him in spite of everything.

"Do you know if Gary ever dated Darla Rodriguez?" I use the word "dated" to try to spare Barbara's feelings, even though she doesn't spare herself.

"You mean from the bank?"

"That's the one."

"Not that I know of. What gave you that idea?"

"Clara said she thought Darla was after Gary."

She grimaces. "Clara said that? It must have taken a lot for her to admit that Gary might play around. She wouldn't have wanted to admit that he was less than a perfect husband to me." She sets her teacup down. "How would she even know who Darla was? I wonder if she was repeating something Alan said?"

"No, she said it was Cookie who mentioned it."

"Hmm. I'm surprised she talks to Cookie. They don't seem cut out to be friends. Anyway, that's all water under the bridge. For the first time in a long time I don't have to wonder who Gary is sleeping with. Is that all you wanted to ask me?"

"There is one more thing. Did Gary ever talk business with you, like mentioning loans he made or business deals?"

She grows still, suddenly wary. "Sometimes."

"Did he tell you he had a business venture going with Slate and Angel?"

"Only the water park, but that was a while back."

"So Gary never mentioned that he and McClusky had a scheme to get Gabe LoPresto to buy McClusky's resort?"

She shakes her head. "I don't know anything about that. As far as I'm concerned LoPresto is no better than my husband. If somebody is scheming against him, he deserves it." Her eyes go to the kitchen cabinets, and I can see that she's impatient to get back to work. "What does that have to do with Gary's death?"

"I'm trying to figure that out. But if he didn't confide in you, there's nothing more I need to ask."

I'm satisfied with what Barbara Dellmore told me, and yet when I get back to the station, I'm itchy. Something she said is echoing at the back of my brain, and I can't quite put my finger on it. I have a feeling it was something about the bank. Did it have to do with Darla Rodriguez?

"The way I figure it, somebody broke into Camille Overton's house to get the key to the McClusky house. And they stole the gun to kill Dellmore and then afterward put the gun back."

"How did they know the McCluskys had a gun in the first place?" Rodell says.

"Even if they didn't know for sure that McClusky kept a gun, they'd know it was likely—after all he owns a hunting resort. McClusky told me himself that he kept the gun for times when Angel was by herself. I imagine it wasn't a secret."

Rodell rubs the side of his jaw. "I don't know if my brain has been addled by alcohol, but I'm having a hard time puzzling this out. How would the killer know that anybody would check McClusky's gun to find out it had been used to kill Dellmore?"

We sit lost in thought for a minute. "Here's a possibility," I say. "I wondered why somebody broke the window when they went to put the gun back, instead of using the key again. Maybe they meant to call attention to the fact that McClusky had a gun."

Rodell snickers. "Or maybe the killer lost the key." Rodell is more alert than I've seen him in years, although his skin still looks like bread dough. "Or," he points a finger at me. "Maybe McClusky broke the window himself to make it look like somebody stole the gun."

"I've pretty much ruled out McClusky as a suspect. He had a lot to lose with Gary Dellmore dead."

"Maybe McClusky thought Dellmore couldn't be trusted to keep quiet about his part in the water park deal. Dellmore was killed after that meeting you all had. Maybe McClusky thought people were getting too close to figuring out that the water park deal was what sent the town's finances into a tailspin, and he was afraid Dellmore would blow the whistle on him for fraud."

"I thought of that, but I only got interested in the water deal *after* Dellmore was killed. If he hadn't been killed, people would have put the blame on Alton Coldwater and moved on. Also, Dellmore was the key to getting Gabe LoPresto interested in buying McClusky's resort to get out from under some of his debts. Without Dellmore, LoPresto is a lost cause. It doesn't make sense for McClusky to kill him."

"I hate to say it," Rodell says, "but the only person you're leaving open is Barbara Dellmore. She had motive and opportunity. Unless you think Alan or Clara killed him, which is going way too far out on a limb."

I describe my last interview with Barbara, hoping that telling him might trigger the elusive thought I had at the time. But when I finish, the idea seems farther away than ever.

Rodell moves restlessly. He seems a little stronger, but he's still on the sofa. At least he is sober. "By God, I wish I could get up and go help you out."

"If you did, what would you do first?"

He screws his face up. "I don't know. Go talk to everybody again, I guess." He sighs. "This is the kind of situation that makes me want to have a beer."

I get up from my seat. "I appreciate getting your input on this."

"I don't know that I was much good to you."

"As matter of fact, you did rattle one thing loose when you said I should talk to everybody again. There is one person I haven't questioned yet. Darla Rodriguez."

He makes a gun out of his hand and shoots. "Good place to start."

So it's back to the bank. I park in the lot and as I've taken to doing lately, I scan the cars parked there to see if there's one that could be taken for Dellmore's Crown Victoria. For once I score and spot a car in the lot that could be mistaken for a Crown Vic in the dark.

I ask several people before I'm directed to a bookkeeper. She's star-tled when I ask to speak to her privately. In her forties, she's plump, with a pleasant, round face. "How well did you know Gary Dellmore?" I ask.

She shakes her head and looks blank. "I can't say I knew him at all." She gets a look of distaste on her face. "I'm not exactly his type. He was more chatty with the younger girls."

"The Buick belongs to you?"

"Actually, no. I'm driving it today. It's my brother's car."

"How long have you been borrowing it?"

She's increasingly puzzled. "Today was the only day. He's visiting from Dallas and he wanted to go fishing, so I lent him my little pickup."

"When did he get here?"

"Why are you asking? Has he done something?"

"I'm not sure. If I know when he got here, I'll be able to judge a little better."

"He got here Sunday. He's taking a week off." Now she's distinctly annoyed.

"I appreciate your help. That's all I needed to know. Your brother's in the clear."

"Wait a minute. It's not right for you to ask me questions and not tell me what's going on. Did somebody complain about my brother? He can get rowdy sometimes."

"No, nothing like that. There was a car like your brother's involved in a little dust-up last week, but if he didn't get here until Sunday, it has nothing to do with him."

Darla's a pretty girl, wearing a curvy black business suit that manages to look professional and sexy at the same time. A little white lace something peeks out from the cleavage of the jacket. She's wearing a necklace with a single diamond that nestles in the hollow of her throat. That's cold, wearing Gabe's birthday gift after declaring the gift wasn't good enough and insisting he take her off for an expensive weekend and then dumping him.

"How can I help you?" Her eyes sparkle as if I'm the very person she was hoping would come to see her.

I introduce myself.

"I know who you are." She says it like she admires me, which I doubt.

"I need to ask you a few questions about Gary Dellmore."

"Like what?"

"Why don't we find a spare office, or I can take you down to the station."

She looks startled. "Oh, that won't be necessary. I think we can find someplace private." She looks out over the lobby. "Let's go over there." She points to an isolated desk over by the wall. Nobody is sitting nearby. The desks are arranged so that customers can consult with bankers about their finances without being overheard.

We sit down, and she turns her whole attention to me. "Now what can I help you with?" By now Slate McClusky has had plenty of time to alert her, so I expect she knows exactly why I'm here. She's a good bluffer; I'll give her that.

"What was your relationship with Gary like?"

The light in her eyes snuffs out. "I loved Gary. He was such a wonderful man. A great boss."

"Did you have any problems with him at all?"

"Problems?"

"Like him being too friendly, harassing you, anything like that?"

She looks like she'd like to laugh. "Absolutely not. He was always professional." Light dawns in her eyes. "Oh, you're thinking about Jessica Reinhardt. That poor girl had such a crush on him. He knew it too, and he was really sweet to her."

"Sweet, like going to her house and trying to seduce her?"

"Did she tell you that? He went over there to apologize."

"Apologize for what?"

"For getting her in trouble with the Dragon Lady—Cookie Travers was on her case."

"Gary's death hit Jessica hard. She seemed to think Gary came by her place because he was interested in her."

She shrugs. "When somebody has a crush like that, anything a guy does can be misunderstood."

"How often did you see Dellmore outside of work?"

She allows herself a tinkly little laugh and cuts me a knowing look. "Oh, I see. Are you a friend of Gabe's? He was so jealous of Gary."

"Just answer the question."

She examines her manicured nails. "We had dinner together sometimes, but it was always to discuss bank business. It was never about sex between us."

"You had a lot of business with him, didn't you? Including a scheme to persuade Gabe LoPresto to invest in Slate McClusky's failing resort."

"Gabe is a grown man. If he doesn't want to take on an investment, he won't. But I think he's missing a great opportunity." Her voice has grown cold.

"How great can the opportunity be to open a big game resort when you can't have big game there?"

Her eyes grow big. "You mean that problem Slate had with the animals? He told me the quarantine was going to be lifted soon. I hope he wasn't fudging."

"You're a pretty ambitious girl, aren't you?"

She giggles. "You say that like it's a bad thing."

"It can be. You've made yourself a few enemies."

"Who? Barbara Dellmore? What can she do to me? Her buddy-buddy Cookie Travers? Cookie has absolutely no power over me. Alan thinks I'm great and he won't let Cookie fire me."

"What is your relationship with Slate McClusky?"

"Slate and I have an understanding. Strictly business."

"Not the same kind of 'understanding' that Gary and Angel Bright had?"

She grins. "So you know about that? These women and their crushes on Gary!"

"You weren't attracted to him?"

"Not the way other women were. Gary and I were too much alike."

"Angel seemed to think Gary was going to leave his wife and marry her."

"God, no." She leans across the desk, eyes glittering. "But I told him he'd better be careful. Angel might be more dangerous than he thought she was if she found out he had no intention of leaving his wife for her."

"Do you think she killed Gary?"

She sits back, staring at me while she thinks about my question. "I can't imagine that she would. She hadn't gotten to that point yet where she thought there was no hope. That's when you have to worry."

Her words echo with me as I drive away from the bank. I keep going over them. When I get to the station, I sit outside and go over my conversation with her again. Something she said triggered the same kind of mental nudge I got when I last talked to Barbara Dellmore. And then it comes to me, what both Darla and Barbara said that snagged my interest. I hope I'm wrong, but I think I know who killed Gary Dellmore.

I hurry into the station and start looking through the reports I've jotted down the last couple of days and finally come to the one I'm looking for. This time I won't be telephoning Mrs. Witz about her missing car, I'll be going out to see her in person.

CHAPTER 32

"Yes, that's my car." Mrs. Witz points out the black Crown Victoria, a vintage model at least ten years older than Gary Dellmore's but with the same general shape and size. It's parked in the driveway in front of the one-car garage. Mrs. Witz lives in the most modest home on the block, but it's well kept, with a tidy yard. "But nobody has driven it since I called you. To tell you the truth, I'm embarrassed I made that phone call to you. I think I got discombobulated." She's in her eighties, but she seems anything but discombobulated.

"Do you ever let anybody borrow it?"

"My son has driven it a time or two when he comes up from Houston. He wants to make sure it's in good working order. He's a good son."

"Does anyone else have a key to it?"

"I don't believe so."

"But you're not sure?"

She hesitates. "My neighbor drove me to the doctor when I had cataract surgery a few weeks ago and we took my car. That's such a good surgery. I can see without glasses now."

"You got the key back from your neighbor after she drove you to the doctor? It was 'she,' I believe."

She frowns. "Yes, I had her use my spare set and I thought I got it back. Let me take a look. Come on in."

While she goes into a back room, I wait in her living room, trying not to choke on the strong scent of potpourri. Despite the smell, I'm happy for her to take her time, because when I leave her, I'm likely going to have to make an arrest I don't want to make.

She comes back looking flustered. "I don't believe I did get the keys back. I suppose I could have put them somewhere else, but I'm pretty good about returning things where they're supposed to stay. You know, when you get as old as I am, you worry that you'll lose track of things."

I ask her the name of the neighbor who drove her to have her surgery, and it's exactly who I feared it would be.

Back at the station, I sit down and write out all the clues that point to the killer, a person who had access to a car to switch with Dellmore's car, who had every reason to despise Gary Dellmore, and who carried a burdensome secret, with a side dose of ambition to boot. I'm stalling to give her time to finish up her business for the day. Alan Dellmore will have a lot on his plate, and it won't hurt to give him one more day to grieve his son before he has to start grieving all over again.

Meanwhile, I drive to the McCluskys' house. Both their cars are in the driveway. I ring the doorbell and Angel opens the door. "Oh, it's you."

"I have one more question, to satisfy my curiosity."

"Great, more questions." She walks away from the door without asking me in, but I follow anyway. "Slate?" Angel yells out. "Your new best friend is here." I don't think it's my imagination that her accent is considerably more west Texas than usual.

We stand in the living room, and I sneak a glance at the Remington. The light that displays it is turned off, and I like it even better that way. I don't know why I like Remington. He has a lot of horses in his paintings, and I'm not fond of horses. But in his paintings horses seem to have a purpose and give a sense of what real frontier life must have been like. The one here in the McClusky living room is one of his brooding pieces, with two horses and a cowboy on foot leading them while a small herd of cows looks on in the background. The colors are muted, like night is coming on.

Slate McClusky comes in, and although his manner is strained he has a businessman's knack for pretending things are okay when they aren't. He's retrieved his smile. "What brings you here?"

"I heard that you and Angel were putting your house on the market."

"I didn't figure it would take long for the news to get out. We've decided we need to start fresh somewhere. Angel never liked it here anyway, so she'll be glad to move on, won't you, honey?"

"You've got that right. Who needs this place anyway?" Although her words sound like she is supporting Slate, the bitter set of her mouth tells me the support is on rocky ground.

"I presume you have something to say besides rubbing my nose in my financial situation?" His smile doesn't go with his harsh words.

I nod toward the Remington. "If you have any interest in selling that painting, I'd make you a fair offer for it."

McClusky blinks. Angel laughs and says, "You know how to twist the knife, don't you?"

"I didn't intend that. If it has sentimental value, then I understand."

"Angel is being sarcastic," McClusky says, "and not doing a very good job of it."

"Is the picture an original?"

"How the hell do I know? I got it from an old boy who was going bankrupt a few years back. He said he could give me that picture or a block of strip mall in a slum section of Colorado Springs. He claimed they were equal value. I kind of liked the picture, so I said yes. These days I'd probably take the mall."

He'd be wrong. I have a feeling he has no idea what this picture is worth. "How much do you want for it?"

"I don't know. You think it's worth fifty thousand dollars?" His voice is hopeful.

He might have saved himself a good bit of trouble and maybe been able to buy himself a little leeway if he'd bothered to find out what this picture was really worth. "I tell you what, I have a man from Houston who can come up and give us an appraisal on it. You got any papers for it?"

Slate is beginning to look interested. "Somewhere around here. I'll look in my files. What do you think it might bring?"

"We'll have to make sure it's genuine before I'd be able to speculate." I'm not going to give him a number. The picture might be nothing more than a good imitation. George Manning can tell me that.

Back at my house I call Manning. He owns a gallery in Houston. Jeanne and I bought a few pieces from him. He says he's busy this weekend, but he'll drive up on Monday. I tell him I don't have a fine restaurant to take him out to, but I can fit him up with some good barbecue or Mexican food, his choice.

It's mid-afternoon when I stop by Loretta's place. She's finishing up the shirts she's making for her grandsons. "I'm glad to put this aside for a while. My eyes are tired."

We go into her kitchen and she brews coffee. She's gotten in the habit of brewing it extra-strong for me and adding water to her own. "You look a little pale. Have you had any lunch?"

I admit to her that I hadn't even thought about it.

"You've got something on your mind."

"Yes, but I can't discuss it."

"That's okay. I'll do the talking." She whips me up a lunch of a tuna fish sandwich with sliced pickles on the side.

Two bites into it, I already feel better. "So talk."

"I found out that Slate and Angel McClusky are leaving here," she says. "They're putting their house on the market. But somebody said it wasn't all on the up-and-up." She looks at me keenly. "Would you know anything about that?"

"Yes, but that's something else I can't discuss. It'll come out eventually."

"Somebody said they also had their house in Vail on the market, and that's why they've stayed in town this winter. But Angel told Camille Overton they planned to consolidate all their places and then maybe they'd buy a house in California. It sounds like Angel has gotten a little bored and maybe she's going to try for a comeback."

"Wouldn't they be going to Nashville for that?" I'm thinking of that poster advertising the comeback tour that never happened and Slate's claim that Angel had lost her singing voice.

"That's what I said, but Camille said she only knows what Angel told her. What kind of name is 'Angel,' anyway?"

I laugh. She's no angel, that's for sure. "What else is on your mind?"

"Oh, that new woman, Ellen Forester, is apparently having problems with her ex-husband. Somebody said he came after her and things got ugly." She looks at me sharply, but I keep quiet.

"Anyway, it turns out she's going to have a big party for the opening of the store. I think that's a nice idea, don't you?"

"I do."

"It will be a welcome change. Everybody's so gloomy with the town having such financial trouble. We need a party to cheer us up."

I listen to Loretta chatter on, glad for a little respite. But eventually I have to go take care of business.

CHAPTER 33

"I usually go straight home after work," Cookie Travers says. "I have my routine. I change clothes and then pour myself a glass of wine and look through my mail."

"The reason I ask is that I need to have a chat with you."

Maybe it's something in my voice, or maybe it's nothing, but she pauses for a minute before she replies. "I'll tell you what. Why don't you follow me to my house and I'll give you a glass of wine, too, and then we can talk."

"I'll wait for you outside."

It's twenty minutes before she comes out the front door of the bank, and after she locks the big double doors, she does an odd thing. She looks the building up and down like she's taking it in to remember it. It's true, even though she'll likely see the bank again, it will never be through the same eyes.

Her house is much nicer than her neighbor's across the street, Mrs. Witz's. It's at least three bedrooms. I wonder if she bought it thinking that one day she'd marry and have children.

Cookie says she'd like to change clothes, and I tell her that will be fine. While I wait I look at the photos she has arranged on a table. There are some with her as a young girl, along with what I take to be her parents and two siblings. And there are several of her with people I know around town, and a formal picture of her taken in her work clothes standing in front of the bank. There are also pictures of Alan Dellmore—one with his bank board, another that is several years old, and then a recent one. It's a curious photo, because it looks like it has been cut. There was someone else in the photo that Cookie didn't want to display.

When Cookie comes back, she has exchanged her suit for slacks and a sweater with a fleece vest, and her high heels for running shoes. It's too warm in here for the vest.

She asks what I want to drink, and I tell her I'll have what she's having.

"I believe I'll open a nice bottle of white wine," she says. She goes into the kitchen and comes back with two pretty crystal stems and a bottle of what I know to be expensive chardonnay. Even though I don't prefer white wine, I recognize the name from the catalog I buy my red wine from. She opens the wine and pours it into the glasses. "Beautiful color," she says, and sniffs. "And a nice nose. It's a special bottle."

When Cookie sits down, I ask her when she moved here.

"I've been with the bank for over twenty years."

"How did you come to settle in Jarrett Creek?"

She smiles, but it's not a smile of pleasure—it's full of sadness. "I met Alan at a banking conference. I was working in Beaumont at the time. We hit it off." She takes a sip of her wine. "He asked me if I'd consider coming to work for him, and I said yes."

"Have you ever regretted the decision?"

"That's a funny question." She smoothes her hair. "I guess everybody regrets some parts of their life. I was engaged to be married, and if I'd stayed in Beaumont, I would've had a different life. Probably kids. I think I would like to have had children, but it didn't work out that way."

"What did Alan promise you if you moved here?"

The bottle of wine may be special, but she slugged the first glass back as if it were water, and now she's staring at her empty glass. "I usually only have one glass of wine, but I think I'm going to have another one tonight." She doesn't ask me if I want another, because I've hardly touched my first. When she sits back down, her eyes are glistening with unshed tears. "You asked me what Alan promised? I wish I could tell you he lied to me and promised me things, but he didn't. It was all on me."

I know from her answer that she's aware of exactly why I'm here. Like me, she's putting off the moment of truth. "It must have been hard when Alan hired Gary at the bank."

She takes a shaky breath. "You have no idea. I helped Alan build that bank to be a fine institution. Do you know that we have people who do business with us all over the county and beyond? Or at least we did."

"Before Gary came along and started working for his dad?"

"And making a mess of things. In more ways than one." She wipes her eyes with the heels of her hands, smearing her mascara.

"So you decided to take care of the problem."

She shudders when I say the words. She sets her glass down very carefully on the coffee table, and when she raises her head, her eyes are dead cold. "Are you suggesting that I killed Gary?"

"Cookie, before we get into that, I'd like you to take off that vest. I don't see how you can stand to wear it. It's too warm in here." As I speak, I pull the .45 out of my holster and point it at her.

She draws a sharp breath. "I'm fine. I'm not too warm."

"Humor me. I know you've got a gun in the pocket and we need to get that out of the way."

I wait while she thinks it over and realizes there's no way she can get to that gun before I shoot her. She shrugs off the vest and lets it fall around her.

"Throw the vest on the floor."

She does so, and it falls with a muffled clunk.

"I didn't kill Gary. You have no evidence," she says, her chin jutting out.

"Well, I do, actually. I have your fingerprint on the gun used to kill him, the one you stole out of the McClusky place to try to frame Angel. People think they've wiped a gun free of fingerprints, but they always forget the trigger."

Her eyes narrow. She's trying to remember whether she wiped the trigger off. I'm bluffing anyway, but I'm hoping she doesn't guess that.

"Can you at least answer one thing for me?" I say. "I can't quite clear it up."

"I don't know whether I can or not."

"I know you stole the McClusky's key out of Camille Overton's utility room so you could get in and steal Angel's gun, but why didn't you use the key when you went back to replace the gun? Why break a window?"

I've got her now. She closes her eyes for a moment, making the decision to maintain dignity. When she opens them I see that she's given in to the process. "That was awful. All that planning, and then I forgot the key. I changed purses that morning when I went to work and I completely forgot that the key was in a side pocket of the other purse. Pure vanity, wanting to be sure my bag matched my shoes." A laugh bubbles up and she clamps a hand over her mouth to keep it from getting out of control.

"Oh, Cookie."

She takes a deep, shuddering breath. "Then when I got to the McCluskys' house and realized I'd forgotten the key, I had to decide whether I'd go back home and get it or break that little window."

"Why did you want to frame Angel for the murder? Or was it Slate you wanted to pin it on?"

"That little bitch thought she was so smart and that nobody would guess she and Gary were sleeping together. She'd come sashaying into the bank and hang all over him. One more humiliation for Barbara Dellmore. What that poor woman had to put up with . . . anyway, I figured if anybody got close to finding out what happened to Gary, I might as well point things in Angel's direction. And if you hadn't butted in, it would have gone fine. Can you imagine James Harley Krueger figuring this out?"

"Probably not."

"And how *did* you figure it out? I thought I had done a pretty good job of covering my tracks."

"You did a damned good job."

"It couldn't have been that good, since you caught me."

I put up my hands. "I mean it. You got lazy though, that's what eventually led me to you."

"I am not a lazy woman by any stretch of the imagination."

"Let me ask you this. Why did you drive Gary's car back to the park where you left Mrs. Witz's car the night you killed him? That was laziness. You could have walked back to the car and driven it away, and I never would have made the connection to you."

Cookie looks truly puzzled. "I don't know what you're talking about."

I tell her that Louis Caton noticed the car in both directions. "He thought it was the same car, but I realized that whoever did the killing parked up on the dam road and walked to the American Legion Hall to shoot Gary and then drove Gary's car back and left it. If you'd just walked back and driven the car away, Louis Caton wouldn't have come along and stolen it, and I wouldn't have wondered whose car had been exchanged for it."

She shakes her head. "Fool. I thought it was a brilliant idea, taking his car up there and leaving it. I thought it would be an extra little mystery for somebody to have to figure out." She frowns. "But how did you connect the car with me?"

"Mrs. Witz. You know how old people are. They worry over every little thing. She called and told me that she thought somebody had driven her car. I didn't pay much attention to it, but when I started wondering whether you might have had something to do with Gary's death, I found out her car was an easy switch for Gary's. It was the last piece I needed to put the puzzle together."

"I thought it was clever to use Mrs. Witz's car instead of mine, so in case anybody saw the car they would never connect it with me." Her eyes glitter with triumph, but she quickly realizes that she wasn't so clever after all. She doubles over as in pain. "I really thought I was going to get away with it. Why did you have to interfere? You said finding out Mrs. Witz lived across the street from me only confirmed your suspicion. What got you thinking it was me in the first place?"

"Something Barbara said. She said you and Clara were unlikely friends. It struck me as odd. Clara seemed glad to have you sit with the family at the funeral, so I wondered why the two of you were unlikely friends. And I began to remember all the times I had talked to you and how you talked about yourself and Alan as if you were partners.

"We were partners!"

"I know you were. Later I talked to Darla Rodriguez, and she said something like it's only when a woman loses hope that she becomes dangerous. The remark had nothing to do with you, but it occurred to me that when Gary came on the scene, you started to lose hope that Alan would reward you for all your years of sticking by him. What I don't understand is why now? Gary has been at the bank for a few years. Surely it wasn't finding out that Gary was fooling around with Angel Bright that made you act."

Cookie looks sick. Her voice is broken. "All those years I loved Alan and stuck by him. I worked so hard to make sure the bank thrived. It was my whole life. I watched Alan and Clara raise their kids and have another whole life. But lately Alan was starting to talk about retiring. I knew he was going to make Gary a vice president. I could see the handwriting on the wall. After all the work I had done, all my sacrifice for the bank, no matter that I deserved to be president of the bank, I knew Alan would see to it that Gary was promoted over me eventually. I couldn't stand it. It wasn't fair."

I don't have the heart to tell her that Dellmore knew the bank board wouldn't allow Gary to head the bank. He might inherit it, but he was never going to be in charge of it. Cookie killed Gary Dellmore for nothing.

I stand up. "Cookie, I'm going to have to take you in. But what I'd like to do is take you to the jail in Bobtail. That way you're not going to have to face people you know here in town. At least not right away. I can keep you here in our jail, though, if you prefer that."

She gets quiet and gradually straightens up. Her lips are trembling, but she has restored some measure of dignity. "Bobtail is better. I appreciate it." She stands up and falters as if her legs won't hold her, but she takes two steps and grabs the back of the sofa to steady herself. She looks around her place like she's never seen it before. "What can I take with me?"

"Put together some personal items, toiletries, any medication you need. They'll confiscate them at first, but you'll get them back."

"What will happen to my house?"

"I'll come by and check on it. You have any pets?"

"No, my dog died last year and I decided not to get another one."

"I'll have to keep an eye on you while you get your things together."

She looks puzzled and then understands. "Oh, I'm not going to kill myself. If it comes to that, the state will have that satisfaction."

When we get outside, Zeke Dibble is sitting in his car out front where I've asked him to wait. He pulls in behind us as I drive away from the curb.

CHAPTER 34

The crowd is upbeat at the opening of Ellen Forester's new art gallery and workshop, nobody more so than Ellen herself. She hugs me when I walk in. "Thank you so much for your help," she whispers.

I don't dare look at Loretta and Jenny, who I've brought with me, but Loretta prods me. "What was that all about?"

"I helped her hang the art and lent her a couple of my paintings." That's not all I did. She called me one night when her husband showed up, and I went out to the little rental house she's staying in while her place is being renovated. I told him if anything happened to Ellen or any of her property, he was going to jail. Period. I don't know if we've seen the last of him, but at least I've put him on notice.

Gabe LoPresto is here with Sandy. She apparently decided she liked the look she adopted when Gabe was gone, and Gabe looks at her like he does, too. He's strutting around like he never did a thing wrong and as if Darla Rodriguez never existed.

The gallery looks good, although, as I feared, I'm not partial to the kind of art Ellen displays. I want her to be successful, that's why I spent the last couple of days helping her hang pictures. I wanted to lend Ellen the Remington as a showpiece, but it's stuck in Houston, waiting for a verdict on the provenance. They can't seem to locate the man Slate McClusky said gave it to him in settlement of debts, and Slate couldn't find any papers. I let Ellen borrow my Melinda Buie instead. It's an abstract, but at least people can recognize it as a cow.

Slate and Angel have mysteriously disappeared. Jenny says it will take some time to put together a case against them, and even then it may not be worth the trouble since they don't appear to have salvaged much from their high-finance days. I expect the only thing we'll see of them for some time to come is if they manage to locate the Remington's former owner. And if he isn't found, I don't know that I'll ever get my hands on it.

Alan and Clara Dellmore haven't shown up, and I doubt that they will. Alan tried in vain to have Cookie let out on bail, her expensive lawyer claiming that she was no threat to the community. But there was the matter of the premeditation that the judge didn't take kindly to. I've gone to see her a couple of times, and she's not doing well.

Once when I went to see her, I stopped at the bar where James Harley Krueger is working. He seems to have settled into his job, but he didn't appreciate my request that he not supply Rodell with any alcohol.

"That's none of your business," he said. "Rodell is a friend of mine and he was good to me when I was a cop. The least I can do for him is see that he's happy."

Patty has come to the opening, but she says Rodell is still not up to such a tiring event. I'll look in on him tomorrow, maybe see if I can get him in the car and down to the station. I've come to enjoy his sense of humor, something he had lost in the bottle.

Barbara Dellmore has shown up tonight looking like a new woman. Most people in her situation wouldn't have shown their face, but she's defiant. She didn't kill her husband, and she stuck by him despite his affairs. She has nothing to be ashamed of, she told me, and she intends to let everybody know it.

ACKNOWLEDGMENTS

I want to acknowledge the amazing members of my high school class at Brazosport Senior High in Texas, many of whom I haven't seen in decades, who rally to celebrate my books in person at signings, put out the word on social media, and generally make me feel like a superstar. In particular, thanks to Sheila Skaggs Hale (she missed her calling—should have been a publicist), Gretchen Muehlberg Williams, Cheryl Hill Dancak, Sandra James Booth, their husbands, and all the people they roped into coming to readings and prodded to read my books.

And then there are my relatives, that crazy Gaines gang, in-laws and outlaws, who read the books and try to guess who the characters are modeled after. No matter our different philosophies and lives, your love surrounds me. How lucky can I be?

A shout-out to Detective Ruben Vasquez of the Georgetown Police Department for his fascinating talk about murder investigation in Texas. He set me straight on some things, forcing me into feverish last-minute edits, but they were worth it to get it right.

A special thank you to my husband, David, for his insights into how financial arrangements work between banks and big business—especially the shady side.

ABOUT THE AUTHOR

TERRY SHAMES is the best-selling author of *A Killing at Cotton Hill*—a finalist for Left Coast Crime's award for best mystery of 2013, for the *Strand Magazine* award for Best First Mystery, and for the Macavity award for Best First Mystery—and *The Last Death of Jack Harbin*. She lives in Berkeley, CA, but her imagination is always stirred by the vast landscape and human drama of Texas, where she grew up. Visit her website at www.Terrryshames.com.

WHERE IT BEGAN – THE FIRST SAMUEL CRADDOCK MYSTERY!

"An amazing read. The poetic, literary quality of the writing draws you into a small town and its interesting, secret-carrying residents."

—RT BOOK REVIEWS

"A very strong start to this series, one worth seeking out."

—MYSTERIOUS REVIEWS

"*A Killing at Cotton Hill* enchants with memorable characters and a Texas backdrop as authentic as bluebonnets and scrub cedars. A splendid debut by a gifted writer."

—CAROLYN HART
Author of *Escape from Paris*

"Terry Shames does small-town Texas crime right, and *A Killing at Cotton Hill* is the real thing. . . . Craddock is a man readers are going to love, and they'll want to visit him and Jarrett Creek, Texas, often."

—BILL CRIDER
Author of *Compound Murder*, a Dan Rhodes mystery

Available in trade paperback and ebook editions wherever books are sold.

SEVENTH STREET BOOKS

Where Fiction Is a Crime
www.seventhstreetbooks.com
An imprint of Prometheus Books

IN A SMALL TEXAS TOWN WHERE SECRETS CAN BE LETHAL, SAMUEL CRADDOCK MUST FIND THE TRUTH.

"Samuel Craddock is a hero worth rooting for."

—SHELDON SIEGEL
New York Times–bestselling author

"A terrific read. Terry Shames brings a fresh, new voice to crime fiction."

—DEBORAH CROMBIE
New York Times–bestselling author

"A gritty take on small-town crime."

—BOOKLIST

"The most engaging new American sleuth in crime fiction."

—TORONTO STAR

"I'm looking forward to visiting Jarrett Creek, Texas, again."

—MYSTERY SCENE